The Country
Beyond
A Romance of
the Wilderness

James Oliver Curwood

Contents

THE COUNTRY BEYOND
A ROMANCE OF THE WILDERNESS

by

James Oliver Curwood

A glass of wine once lost a kingdom, a nail turned the tide of a mighty battle, and a woman's smile once upon a time destroyed the homes of a million people. Thus have trivial things played their potent parts in the history of human lives; yet these things Peter did not know.

THE COUNTRY BEYOND

CHAPTER I

NOT far from the rugged and storm-whipped north shore of Lake Superior, and south of the Kaministiqua, yet not as far south as the Rainy River waterway, there lay a paradise lost in the heart of a wilderness world—and in that paradise "a little corner of hell."

That was what the girl had called it once upon a time, when sobbing out the shame and the agony of it to herself. That was before Peter had come to leaven the drab of her life. But the hell was still there.

One would not have guessed its existence, standing at the bald top of Cragg's Ridge this wonderful thirtieth day of May. In the whiteness of winter one could look off over a hundred square miles of freezing forest and swamp and river country, with the gleam of ice-covered lakes here and there, fringed by their black spruce and cedar and balsam—a country of storm, of deep snows, and men and women whose blood ran red with the thrill that the hardship and the never-ending adventure of the wild.

But this was spring. And such a spring as had not come to the Canadian north country in many years. Until three days ago there had been a deluge of warm rains, and since then the sun had inundated the land with the golden warmth of summer. The last chill was gone from the air, and the last bit of frozen earth and muck from the deepest and blackest swamps, North, south, east and west the wilderness world was a glory of bursting life, of springtime mellowing into summer. Ridge upon ridge of yellows and greens and blacks swept away into the unknown distances like the billows of a vast sea; and between them lay the valleys and swamps, the lakes and waterways, glad with the rippling song of running waters, the sweet scents of early flowering time, and the joyous voice of all mating creatures.

Just under Cragg's Ridge lay the paradise, a meadow-like sweep of plain that reached down to the edge of Clearwater Lake, with clumps of poplars and white birch and darker tapestries of spruce and balsams dotting it like islets in a sea of verdant green. The flowers were two weeks ahead of their time and the sweet perfumes of late June, instead of May, rose up out of the plain, and already there was nesting in the velvety splashes of timber.

In the edge of a clump of this timber, flat on his belly, lay Peter. The love of adventure was in him, and today he had sallied forth on his most desperate enterprise. For the first time he had gone alone to the edge of Clearwater Lake, half a mile away; boldly he had trotted up and down the white strip of beach where the girl's footprints still remained in the sand, and defiantly he had yipped at the shimmering vastness of the water, and at the white gulls circling near him in quest of dead fish flung ashore. Peter was three months old. Yesterday he had been a timid pup, shrinking from the bigness and strangeness of everything about him; but today he had braved the lake trail on his own nerve, and nothing had dared to come near him in spite of his yipping, so that a great courage and a great desire were born in him.

Therefore, in returning, he had paused in the edge of a great clump of balsams and spruce, and lay flat on his belly, his sharp little eyes leveled yearningly at the black mystery of its deeper shadows. The bit of forest filled a cup-like depression in the plain, and was possibly half a rifle-shot distance from end to end—but to Peter it was as vast as life itself. And something urged him to go in.

And as he lay there, desire and indecision struggling for mastery within him, no power could have told Peter that destinies greater than his own were working through the soul of the dog that was in him, and that on his decision to go in or not to go in—on the triumph of courage or cowardice—there rested the fates of lives greater than his own, of men, and women, and of little children still unborn. A glass of wine once lost a kingdom, a nail turned the tide of a mighty battle, and a woman's smile once upon a time destroyed the homes of a million people. Thus have trivial things played their potent parts in the history of human lives, yet these things Peter did not know—nor that his greatest hour had come.

At last he rose from his squatting posture, and stood upon his feet. He was not a beautiful pup, this Peter Pied-Bot—or Peter Club-foot, as Jolly Roger Mc-Kay—who lived over in the big cedar swamp—had named him when he gave Peter to the girl. He was, in a way, an accident and a homely one at that. His father was a blue- blooded fighting Airedale who had broken from his kennel long enough to commit a MESALLIANCE with a huge big footed and peace- loving Mackenzie hound—and Peter was the result. He wore the fiercely bristling whiskers of his Airedale father at the age of three months; his ears were flappy and big, his tail was knotted, and his legs were ungainly and loose, with huge feet at the end of them—so big and heavy that he stumbled frequently, and fell on his nose. One pitied him at first—and then loved him. For Peter, in spite of his homeliness, had the two best bloods of all dog creation in his veins. Yet in a way it was like mixing nitro- glycerin with olive oil, or dynamite and saltpeter with milk and honey.

Peter's heart was thumping rapidly as he took a step toward the deeper shadows. He swallowed hard, as if to clear a knot out of his scrawny throat. But he had made up his mind. Something was compelling him, and he would go in. Slowly the gloom engulfed him, and once again the whimsical spirit of fatalism had chosen a trivial thing to work out its ends in the romance and tragedy of human lives.

Grim shadows began to surround Peter, and his ears shot up, and a scraggly brush stood out along his spine. But he did not bark, as he had barked along the shore of the lake, and in the green opens. Twice he looked back to the shimmer of sunshine that was growing more and more indistinct. As long as he could see this, and knew that his retreat was open, there still remained a bit of that courage which was swiftly ebbing in the thickening darkness. But the third time he looked back the light of the sun was utterly gone! For an instant the knot rose up in his throat and choked him, and his eyes popped, and grew like little balls of fire in his intense desire to see through the gloom. Even the girl, who was afraid of only one thing in the world, would have paused where Peter stood, with a little quickening of her heart. For all the light of the day, it seemed to Peter, had suddenly died out. Over his head the spruce and cedar and balsam tops grew so thick they were like a canopy of night. Through them the snow never came in winter, and under them the light of a blazing sun was only a ghostly twilight.

And now, as he stood there, his whole soul burning with a desire to see his way out, Peter began to hear strange sounds. Strangest of all, and most fearsome, was a hissing that came and went, sometimes very near to him, and always accompanied by a grating noise that curdled his blood. Twice after that he saw the shadow of the great owl as it swooped over him, and he flattened himself down, the knot in his throat growing bigger and more choking. And then he heard the soft and uncanny movement of huge feathered bodies in the thick shroud of boughs overhead, and slowly and cautiously he wormed himself around, determined to get back to sunshine and day as quickly as he could. It was not until he had made this movement that the real chill of horror gripped at his heart. Straight behind him, directly in the path he had traveled, he saw two little green balls of flame!

It was instinct, and not reason or experience, which told Peter there was menace and peril in these two tiny spots blazing in the gloom. He did not know that his own eyes, popping half out of his head, were equally terrifying in that pit of silence, nor that from him emanated a still more terrifying thing—the scent of dog. He trembled on his wobbly legs as the green eyes stared at him, and his back seemed to break in the middle, so that he sank helplessly down upon the soft spruce needles, waiting for his doom. In another flash the twin balls of green fire were gone. In a moment they appeared again, a little farther away. Then a second time they were gone, and a third time they flashed back at him—so distant they appeared like needle-points in the darkness. Something stupendous rose up in Peter. It was the soul of his Airedale father, telling him the other thing was running away! And in the joy of triumph Peter let out a yelp. In that night-infested place, alive with hiding things, the yelp set loose weird rustlings in the tangled treetops, strange murmurings of chortling voices, and the nasty snapping of beaks that held in them the power to rend Peter's skinny body into a hundred bits. From deeper in the thicket came the sudden crash of a heavy body, and with it the chuckling notes of a porcupine, and a HOO-HOO-HOO-EE of startled inquiry that at first Peter took for a human voice. And again he lay shivering close to the foot-deep carpet of needles under him, while his heart thumped against his ribs, and his whiskers stood out in mortal fear. There followed a weird and appalling silence, and in that stillness Peter quested vainly for the sunlight he had lost. And then, indistinctly, but bringing with it a new thrill, he heard another sound. It was a soft and distant rippling of running water. He knew that sound. It was friendly. He had played among the rocks and pebbles and sand where it was made. His courage came back, and he rose up on his legs, and made his way toward it. Something inside him told him to go quietly, but his feet were big and clumsy, and half a dozen times in the next two minutes he stumbled on his nose. At last he came to the stream, scarcely wider than a man might have reached across, rippling and plashing its way through the naked roots of trees. And ahead of him Peter saw light. He quickened his pace, until at the last he was running when he came out into the edge of the meadowy plain, with its sweetness of flowers and green grass and song of birds, and its glory of blue sky and sun.

If he had ever been afraid, Peter forgot it now. The choking went out of his throat, his heart fell back in its place, and the fierce conviction that he had vanquished everything in the world possessed him. He peered back into the dark cavern of evergreen out of which the streamlet gurgled, and then trotted straight away from it, growling back his defiance as he ran. At a safe distance he stopped, and faced about. Nothing was following him, and the importance of his achievements grew upon him. He began to swell; his fore-legs he planted pugnaciously, he hollowed his back, and began to bark with all the puppyish ferocity that was in him. And though he continued to yelp, and pounded the earth with his paws, and tore up the green grass with his sharp little teeth, nothing dared to come out of the black forest in answer to his challenge!

His head was high and his ears cocked jauntily as he trotted up the slope, and for the first time in his three months of existence he yearned to give battle to something that was alive. He was a changed Peter, no longer satisfied with the thought of gnawing sticks or stones or mauling a rabbit skin. At the crest of the slope he stopped, and yelped down, almost determined to go back to that black patch of forest and chase out everything that was in it. Then he turned toward Cragg's Ridge, and what he saw seemed slowly to shrink up the pugnaciousness that was in him, and his stiffened tail drooped until the knotty end of it touched the ground.

Three or four hundred yards away, out of the heart of that cup- like paradise which ran back through a break in the ridge, rose a spiral of white smoke, and with the sight of that smoke Peter heard also the chopping of axe. It made him shiver, and yet he made his way toward it. He was not old enough—nor was it in the gentle blood of his Mackenzie mother—to know the meaning of hate; but something was growing swiftly in Peter's shrewd little head, and he sensed impending danger whenever he heard the sound of the axe. For always there was associated with that sound the cat-like, thin-faced man with the red bristle on his upper lip, and the one eye that never opened but was always closed. And Peter had come to fear this one eyed man more than he feared any of the ghostly monsters hidden in the black pit of the forest he had braved that day.

But the owls, and the porcupine, and the fiery-eyed fox that had run away from him, had put into Peter something which was not in him yesterday, and he did not slink on his belly when he came to the edge of the cup between the broken ridge, but stood up boldly on his crooked legs and looked ahead of him. At the far edge of the cup, under the western shoulder of the ridge, was a thick scattering of tall cedars and green poplars and white birch, and in the shelter of these was a cabin built of logs. A lovelier spot could not have been chosen for the home of man. The hollow, from where Peter stood, was a velvety carpet of green, thickly strewn with flowers and ferns, sweet with the scent of violets and wild honey-suckle, and filled with the song of birds. Through the middle of it purled a tiny creek which disappeared between the ragged shoulders of rock, and close to this creek stood the cabin, its log walls smothered under a luxuriant growth of wood-vine. But Peter's quizzical little eyes were not measuring the beauty of the place, nor were his ears listening to the singing of birds, or the chattering of a red-squirrel on a stub a few yards away. He was looking beyond the cabin, to a chalk-white mass of rock that rose like a giant mushroom in the edge of the trees—and he was listening to the ringing of the axe, and straining his ears to catch the sound of a voice.

It was the voice he wanted most of all, and when this did not come he choked back a whimper in his throat, and went down to the creek, and waded through it, and came up cautiously behind the cabin, his eyes and ears alert and his loosely jointed legs ready for flight at a sign of danger. He wanted to set up his sharp yipping signal for the girl, but the menace of the axe choked back his desire. At the very end of the cabin, where the wood-vine grew thick and dense, Peter had burrowed himself a hiding-place, and into this he skulked with the quickness of a rat getting away from its enemies. From this protecting screen he cautiously poked forth his whiskered face, to make what inventory he could of his chances for supper and a safe home-coming.

And as he looked forth his heart gave a sudden jump.

It was the girl, and not the man who was using the axe today. At the big wood-pile half a stone's throw away he saw the shimmer of her brown curls in the sun, and a glimpse of her white face as it was turned for an instant toward the cabin. In his gladness he would have leaped out, but the curse of a voice he had learned to dread held him back.

A man had come out of the cabin, and close behind the man, a woman. The man was a long, lean, cadaverous-faced creature, and Peter knew that the devil was in him as he stood there at the cabin door. His breath, if one had stood close enough to smell it, was heavy with whiskey. Tobacco juice stained the corners of his mouth, and his one eye gleamed with an animal-like exultation as he nodded toward the girl with the shining curls

"Mooney says he'll pay seven-fifty for her when he gets his tie- money from the Government, an' he paid me fifty down," he said. "It'll help pay for the brat's board these last ten years—an' mebby, when it comes to a show-down, I can stick him for a thousand."

The woman made no answer. She was, in a way, past answering with a mind of her own. The man, as he stood there, was wicked and cruel, every line in his ugly face and angular body a line of sin. The woman was bent, broken, a wreck. In her face there was no sign of a living soul. Her eyes were dull, her heart burned out, her hands gnarled with toil under the slavedom of a beast. Yet even Peter, quiet as a mouse where he lay, sensed the difference between them. He had seen the girl and this woman sobbing in each other's arms. And often he had crawled to the woman's feet, and occasionally her hand had touched him, and frequently she had given him things to eat. But it was seldom he heard her voice when the man was near.

The man was biting off a chunk of black tobacco. Suddenly he asked,

"How old is she, Liz?"

And the woman answered in a strange and husky voice.

"Seventeen the twelfth day of this month."

The man spat.

"Mooney ought to pay a thousand. We've had her better'n ten years —an' Mooney's crazy as a loon to git her. He'll pay!"

"Jed—" The woman's voice rose above its hoarseness. "Jed—it ain't right!"

The man laughed. He opened his mouth wide, until his yellow fangs gleamed in the sun, and the girl with the axe paused for a moment in her work, and flung back her head, staring at the two before the cabin door.

"Right?" jeered the man. "Right? That's what you been preachin' me these last ten years 'bout whiskey-runnin,' but it ain't made me stop sellin' whiskey, has it? An' I guess it ain't a word that'll come between Mooney and me—not if Mooney gits his thousand." Suddenly he turned upon her, a hand half raised to strike. "An' if you whisper a word to her—if y' double-cross me so much as the length of your little finger—I'll break every bone in your body, so help me God! You understand? You won't say anything to her?"

The woman's uneven shoulders drooped lower.

"I won't say ennything, Jed. I—promise."

The man dropped his uplifted hand with a harsh grunt.

"I'll kill y' if you do," he warned.

The girl had dropped her axe, and was coming toward them. She was a slim, bird-like creature, with a poise to her head and an up- tilt to her chin which warned that the man had not yet beaten her to the level of the woman. She was dressed in a faded calico, frayed at the bottom, and with the sleeves bobbed off just above the elbows of her slim white arms. Her stockings were mottled with patches and mends, and her shoes were old, and worn out at the toes.

But to Peter, worshipping her from his hiding place, she was the most beautiful thing in the world. Jolly Roger had said the same thing, and most men—and women, too—would have agreed that this slip of a girl possessed a beauty which it would take a long time for unhappiness and torture to crush entirely out of her. Her eyes were as blue as the violets Peter had thrust his nose among that day. And her hair was a glory, loosed by her exertion from its bondage of faded ribbon, and falling about her shoulders and nearly to her waist in a mass of curling brown tresses that at times had made even Jed Hawkins' one eye light of with admiration. And yet, even in those times, he hated her, and more than once his bony fingers had closed viciously in that mass of radiant hair, but seldom could he wring a scream of pain from Nada. Even now, when she could see the light of the devil in his one gleaming eye, it was only her flesh—and not her soul—that was afraid.

But the strain had begun to show its mark. In the blue of her eyes was the look of one who was never free of haunting visions, her cheeks were pallid, and a little too thin, and the vivid redness of her lips was not of health and happiness, but a touch of the color which should have been in her face, and which until now had refused to die.

She faced the man, a little out of the reach of his arm.

"I told you never again to raise your hand to strike her," she cried in a fierce, suppressed little voice, her blue eyes flaming loathing and hatred at him. "If you hit her once more—something is going to happen. If you want to hit anyone, hit me. I kin stand it. But—look at her! You've broken her shoulder, you've crippled her—an' you oughta die!"

The man advanced half a step, his eye ablaze. Deep down in him Peter felt something he had never felt before. For the first time in his life he had no desire to run away from the man. Something rose up from his bony little chest, and grew in his throat, until it was a babyish snarl so low that no human ears could hear it. And in his hiding-place his needle-like fangs gleamed under snarling lips.

But the man did not strike, nor did he reach out to grip his fingers in the silken mass of Nada's hair. He laughed, as if something was choking him, and turned away with a toss of his arms.

"You ain't seein' me hit her any more, are you, Nady?" he said, and disappeared around the end of the cabin.

The girl laid a hand on the woman's arm. Her eyes softened, but she was trembling.

"I've told him what'll happen, an' he won't dare hit you any more," she comforted. "If he does, I'll end him. I will! I'll bring the police. I'll show 'em the places where he hides his whiskey. I'll—I'll put him in jail, if I die for it!"

The woman's bony hands clutched at one of Nada's.

"No, no, you mustn't do that," she pleaded. "He was good to me once, a long time ago, Nada. It ain't Jed that's bad—it's the whiskey. You mustn't tell on him, Nada—you mustn't!"

"I've promised you I won't—if he don't hit you any more. He kin shake me by the hair if he wants to. But if he hits you—"

She drew a deep breath, and also passed around the end of the cabin.

For a few moments Peter listened. Then he slipped back through the tunnel he had made under the wood-vine, and saw Nada walking swiftly toward the break in the ridge. He followed, so quietly that she was through the break, and was picking her way among the tumbled masses of rock along the farther foot of the ridge, before she discovered his presence. With a glad cry she caught him up in her arms and hugged him against her breast.

"Peter, Peter, where have you been?" she demanded. "I thought something had happened to you, and I've been huntin' for you, and so has Roger—I mean Mister Jolly Roger."

Peter was hugged tighter, and he hung limply until his mistress came to a thick little clump of dwarf balsams hidden among the rocks. It was their "secret place," and Peter had come to sense the fact that its mystery was not to be disclosed. Here Nada had made her little bower, and she sat down now upon a thick rug of balsam boughs, and held Peter out in front of her, squatted on his haunches. A new light had come into her eyes, and they were shining like stars. There was a flush in her cheeks, her red lips were parted, and Peter, looking up—and being just dog—could scarcely measure the beauty of her. But he knew that something had happened, and he tried hard to understand.

"Peter, he was here ag'in today—Mister Roger—Mister Jolly Roger," she cried softly, the pink in her cheeks growing brighter. "And he told me I was pretty!"

She drew a deep breath, and looked out over the rocks to the valley and the black forest beyond. And her fingers, under Peter's scrawny armpits, tightened until he grunted.

"And he asked me if he could touch my hair—mind you he asked me that, Peter!—And when I said 'yes' he just put his hand on it, as if he was afraid, and he said it was beautiful, and that I must take wonderful care of it!"

Peter saw a throbbing in her throat.

"Peter—he said he didn't want to do anything wrong to me, that he'd cut off his hand first. He said that! And then he said—if I didn't think it was wrong—he'd like to kiss me—"

She hugged Peter up close to her again.

"And—I told him I guessed it wasn't wrong, because I liked him, and nobody else had ever kissed me, and—Peter—he didn't kiss me! And when he went away he looked so queer—so white-like—and somethin' inside me has been singing ever since. I don't know what it is, Peter. But it's there!"

And then, after a moment.

"Peter," she whispered, "I wish Mister Jolly Roger would take us away!"

The thought drew a tightening to her lips, and the pucker of a frown between her eyes, and she sat Peter down beside her and looked over the valley to the black forest, in the heart of which was Jolly Roger's cabin.

"It's funny he don't want anybody to know he's there, ain't it—I mean—isn't it, Peter?" she mused. "He's livin' in the old shack Indian Tom died in last winter, and I've promised not to tell. He says it's a great secret, and that only you, and I, and the Missioner over at Sucker Creek know anything about it. I'd like to go over and clean up the shack for him. I sure would."

Peter, beginning to nose among the rocks, did not see the flash of fire that came slowly into the blue of the girl's eyes. She was looking at her ragged shoes, at the patched stockings, at the poverty of her faded dress, and her fingers clenched in her lap.

"I'd do it—I'd go away—somewhere—and never come back, if it wasn't for her," she breathed. "She treats me like a witch most of the time, but Jed Hawkins made her that way. I kin remember—"

Suddenly she jumped up, and flung back her head defiantly, so that her hair streamed out in a sun-filled cloud in a gust of wind that came up the valley.

"Some day, I'll kill 'im," she cried to the black forest across the plain. "Some day—I will!"

CHAPTER II

S HE followed Peter. For a long time the storm had been gathering in her
brain, a storm which she had held back, smothered under her unhappiness,
so that only Peter had seen the lightning-flashes of it. But today the betrayal
had forced itself from her lips, and in a hard little voice she had told Jolly
Roger—the stranger who had come into the black forest—how her mother and
father had died of the same plague more than ten years ago, and how Jed Hawkins
and his woman had promised to keep her for three silver fox skins which her father
had caught before the sickness came. That much the woman had confided in her,
for she was only six when it happened. And she had not dared to look at Jolly Roger
when she told him of what had passed since then, so she saw little of the hardening
in his face as he listened. But he had blown his nose— hard. It was a way with Jolly
Roger, and she had not known him long enough to understand what it meant. And
a little later he had asked her if he might touch her hair—and his big hand had lain
for a moment on her head, as gently as a woman's.

Like a warm glow in her heart still remained the touch of that hand. It had
given her a new courage, and a new thrill, just as Peter's vanquishment of unknown
monsters that day had done the same for him. Peter was no longer afraid, and the
girl was no longer afraid, and together they went along the slope of the ridge, until
they came to a dried-up coulee which was choked with a wild upheaval of rock.
Here Peter suddenly stopped, with his nose to the ground, and then his legs stiffened, and for the first time the girl heard the babyish growl in his throat. For a moment she stood very still, and listened, and faintly there came to her a sound, as if
someone was scraping rock against rock. The girl drew in a quick breath; she stood

straighter, and Peter—looking up—saw her eyes flashing, and her lips apart. And then she bent down, and picked up a jagged stick.

"We'll go up, Peter," she whispered. "It's one of his hiding- places!"

There was a wonderful thrill in the knowledge that she was no longer afraid, and the same thrill was in Peter's swiftly beating little heart as he followed her. They went very quietly, the girl on tip-toe, and Peter making no sound with his soft footpads, so that Jed Hawkins was still on his knees, with his back toward them, when they came out into a square of pebbles and sand between two giant masses of rock. Yesterday, or the day before, both Peter and Nada would have slunk back, for Jed was at his devil's work, and only evil could come to the one who discovered him at it. He had scooped out a pile of sand from under the edge of the biggest rock, and was filling half a dozen grimy leather flasks from a jug which he had pulled from the hole. And then he paused to drink. They could hear the liquor gurgling down his throat.

Nada tapped the end of her stick against the rock, and like a shot the man whirled about to face them. His face turned livid when he saw who it was, and he drew himself up until he stood on his feet, his two big fists clenched, his yellow teeth snarling at her.

"You damned—spy!" he cried chokingly. "If you was a man—I'd kill you!"

The girl did not shrink. Her face did not whiten. Two bright spots flamed in her cheeks, and Hawkins saw the triumph shining in her eyes. And there was a new thing in the odd twist of her red lips, as she said tauntingly.

"If I was a man, Jed Hawkins—you'd run!"

He took a step toward her.

"You'd run," she repeated, meeting him squarely, and taking a tighter grip of her stick. "I ain't ever seen you hit anything but a woman, an' a girl, or some poor animal that didn't dare bite back. You're a coward, Jed Hawkins, a low-down, sneakin,' whiskey- sellin' coward—and you oughta die!"

Even Peter sensed the cataclysmic change that had come in this moment between the two big rocks. It held something in the air, like the impending crash of dynamite, or the falling down of the world. He forgot himself, and looked up at his mistress, a wonderful, slim little thing standing there at last unafraid before the future—and in his dog heart and soul a part of the truth came to him, and he planted his big feet squarely in front of Jed Hawkins, and snarled at him as he had never snarled before in his life.

And the bootlegger, for a moment, was stunned, For a while back he had humored the girl a little, to hold her in peace and without suspicion until Mooney was able to turn over her body-money. After that—after he had delivered her to the other's shack—it would all be up to Mooney, he figured. And this was what had come of his peace-loving efforts! She was taking advantage of him, defying him, spying upon him—the brat he had fed and brought up for ten years! Her beauty as she stood there did not hold him back. It was punishment she needed, a beating, a hair-pulling, until there was no breath left in her impudent body. He sprang forward, and Peter let out a wild yip as he saw Nada raise her stick. But she was a moment too slow. The man's hand caught it, and his right hand shot forward and buried itself in the thick, soft mass of her hair.

It was then that something broke loose in Peter. For this day, this hour, this minute the gods of destiny had given him birth. All things in the world were blotted out for him except one—the six inches of naked shank between the bootlegger's trouser-leg and his shoe. He dove in. His white teeth, sharp as stiletto-points, sank into it. And a wild and terrible yell came from Jed Hawkins as he loosed the girl's hair. Peter heard the yell, and his teeth sank deeper in the flesh of the first thing he had ever hated. It was the girl, more than Peter, who realized the horror of what followed. The man bent down and his powerful fingers closed round Peter's scrawny neck, and Peter felt his wind suddenly shut off, and his mouth opened. Then Jed Hawkins drew back the arm that held him, as he would have drawn it back to fling a stone.

With a scream the girl tore at him as his arm straightened out, and Peter went hurtling through the air. Her stick struck him fiercely across the face, and in that same moment there was a sickening, crushing thud as Peter's loosely-jointed little body struck against the face of the great rock. When Nada turned Peter was groveling in the sand, his hips and back broken down, but his bright eyes were on her, and without a whimper or a whine he was struggling to drag himself toward her. Only Jolly Roger could tell the story of how Peter's mother had died for a woman, and in this moment it must have been that her spirit entered into Peter's soul, for the pain of his terrible hurt was forgotten in his desire to drag himself back to the feet of the girl, and die facing her enemy—the man. He did not know that he was dragging his broken body only an inch at a time through the sand. But the girl saw the terrible truth, and with a cry of agony which all of Hawkin's torture could not have wrung from her she ran to him, and fell upon her knees, and gathered him tenderly in her arms. Then, in a flash, she was on her feet, facing Jed Hawkins like a little demon.

"For that—I'll kill you!" she panted. "I will. I'll kill you!"

The blow of her stick had half blinded the bootlegger's one eye, but he was coming toward her. Swift as a bird Nada turned and ran, and as the man's footsteps crunched in the gravel and rock behind her a wild fear possessed her—fear for Peter, and not for herself. Very soon Hawkins was left behind, cursing at the futility of the pursuit, and at the fate that had robbed him of an eye.

Down the coulee and out into the green meadowland of the plain ran Nada, her hair streaming brightly in the sun, her arms clutching Peter to her breast. Peter was whimpering now, crying softly and piteously, just as once upon a time she had heard a baby cry—a little baby that was dying. And her soul cried out in agony, for she knew that Peter, too, was dying. And as she stumbled onward— on toward the black forest, she put her face down to Peter and sobbed over and over again his name.

"Peter—Peter—Peter—"

And Peter, joyous and grateful for her love and the sound of her voice even in these moments, thrust out his tongue and caressed her cheek, and the girl's breath came in a great sob as she staggered on.

"It's all right now, Peter," she crooned. "It's all right, baby. He won't hurt you any more, an' we're goin' across the creek to Mister Roger's cabin, an' you'll be happy there. You'll be happy— "

Her voice choked full, and her mother-heart seemed to break inside her, just as life had gone out of that other mother's heart when the baby died. For their grief, in God's reckoning of things, was the same; and little Peter, sensing the greatness of this thing that had made them one in flesh and blood, snuggled his wiry face closer in her neck, crying softly to her, and content to die there close to the warmth of the creature he loved.

"Don't cry, baby," she soothed. "Don't cry, Peter, dear. It'll soon be all right—all right— " And the sob came again into her throat, and clung there like a choking fist, until they came to the edge of the big forest.

She looked down, and saw that Peter's eyes were closed; and not until then did the miracle of understanding come upon her fully that there was no difference at all between the dying baby's face and dying Peter's, except that one had been white and soft, and Peter's was different—and covered with hair.

"God'll take care o' you, Peter," she whispered. "He will—God, 'n' me, and Mister Roger—"

She knew there was untruth in what she was saying for no one, not even God, would ever take care of Peter again—in life. His still little face and the terrible grief in her own heart told her that. For Peter's back was broken, and he was going—going even now—as she ran moaningly with him through the deep aisles of the forest. But before he died, before his heart stopped beating in her arms, she wanted to reach Jolly Roger's friendly cabin, in the big swamp beyond the creek. It was not that he could save Peter, but something told her that Jolly Roger's presence would make Peter's dying easier, both for Peter and for her, for in this first glad spring of her existence the stranger in the forest shack had brought sunshine and hope and new dreams into her life; and they had set him up, she and Peter, as they would have set up a god on a shrine.

So she ran for the fording place on Sucker Creek, which was a good half mile above the shack in which the stranger was living. She was staggering, and short of wind, when she came to the ford, and when she saw the whirl and rush of water ahead of her she remembered what Jolly Roger had said about the flooding of the creek, and her eyes widened. Then she looked down at Peter, piteously limp and still in her arms, and she drew a quick breath and made up her mind. She knew that at this shallow place the water could not be more than up to her waist, even at the flood- tide. But it was running like a mill-race.

She put her lips down to Peter's fuzzy little face, and held them there for a moment, and kissed him.

"We'll make it, Peter," she whispered. "We ain't afraid, are we, baby? We'll make it—sure—sure—we'll make it—"

She set out bravely, and the current swished about her ankles, to her knees, to her hips. And then, suddenly, unseen hands under the water seemed to rouse themselves, and she felt them pulling and tugging at her as the water deepened to her waist. In another moment she was fighting, fighting to hold her feet, struggling to keep the forces from driving her downstream. And then came the supreme moment, close to the shore for which she was striving. She felt herself giving away, and she cried out brokenly for Peter not to be afraid. And then something drove pitilessly against her body, and she flung out one arm, holding Peter close with the other—and caught hold of a bit of stub that protruded like a handle from the black and slippery log the flood-water had brought down upon her.

"We're all right, Peter," she cried, even in that moment when she knew she had lost. "We're all ri—"

And then suddenly the bright glory of her head went down, and with her went Peter, still held to her breast under the sweeping rush of the flood.

Even then it was thought of Peter that filled her brain. Somehow she was not afraid. She was not terrified, as she had often been of the flood-rush of waters that smashed down the creeks in springtime. An inundating roar was over her, under her, and all about her; it beat in a hissing thunder against the drums of her ears, yet it did not frighten her as she had sometimes been frightened. Even in that black chaos which was swiftly suffocating the life from her, unspoken words of cheer for Peter formed in her heart, and she struggled to hold him to her, while with her other hand she fought to raise herself by the stub of the log to which she clung. For she was not thinking of him as Peter, the dog, but as something greater—something that had fought for her that day, and because of her had died.

Suddenly she felt a force pulling her from above. It was the big log, turning again to that point of equilibrium which for a space her weight had destroyed. In the edge of a quieter pool where the water swirled but did not rush, her brown head appeared, and then her white face, and with a last mighty effort she thrust up Peter so that his dripping body was on the log. Sobbingly she filled her lungs with air. But the drench of water and her hair blinded her so that she could not see. And she found all at once that the strength had gone from her body. Vainly she tried to drag herself up beside Peter, and in the struggle she raised herself a little, so that a low-hanging branch of a tree swept her like a mighty arm from the log.

With a cry she reached out for Peter. But he was gone, the log was gone, and she felt a vicious pulling at her hair, as Jed Hawkins himself had often pulled it, and for a few moments the current pounded against her body and the tree-limb swayed back and forth as it held her there by her hair.

If there was pain from that tugging, Nada did not feel it. She could see now, and thirty yards below her was a wide, quiet pool into which the log was drifting. Peter was gone. And then, suddenly, her heart seemed to stop its beating, and her eyes widened, and in that moment of astounding miracle she forgot that she was hanging by her hair in the ugly lip of the flood, with slippery hands beating and pulling at her from below. For she saw Peter—Peter in the edge of the pool—making his way toward the shore! For a space she could not believe. It must be his dead body drifting. It could not be Peter—swimming! And yet—his head was above the water—he was moving shoreward—he was struggling—

Frantically she tore at the detaining clutch above her. Something gave way. She felt the sharp sting of it, and then she plunged into the current, and swept down with it, and in the edge of the pool struck out with all her last strength until her feet touched bottom, and she could stand. She wiped the water from her eyes, sobbing in her breathless fear—her mighty hope. Peter had reached the shore. He had dragged himself out, and had crumpled down in a broken heap—but he was facing her, his bright eyes wide open and questing for her. Slowly Nada went to him. Until now, when it was all over, she had not realized how helplessly weak she was. Something was turning round and round in her head, and she was so dizzy that the shore swam before her eyes, and it seemed quite right to her that Peter should be alive—and not dead. She was still in a foot of water when she fell on her knees and dragged herself the rest of the way to him, and gathered him in her arms again, close up against her wet, choking breast.

And there the sun shone down upon them, without the shade of a twig overhead; and the water that a little while before had sung of death rippled with its old musical joy, and about them the birds sang, and very near to them a pair of mating red-squirrels chattered and played in a mountain-ash tree. And Nada's hair brightened in the sun, and began to ripple into curls at the end, and Peter's bristling whiskers grew dry—so that half an hour after she had dragged herself out of the water there was a new light in the girl's eyes, and a color in her cheeks that was like the first dawning of summer pink in the heart of a rose.

"We're a'most dry enough to go to Mister Jolly Roger, Peter," she whispered, a little thrill in her voice.

She stood up, and shook out her half dry hair, and then picked up Peter—and winced when he gave a little moan.

"He'll fix you, Peter," she comforted. "An' it'll be so nice over here—with him."

Her eyes were looking ahead, down through the glory of the sun- filled forest, and the song of birds and the beauty of the world filled her soul, and a new and wonderful freedom seemed to thrill in the touch of the soft earth under her feet.

"Flowers," she cried softly. "Flowers, an' birds, an' the sun, Peter—" She paused a moment, as if listening to the throb of light and life about her. And then, "I guess we'll go to Mister Jolly Roger now," she said.

She shook her hair again, so that it shone in a soft and rebellious glory about her, and the violet light grew a little darker in her eyes, and the color a bit deeper in her cheeks as she walked on into the forest over the faintly worn foot-trail that led to the old cabin where Jolly Roger was keeping himself away from the eyes of men.

CHAPTER III

FROM the little old cabin of dead Indian Tom, built in a grassy glade close to the shore of Sucker Creek, came the sound of a man's laughter. In this late afternoon the last flooding gold of the sun filled the open door of the poplar shack. The man's laughter, like the sun on the mottled tapestry of the poplar-wood, was a heart-lightening thing there on the edge of the great swamp that swept back for miles to the north and west. It was the sort of laughter one seldom hears from a man, not riotous of over-bold, but a big, clean laughter that came from the soul out. It was an infectious thing. It drove the gloom out of the blackest night. It dispelled fear, and if ever there were devils lurking in the edge of old Indian Tom's swamp they slunk away at the sound of it. And more than once, as those who lived in tepee and cabin and far-away shack could testify, that laugh had driven back death itself.

In the shack, this last day of May afternoon, stood leaning over a rough table the man of the laugh—Roger McKay, known as Jolly Roger, outlaw extraordinary, and sought by the men of every Royal Northwest Mounted Police patrol north of the Height of Land.

It was incongruous and inconceivable to think of him as an outlaw, as he stood there in the last glow of the sun—an outlaw with the weirdest and strangest record in all the northland hung up against his name. He was not tall, and neither was he short, and he was as plump as an apple and as rosy as its ripest side. There was something cherubic in the smoothness and the fullness of his face, the clear gray of his eyes, the fine-spun blond of his short- cropped hair, and the plumpness of his hands and half-bared arms. He was a priestly, well-fed looking man, was this Jolly

Roger, rotund and convivial in all his proportions, and some in great error would have called him fat. But it was a strange kind of fatness, as many a man on the trail could swear to. And as for sin, or one sign of outlawry, it could not be found in any mark upon him—unless one closed his eyes to all else and guessed it by the belt and revolver holster which he wore about his rotund waist. In every other respect Jolly Roger appeared to be not only a harmless creature, but one especially designed by the Creator of things to spread cheer and good-will wherever he went. His age, if he had seen fit to disclose it, was thirty-four.

There seemed, at first, to be nothing that even a contented man might laugh at in the cabin, and even less to bring merriment from one on whose head a price was set—unless it was the delicious aroma of a supper just about ready to be served. On a little stove in the farthest corner of the shack the breasts of two spruce partridges were turning golden brown in a skittle, and from the broken neck of a coffee pot a rich perfume was rising with the steam. Piping hot in the open oven half a dozen baked potatoes were waiting in their crisp brown jackets.

From the table Jolly Roger turned, rubbing his hands and chuckling as he went for a third time to a low shelf built against the cabin wall. There he carefully raised a mass of old papers from a box, and at the movement there came a protesting squeak, and a little brown mouse popped up to the edge of it and peered at him with a pair of bright little questioning eyes.

"You little devil!" he exulted. "You nervy little devil!"

He raised the papers higher, and again looked upon his discovery of half an hour ago. In a soft nest lay four tiny mice, still naked and blind, and as he lowered the mass of papers the mother burrowed back to them, and he could hear her squeaking and chirruping to the little ones, as if she was trying to tell them not to be afraid of this man, for she knew him very well, and it wasn't in his mind to hurt them. And Jolly Roger, as he returned to the setting of his table, laughed again—and the laugh rolled out into the golden sunset, and from the top of a spruce at the edge of the creek a big blue-jay answered it in a riotous challenge.

But at the bottom of that laugh, if one could have looked a bit deeper, was something more than the naked little mice in the nest of torn-up paper. Today happiness had strangely come this gay- hearted freebooter's way, and he might have reached out, and seized it, and have kept it for his own. But in the hour of his opportunity he had refused it—because he was an outlaw—because strong within him was a peculiar code of honor all his own. There was nothing of man-made religion in the soul of Roger McKay. Nature was his god; its manifestations, its life, and the air it gave him to breathe were the pages which made up the Book that guided him. And within the last hour, since the sun had begun to drop behind the tips of the tallest trees, these things had told him that he was a fool for turning away from the one great thing in all life—simply because his own humors of existence had made him an outcast and hunted by the laws of men. So the change had come, and for a space his soul was filled with the thrill of song and laughter.

Half an hour ago he believed that he had definitely made up his mind. He had forced himself into forgetfulness of laws he had broken, and the scarlet-coated men who were ever on the watch for his trail. They would never seek him here, in the wilderness country close to the edge of civilization, and time, he had told himself in that moment of optimism, would blot out both his identity and his danger. Tomorrow he would go over to Cragg's Ridge again, and then—

His mind was crowded with a vision of blue eyes, of brown curls glowing in the pale sun, of a wistful, wide-eyed little face turned up to him, and red lips that said falteringly, "I don't think it's wrong for you to kiss me—if you want to, Mister Jolly Roger!"

Boldly he had talked about it to the bright-eyed little mother- mouse who peered at him now and then over the edge of her box.

"You're a little devil of iniquity yourself," he told her. "You're a regular Mrs. Captain Kidd, and you've eaten my cheese, and chawed my snowshoe laces, and robbed me of a sock to make your nest. I ought to catch you in a trap, or blow your head off. But I don't. I let you live—and have a fam'ly. And it's you who have given me the Big Idea, Mrs. Captain Kidd. You sure have! You've told me I've got a right to have a nest of my own, and I'm going to have it—an' in that nest is going to be the sweetest, prettiest little angel that God Almighty ever forgot to make into a flower! Yessir. And if the law comes—"

And then, suddenly, the vision clouded, and there came into Jolly Roger's face the look of a man who knew—when he stood the truth out naked—that he was facing a world with his back to the wall.

And now, as the sun went down, and his supper waited—that cloud which came to blot out his picture grew deeper and more sinister, and the chill of it entered his heart. He turned from his table to the open door, and his fingers drew themselves slowly into clenched fists, and he looked out quietly and steadily into his world. The darkening depths of the forest reached out before his eyes, mottled and painted in the fading glory of the sun. It was his world, his everything—father, mother, God. In it he was born, and in it he knew that some day he would die. He loved it, understood it, and night and day, in sunshine and storm, its mighty spirit was the spirit that kept him company. But it held no message for him now. And his ears scarcely heard the raucous scolding of the blue-jay in the fire-tipped crest of the tall black spruce.

And then that something which was bigger than desire came up within him, and forced itself in words between his grimly set lips.

"She's only a—a kid," he said, a fierce, low note of defiance in his voice. "And I—I'm a damned pirate, and there's jails waiting for me, and they'll get me sooner or later, sure as God lets me live!"

He turned from the sun to his shadowing cabin, and for a moment a ghost of a smile played in his face as he heard the little mother- mouse rustling among her papers.

"We can't do it," he said. "We simply can't do it, Mrs. Captain Kidd. She's had hell enough without me taking her into another. And it'd be that, sooner or later. It sure would, Mrs. Captain Kidd. But I'm glad, mighty glad, to think she'd let me kiss her— if I wanted to. Think of that, Mrs. Captain Kidd!—if I wanted to. Oh, Lord!"

And the humor of it crept in alongside the tragedy in Jolly Roger's heart, and he chuckled as he bent over his partridge breasts.

"If I wanted to," he repeated. "Why, if I had a life to give, I'd give it—to kiss her just once! But, as it happens, Mrs. Captain Kidd—"

Jolly Roger's breath cut itself suddenly short, and for an instant he grew tense as he bent over the stove. His philosophy had taught him one thing above all others, that he was a survival of the fittest—only so long as he survived. And he was always guarding against the end. His brain was keen, his ears quick, and every fibre in him trained to its duty of watchfulness. And he knew, without turning his head, that someone was standing in the doorway behind him. There had come a faint noise, a shadowing of the fading sun-glow on the wall, the electrical disturbance of another presence, gazing at him quietly, without motion, and without sound. After that first telegraphic shock of warning he stabbed his fork into a partridge breast, flopped it over, chuckled loudly—and then with a lightning movement was facing the door, his forty-four Colt leveled waist-high at the intruder.

Almost in the same movement his gun-arm dropped limply to his side.

"Well, I'll be—"

He stared. And the face in the doorway stared back at him.

"Nada!" he gasped. "Good Lord, I thought—I thought—" He swallowed as he tried to lie. "I thought—it might be a bear!"

He did not, at first, see that the slim, calico-dressed little figure of Jed Hawkins' foster-girl was almost dripping wet. Her blue eyes were shining at him, wide and startled. Her cheeks were flushed. A strange look had frozen on her parted red lips, and her hair was falling loose in a cloud of curling brown tresses about her shoulders. Jolly Roger, dreaming of her in his insane happiness of a few minutes ago, sensed nothing beyond the beauty and the unexpectedness of her in this first moment. Then—swiftly —he saw the other thing. The last glow of the sun glistened in her wet hair, her dress was sodden and clinging, and little pools of water were widening slowly about her ragged shoes. These things he might have expected, for she had to cross the creek. But it was the look in her eyes that startled him, as she stood there with Peter, the mongrel pup, clasped tightly in her arms.

"Nada, what's happened?" he asked, laying his gun on the table. "You fell in the creek—"

"It—it's Peter," she cried, with a sobbing break in her voice. "We come on Jed Hawkins when he was diggin' up some of his whiskey, and he was mad, and pulled my hair, and Peter bit him— and then he picked up Peter and threw him against a rock—and he's terribly hurt! Oh, Mister Jolly Roger—"

She held out the pup to him, and Peter whimpered as Jolly Roger took his wiry little face between his hands, and then lifted him gently. The girl was sobbing, with passionate little catches in her breath, but there were no tears in her eyes as they turned for an instant from Peter to the gun on the table.

"If I'd had that," she cried, "I'd hev killed him!"

Jolly Roger's face was coldly gray as he knelt down on the floor and bent over

Peter.

"He—pulled your hair, you say?"

"I—forgot," she whispered, close at his shoulder. "I wasn't goin' to tell you that. But it didn't hurt. It was Peter—"

He felt the damp caress of her curls upon his neck as she bent over him.

"Please tell me, Mister Jolly Roger—is he hurt—bad?"

With the tenderness of a woman Jolly Roger worked his fingers over Peter's scrawny little body. And Peter, whimpering softly, felt the infinite consolation of their touch. He was no longer afraid of Jed Hawkins, or of pain, or of death. The soul of a dog is simple in its measurement of blessings, and to Peter it was a great happiness to lie here, broken and in pain, with the face of his beloved mistress over him and Jolly Roger's hands working to mend his hurt. He whimpered when Jolly Roger found the broken place, and he cried out like a little child when there came the sudden quick snapping of a bone—but even then he turned his head so that he could thrust out his hot tongue against the back of his man-friend's hand. And Jolly Roger, as he worked, was giving instructions to the girl, who was quick as a bird to bring him cloth which she tore into bandages, so that at the end of ten minutes Peter's right hind leg was trussed up so tightly that it was as stiff and as useless as a piece of wood.

"His hip was dislocated and his leg-bone broken," said Jolly Roger when he had finished. "He is all right now, and inside of three weeks will be on his feet again."

He lifted Peter gently, and made him a nest among the blankets in his bunk. And then, still with that strange, gray look in his face, he turned to Nada.

She was standing partly facing the door, her eyes straight on him. And Jolly Roger saw in them that wonderful something which had given his storm-beaten soul a glimpse of paradise earlier that day. They were blue, so blue that he had never seen violets like them—and he knew that in her heart there was no guile behind which she could hide the secret they were betraying. A yearning such as had never before come into his life urged him to open his arms to her, and he knew that she would have come into them; but a still mightier will held them tense and throbbing at his side. Her cheeks were aflame as she looked at him, and he told himself that God could not have made a lovelier thing, as she stood there in her worn dress and her ragged shoes, with that light of glory in her face, and her damp hair waving and curling about her in the last light of the day.

"I knew you'd fix him, Mister-Roger," she whispered, a great pride and faith and worship in the low thrill of her voice. "I knew it!"

Something choked Jolly Roger, and he turned to the stove and began spearing the crisp brown potatoes on the end of a fork. And he said, with his back toward her,

"You came just in time for supper, Nada. We'll eat—and then I'll go home with you, as far as the Ridge."

Peter watched them. His pain was gone, and it was nice and comfortable in Jolly Roger's blanket, and with his whiskered face on his fore-paws his bright eyes followed every movement of these two who so completely made up his world. He heard that sweet little laugh which came only now and then from Nada's lips, when for a moment she was happy; he saw her shake out her hair in the glow of the lamp which Jolly Roger lighted, and he observed Jolly Roger standing at the stove—looking at her as she did it—a worship in his face which changed the instant her eyes turned toward him. In Peter's active little brain this gave birth to nothing of definite understanding, except that in it all he sensed happiness, for—somehow—there was always that feeling when they were with Jolly Roger, no matter whether the sun was shining or the day was dark and filled with gloom. Many times in his short life he had seen grief and tears in Nada's face, and had seen her cringe and hide herself at the vile cursing and witch-like voice of the man and woman back in the other cabin. But there was nothing like that in Jolly Roger's company. He had two eyes, and he was not always cursing, and he did not pull Nada's hair—and Peter loved him from the bottom of his soul. And he knew that his mistress loved him, for she had told him so, and there was always a different look in her eyes when she was with Jolly Roger, and it was only then that she laughed in that glad little way—as she was laughing now.

Jolly Roger was seated at the table, and Nada stood behind him, her face flushed joyously at the wonderful privilege of pouring his coffee. And then she sat down, and Jolly Roger gave her the nicest of the partridge breasts, and tried hard to keep his eyes calm and quiet as he looked at the adorable sweetness of her across the table from him. To Nada there was nothing of shame in what lay behind the happiness in the violet radiance of her eyes. Jolly Roger had brought to her the only happiness that had ever come into her life. Next to her God, which Jed Hawkins and his witch-woman had not destroyed within her, she thought of this stranger who for three months had been hiding in Indian Tom's cabin. And, like Peter, she loved him. The innocence of it lay naked in her eyes.

"Nada," said Jolly Roger. "You're seventeen—"

"Goin' on eighteen," she corrected quickly. "I was seventeen two weeks ago!"

The quick, undefined little note of eagerness in her voice made his heart thump. He nodded, and smiled.

"Yes, going on eighteen," he said. "And pretty soon some young fellow will come along, and see you, and marry you—"

"O-o-o-h-h-h!"

It was a little, strange cry that came to her lips, and Jolly Roger saw a quick throbbing in her bare throat. and her eyes were so wide-open and startled as she looked at him that he felt, for a moment, as if the resolution in his soul was giving way.

"Where are you goin', Mister Roger?"

"Me? Oh, I'm not going anywhere—not for a time, at least. But you—you'll surely be going away with some one—some day."

"I won't," she denied hotly. "I hate men! I hate all but you, Mister Jolly Roger. And if you go away—"

"Yes, if I go away—

"I'll kill Jed Hawkins!"

Involuntarily she reached out a slim hand to the big gun on the corner of the table.

"I'll kill 'im, if you go away," she threatened again, "He's broken his wife, and crippled her, and if it wasn't for her I'd have gone long ago. But I've promised, and I'm goin' to stay— until something happens. And if you go—now—"

At the choking throb in her throat and the sudden quiver that came to her lips, Jolly Roger jumped up for the coffee pot, though his cup was still half full.

"I won't go, Nada," he cried, trying to laugh. "I promise—cross my heart and hope to die! I won't go—until you tell me I can."

And then, feeling that something had almost gone wrong for a moment, Peter yipped from his nest in the bunk, and the gladness in Nada's eyes thanked Jolly

Roger for his promise when he came back with the coffee pot. Standing behind her, he made pretense of refilling her cup, though she had scarcely touched it, and all the time his eyes were looking at her beautiful head, and he saw again the dampness in her hair.

"What happened in the creek, Nada?" he asked.

She told him, and at the mention of his name Peter drew his bristling little head erect, and waited expectantly. He could see Jolly Roger's face, now staring and a bit shocked, and then with a quick smile flashing over it; and when Nada had finished, Jolly Roger leaned a little toward her in the lampglow, and said,

"You've got to promise me something, Nada. If Jed Hawkins ever hits you again, or pulls your hair, or even threatens to do it— will you tell me?" Nada hesitated.

"If you don't—I'll take back my promise, and won't stay," he added.

"Then—I'll promise," she said. "If he does it, I'll tell you. But I ain't—I mean I am not afraid, except for Peter. Jed Hawkins will sure kill him if I take him back, Mister Roger. Will you keep him here? And—o-o-o-h!—if I could only stay, too—"

The words came from her in a frightened breath, and in an instant a flood of color rushed like fire into her cheeks. But Jolly Roger turned again to the stove, and made as if he had not seen the blush or heard her last words, so that the shame of her embarrassment was gone as quickly as it had come.

"Yes, I'll keep Peter," he said over his shoulder. And in his heart another voice which she could not hear, was crying, "And I'd give my life if I could keep you!"

Devouring his bits of partridge breast, Peter watched Jolly Roger and Nada out of the corner of his eye as they left the cabin half an hour later. It was dark when they went, and Jolly Roger closed only the mosquito-screen, leaving the door wide open, and Peter could hear their footsteps disappearing slowly into the deep gloom of the forest. It was a little before moonrise, and under the spruce and cedar and thick balsam the world was like a black pit. It was very still, and except for the soft tread of their own feet and the musical ripple of water in the creek there was scarcely a sound in this first hour of the night. In Jolly Roger there rose something of exultation, for Nada's warm little hand lay in his as he guided her through the darkness, and her fingers had clasped themselves tightly round his thumb. She was very close to him when he paused to make sure of the unseen trail, so close that her cheek rested against his arm, and—bending a little—his lips touched the soft ripples of her hair. But he could not see her in the gloom, and his heart pounded fiercely all the way to the ford.

Then he laughed a strange little laugh that was not at all like Jolly Roger.

"I'll try and not let you get wet again, Nada," he said.

Her fingers still held to his thumb, as if she was afraid of losing him there in the blackness that lay about them like a great ink-blotch. And she crept closer to him, saying nothing, and all the power in his soul fought in Jolly Roger to keep him from putting his arms about her slim little body and crying out the worship that was in him.

"I ain't—I mean I'm not afraid of gettin' wet," he heard her whisper then. "You're so big and strong, Mister Roger—"

Gently he freed his thumb from her fingers, and picked her up, and held her high, so that she was against his breast and above the deepest of the water. Lightly at first Nada's arms lay about his shoulders, but as the flood began to rush higher and she felt him straining against it,—her arms tightened, until the clasp of them was warm and thrilling round Jolly Roger's neck. She gave a big gasp of relief when he stood her safely down upon her feet on the other side. And then again she reached out, and found his hand, and twined her fingers about his big thumb—and Jolly Roger went on with her over the plain toward Cragg's Ridge, dripping wet, just as the rim of the moon began to rise over the edge of the eastern forests.

CHAPTER IV

IT seemed an interminable wait to Peter, back in the cabin. Jolly Roger had put out the light, and when the moon came up the glow of it did not come into the dark room where Peter lay, for the open door was to the west, and curtains were drawn closely at both windows. But through the door he could see the first mellowing of the night, and after that the swift coming of a soft, golden radiance which swallowed all darkness and filled his world with the ghostly shadows which seemed alive, yet never made a sound. It was a big, splendid moon this night, and Peter loved the moon, though he had seen it only a few times in his three months of life. It fascinated him more than the sun, for it was always light when the sun came, and he had never seen the sun eat up darkness, as the moon did. Its mystery awed him, but did not frighten. He could not quite understand the strange, still shadows which were always unreal when he nosed into them, and it puzzled him why the birds did not fly about in the moon glow, and sing as they did in the day-time. And something deep in him, many generations older than himself, made his blood run faster when this thing that ate up darkness came creeping through the sky, and he was filled with a yearning to adventure out into the strange glow of it, quietly and stealthily, watching and listening for things he had never seen or heard.

In the gloom of the cabin his eyes remained fixed steadily upon the open door, and for a long time he listened only for the returning footsteps of Jolly Roger and Nada. Twice he made efforts to drag himself to the edge of the bunk, but the movement sent such a cutting pain through him that he did not make a third. And outside, after a time, he heard the Night People rousing themselves. They were very cautious, these Night People, for unlike the creatures of the dawn, waking to greet the sun with song and happiness, most of them were sharp-fanged and long-clawed-rovers and pirates of the great wilderness, ready to kill. And this, too, Peter sensed through the generations of northland dog that was in him. He heard a wolf howl, coming faintly through the night from miles away, and something told him it was not a dog. From nearer came the call of a moose, and that same sense told him he had heard a monster bear which his eyes had never seen. He did not know of the soft-footed, night-eyed creatures of prey—the fox, the lynx, the fisher-cat, the mink and the ermine, nor of the round-eyed, feathered murderers in the tree-tops—yet that same something told him they were out there among the shadows, under the luring glow of the moon. And a thing happened, all at once, to stab the truth home to him. A baby snowshoe rabbit, a third grown, hopped out into the open close to the cabin door, and as it nibbled at the green grass, a gray catapult of claw and feathers shot out of the air, and Peter heard the crying agony of the rabbit as the owl bore it off into the thick spruce tops. Even then—unafraid—Peter wanted to go out into the moon glow!

At last, there was an end to his wait. He heard footsteps, and Jolly Roger came from out of the yellow moon-mist of the night and stopped in front of the door. There he stood, making no sound, and looking into the west, where the sky was ablaze with stars over the tree-tops. There was a glad little yip in Peter's throat, but he choked it back. Jolly Roger was strangely quiet, and Peter could not hear Nada, and as he sniffed, and gulped the lump in his throat, he seemed to catch the breath of something impending in the air. Then Jolly Roger came in, and sat down in darkness near the table, and for a long time Peter kept his eyes fixed on the shadowy blotch of him there in the gloom, and listened to his breathing, until he could stand it no longer, and whined.

The sound stirred Jolly Roger. He got up, struck a match—and then blew the match out, and came and sat down beside Peter, and stroked him with his hand.

"Peter," he said in a low voice, "I guess we've got a job on our hands. You began it today—and I've got to finish it. We're goin' to kill Jed Hawkins!"

Peter snuggled closer.

"Mebby I'm bad, and mebby the law ought to have me," Jolly Roger went on in the darkness, "but until tonight I never made up my mind to kill a man. I'm ready—now. If Jed Hawkins hurts her again we're goin' to kill him! Understand, Pied-Bot?"

He got up, and Peter could hear him undressing. Then he made a nest for Peter on the floor, and stretched himself out in the bunk; and after that, for a long time, there seemed to be something heavier than the gloom of night in the cabin for Peter, and he listened and waited and prayed in his dog way for Nada's return, and wondered why it was that she left him so long. And the Night People held high carnival under the yellow moon, and there was flight and terror and slaughter in the glow of it—and Jolly Roger slept, and the wolf howled nearer, and the creek chortled its incessant song of running water, and in the end Peter's eyes closed, and a red-eyed ermine peeped over the sill into the man- and dog-scented stillness of the outlaw's cabin.

For many days after this first night in the cabin, Peter did not see Nada. There was more rain, and the creek flooded higher, so that each time Jolly Roger went over to Cragg's Ridge he took his life in his hands in fording the stream. Peter saw no one but Jolly Roger, and at the end of the second week he was going about on his mended leg. But there would always be a limp in his gait, and always his right hind-foot would leave a peculiar mark in the trail.

These two weeks of helplessness were an education in Peter's life and were destined to leave their mark upon him always. He learned to know Jolly Roger, not alone from seeing events, but through an intuitive instinct that grew swiftly somewhere in his shrewd head. This instinct, given widest scope in these weeks of helplessness, developed faster than any other in him, until in the end, he could judge Jolly Roger's humor by the sound of his approaching footsteps. Never was there a waking hour in which he was not fighting to comprehend the mystery of the change that had come over his life. He knew that Nada was gone, and each day that passed put her farther away from him, yet he also sensed the fact that Jolly Roger went to her, and when the outlaw returned to the cabin Peter was filled with a yearning hope that Nada was returning with him.

But gradually Peter came to think less about Nada, and more about Jolly Roger, until at last his heart beat with a love for this man which was greater than all other things in his world. And in these days Jolly Roger found in Peter's comradeship and growing understanding a comforting outlet for the things which at times consumed him. Peter saw it all—hours when Jolly Roger's voice and laughter filled the cabin with cheer and happiness, and others when his face was set in grim lines, with that hard, far-away look in his eyes that Peter could never quite make out. It was at such times, when Jolly Roger held a choking grip on the love in his heart, that he told Peter things which he had never revealed to a human soul.

In the dusk of one evening, as he sat wet with the fording of the creek, he said to Peter,

"We ought to go, Peter. We ought to pack up—and go tonight. Because—sometimes I'm afraid of myself, Pied-Bot. I'd kill for her. I'd die for her. I'd give up the whole world, and live in a prison cell—if I could have her with me. And that's dangerous, Peter, because we can't have her. It's impossible, boy. She doesn't guess why I'm here. She doesn't know I've been outlawin' it for years, and that I'm hiding here because the Police would never think of looking for Jolly Roger McKay this close to civilization. If I told her, she would think I was worse than Jed Hawkins, and she wouldn't believe me if I told her I've outlawed with my wits instead of a gun, and that I've never criminally hurt a person in my life. No, she wouldn't believe that, Peter. And she—she cares for me, Pied-Bot. That's the hell of it! And she's got faith in me, and would go with me to the Missioner's tomorrow. I know it. I can see it, feel it, and I—"

His fingers tightened in the loose hide of Peter's neck.

"Peter," he whispered in the thickening darkness. "I believe there's a God, but He's a different sort of God than most people believe in. He lives in the trees out there, in the flowers, in the birds, the sky, in everything—and I hope that God will strike me dead if I do what isn't right with her, Peter! I do. I hope he strikes me dead!"

And that night Peter knew that Jolly Roger tossed about restlessly in his bunk, and slept but little

But the next morning he was singing, and the warm sun flooding over the wilderness was not more cheerful than his voice as he cooked their breakfast. That, to Peter, was the most puzzling thing about this man. With gloom and oppression fastened upon him he would rise up suddenly, and start whistling or singing, and once he said to Peter,

"I take my cue from the sun, Peter Clubfoot. It's always shining, no matter if the clouds are so thick underneath that we can't see it. A laugh never hurts a man, unless he's got a frozen lung."

Jolly Roger did not cross the ford that day.

CHAPTER V

IT was in the third week after his hurt that Peter saw Nada. By that time he could easily follow Jolly Roger as far as the fording-place, and there he would wait, sometimes hours at a stretch, while his comrade and master went over to Cragg's Ridge. But frequently Jolly Roger would not cross, but remained with Peter, and would lie on his back at the edge of a grassy knoll they had found, reading one of the little old-fashioned red books which Peter knew were very precious to him. Often he wondered what was between the faded red covers that was so interesting, and if he could have read he would have seen such titles as "Margaret of Anjou," "History of Napoleon," "History of Peter the Great," "Caesar," "Columbus the Discoverer," and so on through the twenty volumes which Jolly Roger had taken from a wilderness mail two years before, and which he now prized next to his life.

This afternoon, as they lay in the sleepy quiet of June, Jolly Roger answered the questioning inquisitiveness in Peter's face and eyes.

"You see, Pied-Bot, it was this way," he said, beginning a little apologetically. "I was dying for something to read, and I figgered there'd be something on the Mail—newspapers, you know. So I stopped it, and tied up the driver, and found these. And I swear I didn't take anything else—that time. There's twenty of them, and they weigh nine pounds, and in the last two years I've toted them five thousand miles. I wouldn't trade them for my weight in gold, and I'm pretty heavy. I named you after one of them—Peter. I pretty near called you Christopher Columbus. And some day we've got to take these books to the man they were going to, Peter. I've promised myself that. It seems sort of like stealing the soul out of someone. I just borrowed them, that's all. And I've kept the address of the owner, away up on the edge of the Barrens. Some day we're going to make a special trip to take the books home."

Peter, all at once, had become interested in something else, and following the direction of his pointed nose Jolly Roger saw Nada standing quietly on the opposite side of the stream, looking at them. In a moment Peter knew her, and he was trembling in every muscle when Jolly Roger caught him up under his arm, and with a happy laugh plunged through the creek with him. For a good five minutes after that Jolly Roger stood aside watching Peter and Nada, and there was a glisten of dampness in his eyes when he saw the wet on Nada's cheeks, and the whimpering joy of Peter as he caressed her face and hands. Three weeks had been a long time to Peter, but he could see no difference in the little mistress he worshipped. There were still the radiant curls to hide his nose in, the gentle hands, the sweet voice, the warm thrill of her body as she hugged him in her arms. He did not know that she had new shoes and a new dress, and that some of the color had gone from her red lips, and that her cheeks were paler, and that she could no longer hide the old haunted look in her eyes.

But Jolly Roger saw the look, and the growing pallor, and had noted them for two weeks past. And later that afternoon, when Nada returned to Cragg's Ridge, and he re-crossed the stream with Peter, there was a hard and terrible look in his eyes which Peter had caught there more and more frequently of late. And that evening, in the twilight of their cabin, Jolly Roger said,

"It's coming soon, Peter. I'm expecting it. Something is happening which she won't tell us about. She is afraid for me. I know it. But I'm going to find out—soon. And then, Pied-Bot, I think we'll probably kill Jed Hawkins, and hit for the North."

The gloom of foreboding that was in Jolly Roger's voice and words seemed to settle over the cabin for many days after that, and more than ever Peter sensed the thrill and warning of that mysterious something which was impending. He was developing swiftly, in flesh and bone and instinct, and there began to possess him now the beginning of that subtle caution and shrewdness which were to mean so much to him later on. An instinct greater than reason, if it was not reason itself, told him that his master was constantly watching for something which did not come.

And that same instinct, or reason, impinged upon him the fact that it was a thing to be guarded against. He did not go blindly into the mystery of things now. He circumvented them, and came up from behind. Craft and cunning replaced mere curiosity and puppyish egoism. He was quick to learn, and Jolly Roger's word became his law, so that only once or twice was he told a thing, and it became a part of his understanding. While the keen, shrewd brain of his Airedale father developed inside Peter's head, the flesh and blood development of his big, gentle, soft-footed Mackenzie hound mother kept pace in his body. His legs and feet began to lose their grotesqueness. Flesh began to cover the knots in his tail. His head, bristling fiercely with wiry whiskers, seemed to pause for a space to give his lanky body a chance to catch up with it. And in spite of his big feet, so clumsy that a few weeks ago they had stumbled over everything in his way, he could now travel without making a sound.

So it came to pass, after a time, that when Peter heard footsteps approaching the cabin he made no effort to reveal himself until he knew it was Jolly Roger who was coming. And this was strangely in spite of the fact that in the five weeks since Nada had brought him from Cragg's Ridge no one but Jolly Roger and Nada had set foot within sight of the shack. It was an inborn caution, growing stronger in him each day. There came one early evening when Peter made a discovery. He had returned with Jolly Roger from a fishing trip farther down the creek, and scarcely had he set nose to the little clearing about the cabin when he caught the presence of a strange scent. He investigated it swiftly, and found it all about the cabin, and very strong close up against the cabin door. There were no doubts in Peter's mind. A man had been there, and this man had gone around and around the cabin, and had opened the door, and had even gone inside, for Peter found the scent of him on the floor. He tried, in a way, to tell Jolly Roger. He bristled, and whined, and looked searchingly into the darkening edge of the forest. Jolly Roger quested with him for a few moments, and when he failed to find marks in the ground he began cleaning a fish for supper, and said.

"Probably a wolverine, Pied-Bot. The rascal came to see what he could find while we were away."

But Peter was not satisfied. He was restless all that night. Sounds which had been familiar now held a new significance for him. The next day he was filled with a quiet but brooding expectancy. He resented the intrustion of the strange footprints. It was, in his process of instinctive reasoning, an encroachment upon the property rights of his master, and he was—true to the law of his species—the guardian of those rights.

The fourth evening after the stranger's visit to the cabin Jolly Roger was later than usual in returning from Cragg's Ridge. Peter had been on a hunting adventure of his own, and came to the cabin at sunset. But he never came out of cover now without standing quietly for a few moments, getting the wind, and listening. And tonight, poking his head between some balsams twenty yards from the shack, he was treated to a sudden thrill. The cabin door was open. And standing close to this door, looking quietly and cautiously about, stood a stranger. He was not like Jed Hawkins, was Peter's first impression. He was tall, with a wide-brimmed hat, and wore boots with striped trousers tucked into them, and on his coat were bits of metal which caught the last gleams of the sun. Peter knew nothing of the Royal Northwest Mounted Police. But he sensed danger, and he remained very quiet, without moving a muscle of his head or body, while the stranger looked about, with a hand on his unbuttoned pistol holster. Not until he entered the cabin, and closed the door after him, did Peter move back into the deeper gloom of the forest. And then, silent as a fox, he skulked through cover to the foot-trail, and down the trail to the ford, across which Jolly Roger would come from Cragg's Ridge.

There was still half an hour of daylight when Jolly Roger arrived. Peter did not, as usual, run to the edge of the bank to meet him. He remained sitting stolidly on his haunches, with his ears flattened, and in his whole attitude no sign of gladness at his master's coming. With every instinct of caution developed to the highest degree within him, Jolly Roger was lightning quick to observe the significance of small things. He spoke to Peter, caressed him with his hand, and moved on along the foot-trail toward the cabin. Peter fell in behind him moodily, and after a few moments stopped, and squatted on his haunches again. Jolly Roger was puzzled.

"What is it, Peter?" he asked. "Are you afraid of that wolverine— "

Peter whined softly; but even as he whined, his ears were flat, and his eyes filled with a red light as they glared down the trail beyond the outlaw. Jolly Roger turned and went on, until he disappeared around a twist in the path. There he stopped, and peered back. Peter was not following him, but still sat where he had left him. A quicker breath came to Jolly Roger's lips, and he went back to Peter. For fully a minute he stood beside him, watching and listening, and not once did the reddish glare in Peter's eyes leave the direction of the cabin. Jolly Roger's eyes had grown very bright, and suddenly he dropped on his knees beside Peter, and spoke softly, close up to his flattened ear.

"You say it isn't a wolverine, Peter? Is that what you're trying to tell me?"

Peter's teeth clicked, and he whimpered, never taking his eyes from ahead.

There was a cold light in Jolly Roger's eyes as he rose to his feet, and he turned swiftly and quietly into the edge of the forest, and in the gloom that was gathering there his hand carried the big automatic. Peter followed him now, and Jolly Roger swung in a wide circle, so that they came up on that forest side of the cabin where there was no window. And here Jolly Roger knelt down beside Peter again, and whispered to him.

"You stay here, Pied-Bot. Understand? You stay here."

He pressed him down gently with his hand, so that Peter understood. Then, slinking low, and swift as a cat, Jolly Roger ran to the end of the cabin where there was no window. With his head close to the ground he peered out cautiously at the door. It was closed. Then he looked at the windows. To the west the curtains were up, as he had left them. And to the east—

A whimsical smile played at the corners of his mouth. Those curtains he had kept tightly drawn. One of them was down now. But the other was raised two inches, so that one hidden within the cabin could watch the approach from the trail!

He drew back, and under his breath he chuckled. He recognized the sheer nerve of the thing, the clever handiwork of it. Someone was inside the cabin, and he was ready to stake his life it was Cassidy, the Irish bloodhound of "M" Division. If anyone ferreted him out way down here on the edge of civilization he had gambled with himself that it would be Cassidy. And Cassidy had come— Cassidy, who had hung like a wolf to his trails for three years, who had chased him across the Barren Lands, who had followed him up the Mackenzie, and back again—who had fought with him, and starved with him, and froze with him, yet had never brought him to prison. Deep down in his heart Jolly Roger loved Cassidy. They had played, and were still playing, a thrilling game, and to win that game had become the life's ambition of each. And now Cassidy was in there, confident that at last he had his man, and waiting for him to step into the trap.

To Jolly Roger, in the face of its possible tragedy, there was a deep-seated humor in the situation. Three times in the last year and a half had he turned the tables on Cassidy, leaving him floundering in the cleverly woven webs which the man-hunter had placed for his victim. This was the fourth time. And Cassidy would be tremendously upset!

Praying that Peter would remain quiet, Jolly Roger took off his shoes. After that he made no more sound than a ferret as he crept to the door. An inch at a time he raised himself, until he was standing up, with his ear half an inch from the crack that ran lengthwise of the frame. Holding his breath, he listened. For an interminable time, it seemed to him, there was no sound from within. He guessed what Cassidy was doing—peering through that slit of window under the curtain. But he was not absolutely sure. And he knew the necessity of making no error, with Cassidy in there, gripping the butt of his gun.

Suddenly he heard a movement. A man's steps, subdued and yet distinct, were moving from the window toward the door. Half way they paused, and turned to one of the windows looking westward. But it was evident the watcher was not expecting his game from that direction, for after a moment's silence he returned to the window through which he could see the trail. This time Jolly Roger was sure. Cassidy was again peering through the window, with his back toward him, and every muscle in the forest rover's body gathered for instant action. In another moment he had flung open the door, and the watcher at the window whirled about to find himself looking straight into the muzzle of Jolly Roger's gun.

For several minutes after that last swift movement of Jolly Roger's, Peter lay where his master had left him, his eyes fairly popping from his head in his eagerness to see what was happening. He heard voices, and then the wild thrill of Jolly Roger's laughter, and restraining himself no longer he trotted cautiously to the open door of the cabin. In a chair sat the stranger with the broad-brimmed hat and high boots, with his hands securely tied behind him. And Jolly Roger was hustling about, filling a shoulder-pack in the last light of the day.

"Cassidy, I oughta kill you," Jolly Roger was saying as he worked, an exultant chuckle in his voice. "You don't give me any peace. No matter where I go you're sure to come, and I can't remember that I ever invited you. I oughta put you out of the way, and plant flowers over you, now that I've got the chance. But I'm too chicken-hearted. Besides, I like you. By the time you get tired of chasing me you should be a pretty good man-hunter. But just now you lack finesse, Cassidy—you lack finesse. "And Jolly Roger's chuckle broke into another laugh.

Cassidy heaved out a grunt.

"It's luck—just damned luck!" he growled.

"If it is, I hope it keeps up," said Jolly Roger. "Now, look here, Cassidy! Let's make a man's bet of it. If you don't get me next time—if you fail, and I turn the trick on you once more—will you quit?"

Cassidy's eyes gleamed in the thickening dusk.

"If I don't get you next time—I'll hand in my resignation!"

The laughter went out of Jolly Roger's voice.

"I believe you, Cassidy. You've played square—always. And now—if I free your hands—will you swear to give me a two hours' start before you leave this cabin?"

"I'll give you the start," said Cassidy.

His lean face was growing indistinct in the gloom.

Jolly Roger came up behind him. There was the slash of a knife. Then he picked up his shoulder-pack. At the door he paused.

"Look at your watch when I'm gone, Cassidy, and be sure you make it a full two hours."

"I'll make it two hours and five minutes," said Cassidy. "Hittin' north are you, Jolly Roger?"

"I'm hittin'—bushward," replied the outlaw. "I'm going where it's plenty thick and hard to travel, Cassidy. Goodby—"

He was gone. He hit straight north, making noise as he went, but once in the timber he swung southward, and plunged through the creek with Peter under his arm. Not until they had traveled a good half mile over the plain did Jolly Roger speak. Then he said, speaking directly at Peter,

"Cassidy thinks I'll sure hit for the North country again, Pied- Bot. But we're foolin' him. I've sort of planned on something like this happening, and right now we're hittin' for the tail-end of Cragg's Ridge where there's a mess of rock that the devil himself can hardly get into. We've got to do it, boy. We can't leave the girl—just now. We can't leave—her—"

Jolly Roger's voice choked. Then he paused for a moment, and bent over to put his hand on Peter.

"If it hadn't been for you, Peter—Cassidy would have got me— sure. And I'm wondering, Peter—I'm wondering—why did God forget to give a dog speech?"

Peter whined in answer, and through the darkness of the night they went on together.

CHAPTER VI

A frosty mist dulled the light of the stars, but this cleared away as Jolly Roger and Peter crossed the plain between the creek and Cragg's Ridge. They did not hurry, for McKay had faith in Cassidy's word. He knew the red-headed man-hunter would not break his promise—he would wait the full two hours in Indian Tom's cabin, and another five minutes after that. In Jolly Roger, as the minutes passed, exultation at his achievement died away, and there filled him again the old loneliness—the loneliness which called out against the fate which had made of Cassidy an enemy instead of a friend. And yet—what an enemy!

He reached down, and touched Peter's bushy head with his hand.

"Why didn't the Law give another man the assignment to run us down," he protested. "Someone we could have hated, and who would have hated us! Why did they send Cassidy—the fairest and squarest man that ever wore red? We can't do him a dirty turn—we can't hurt him, Pied-Bot, even at the worst. And if ever he takes us in to Headquarters, and looks at us through the bars, I feel it's going to be like a knife in his heart. But he'll do it, Peter, if he can. It's his job. And he's honest. We've got to say that of Cassidy."

The Ridge loomed up at the edge of the level plain, and for a few moments Jolly Roger paused, while he looked off through the eastward gloom. A mile in that direction, beyond the cleft that ran like a great furrow through the Ridge, was Jed Hawkins' cabin, still and dark under the faint glow of the stars. And in that cabin was Nada. He felt that she was sitting at her little window, looking out into the night, thinking of him—and a great desire gripped at his heart, tugging him in its direction. But he turned toward the west.

"We can't let her know what has happened, boy," he said, feeling the urge of caution. "For a little while we must let her think we have left the country. If Cassidy sees her, and talks with her, something in those blue-flower eyes of hers might give us away if she knew we were hiding up among the rocks of the Stew-Kettle. But I'm hopin' God A'mighty won't let her see Cassidy. And I'm thinking He won't, Pied-Bot, because I've a pretty good hunch He wants us to settle with Jed Hawkins before we go."

It was a habit of his years of aloneness, this talking to a creature that could make no answer. But even in the darkness he sensed the understanding of Peter.

Rocks grew thicker and heavier under their feet, and they went more slowly, and occasionally stumbled in the gloom. But, after a fashion, they knew their way even in darkness. More than once Peter had wondered why his master had so carefully explored this useless mass of upheaved rock at the end of Cragg's Ridge. They had never seen an animal or a blade of grass in all its gray, sun- blasted sterility. It was like a hostile thing, overhung with a half-dead, slow-beating something that was like the dying pulse of an evil thing. And now darkness added to its mystery and its unfriendliness as Peter nosed close at his master's heels. Up and up they picked their way, over and between ragged upheavals of rock, twisting into this broken path and that, feeling their way, partly sensing it, and always ascending toward the stars. Roger McKay did not speak again to Peter. Each time he came out where the sky was clear he looked toward the solitary dark pinnacle, far up and ahead, strangely resembling a giant tombstone in the star- glow, that was their guide. And after many minutes of strange climbing, in which it seemed to Jolly Roger the nail-heads in the soles of his boots made weirdly loud noises on the rocks, they came near to the top.

There they stopped, and in a deeply shadowed place where there was a carpet of soft sand, with walls of rock close on either side, Jolly Roger spread out his blankets. Then he went out from the black shadow, so that a million stars seemed not far away over their heads. Here he sat down, and began to smoke, thinking of what tomorrow would hold for him, and of the many days destined to follow that tomorrow. Nowhere in the world was there to be—for him—the peace of an absolute certainty. Not until he felt the cold steel of iron bars with his two hands, and the fatal game had been played to the end.

There was no corrosive bitterness of the vengeful in Jolly Roger's heart. For that reason even his enemies, the Police, had fallen into the habit of using the nickname which the wilderness people had given him. He did not hate these police. Curiously, he loved them. Their type was to him the living flesh and blood of the finest manhood since the Crusaders. And he did not hate the law. At times the Law, as personified in all of its unswerving majesty, amused him. It was so terribly serious over such trivial things— like himself, for instance. It could not seem to sleep or rest until a man was hanged, or snugly put behind hard steel, no matter how well that man loved his human-kind—and the world. And Jolly Roger loved both. In his heart he believed he had not committed a crime by achieving justice where otherwise there would have been no justice. Yet outwardly he cursed himself for a lawbreaker. And he loved life. He loved the stars silently glowing down at him tonight. He loved even the gray, lifeless rock, which recalled to his imaginative genius the terrific and interesting life that had once existed—he loved the ghostly majesty of the grave-like pinnacle that rose above him, and beyond that he loved all the world.

But most of all, more than his own life or all that a thousand lives might hold for him, he loved the violet-eyed girl who had come into his life from the desolation and unhappiness of Jed Hawkins' cabin.

Forgetting the law, forgetting all but her, he went at last into the dungeon-like gloom between the rocks, and after Peter had wallowed himself a bed in the carpet of sand they fell asleep.

They awoke with the dawn. But for three days thereafter they went forth only at night, and for three days did not show themselves above the barricade of rocks. The Stew-Kettle was what Jolly Roger had called it, and when the sun was straight above, or descending with the last half of the day, the name fitted.

It was a hot place, so hot that at a distance its piled-up masses of white rock seemed to simmer and broil in the blazing heat of the July sun. Neither man nor beast would look into the heart of it, Jolly Roger had assured Peter, unless the one was half-witted and the other a fool. Looking at it from the meadowy green plain that lay between the Ridge and the forest their temporary retreat was anything but a temptation to the eye. Something had happened there a few thousand centuries before, and in a moment of evident spleen and vexation the earth had vomited up that pile of rock debris, and Jolly Roger good humoredly told himself and Peter that it was an act of Providence especially intended for them, though planned and erupted some years before they were born.

The third afternoon of their hiding, Jolly Roger decided upon action.

This afternoon all of the caloric guns of an unclouded sun had seemed to concentrate themselves on the gigantic rock-pile. Though it was now almost sunset, a swirling and dizzying incandescence still hovered about it. The huge masses of stone were like baked things to the touch of hand and foot, and one breathed a smoldering air in between their gray and white walls.

Thus forbidding looked the Stew-Kettle, when viewed from the plain. But from the top-most crag of the mass, which rose a hundred feet high at the end of the Ridge, one might find his reward for a blistering climb. On all sides, a paradise of green and yellow and gold, stretched the vast wilderness, studded with shimmering lakes that gleamed here and there from out of their rich dark frames of spruce and cedar and balsam. And half way between the edge of the plain and this highest pinnacle of rock, utterly hidden from the eyes of both man and beast, nestled the hiding place which Jolly Roger and Peter had found.

It was a cool and cavernous spot, in spite of the Sahara-like heat of the great pile. In the very heart of it two gigantic masses of rock had put their shoulders together, like Gog and Magog, so that under their ten thousand tons of weight was a crypt-like tunnel as high as a man's head, into which the light and the glare of the sun never came.

Peter, now that he had grown accustomed to the deadness of it, liked this change from Indian Tom's cabin. He liked his wallow of soft sand during the day, and he liked still more the aloneness and the aloofness of their ramparted stronghold when the cool of evening came. He did not, of course, understand just what their escape from Cassidy had meant, but instinct was shrewdly at work within him, and no wolf could have guarded the place more carefully than he. And he had all creation in mind when he guarded the rock-pile.

All but Nada. Many times he whimpered for her, just as the great call for her was in Jolly Roger's own heart. And on this third afternoon, as the hot July sun dipped half way to the western forests, both Peter and his master were looking yearningly, and with the same thought, toward the east, where over the back-bone of Cragg's Ridge Jed Hawkins' cabin lay.

"We'll let her know tonight," Roger McKay said at last, with something very slow and deliberate in his voice. "We'll take the chance—and let her know."

Peter's bristling Airedale whiskers, standing out like a bunch of broom splints about his face, quivered sympathetically, and he thumped his tail in the sand. He was an artful hypocrite, was Peter, because he always looked as if he understood, whether he did or not. And Jolly Roger, staring at the gray rock-backs outside their tunnel door, went on.

"We must play square with her, Pied-Bot, and it's a crime worse than murder not to let her know the truth. If she wasn't a kid, Peter! But she's that—just a kid—the sweetest, purest thing God A'mighty ever made, and it isn't fair to live this lie any longer, no matter how we love her. And we do love her, Peter."

Peter lay very quiet, watching the strange gray look that had settled in Jolly Roger's face.

"I've got to tell her that I'm a damned highwayman," he added, in a moment. "And she won't understand, Peter. She can't. But I'm going to do it. I'm going to tell her—today. And then—I think we'll be hittin' north pretty soon, Pied-Bot. If it wasn't for Jed Hawkins—" He rose up out of the sand, his hands clenched.

"We ought to kill Jed Hawkins before we go. It would be safer for her," he finished.

He went out, forgetting Peter, and climbed a rock-splintered path until he stood on the knob of a mighty boulder, looking off into the northern wilderness. Off there, a hundred, five hundred, a thousand miles—was home. It was ALL his home, from Hudson's Bay to the Rockies, from the Height of Land to the Arctic plains, and in it he had lived the thrill of life according to his own peculiar code. He knew that he had loved life as few had ever loved it. He had worshipped the sun and the moon and the stars. The world had been a glorious place in which to live, in spite of its ceaseless peril for him.

But there was nothing of cheer left in his heart now as he stood in the blaze of the setting sun. Paradise had come to him for a little while, and because of it he had lived a lie. He had not told Jed Hawkins' foster-girl that he was an outlaw, and that he had come to the edge of civilization because he thought it was the last place the

Royal Mounted would look for him. When he went to her this evening it would probably be for the last time. He would tell her the truth. He would tell her the police were after him from one end of the Canadian northland to the other. And that same night, with Peter, he would hit the trail for the Barren Lands, a thousand miles away. He was sure of himself now—sure—even as the dark wall of the forest across the plain faded out, and gave place to a pale, girlish face with eyes blue as flowers, and brown curls filled with the lustre of the sun—a face that had taken the place of mother, sister and God deep down in his soul. Yes, he was sure of himself—even with that face rising lo give battle to his last great test of honor. He was an outlaw, and the police wanted him, but—

Peter was troubled by the grimness that settled in his master's face. They waited for dusk, and when deep shadows had gathered in the valley McKay led the way out of the rock-pile.

An hour later they came cautiously through the darkness that lay between the broken shoulders of Cragg's Ridge. There was a light in the cabin, but Nada's window was dark. Peter crouched down under the warning pressure of McKay's hand.

"I'll go on alone," he said. "You stay here."

It seemed a long time that he waited in the darkness. He could not hear the low tap, tap, tap of his master's fingers against the glass of Nada's darkened window. And Jolly Roger, in response to that signal-tapping, heard nothing from within, except a monotone of voice that came from the outer room. For half an hour he waited, repeating the signals at intervals. At last a door opened, and Nada stood silhouetted against the light of the room beyond.

McKay tapped again, very lightly, and the door closed quickly behind the girl. In a moment she was at the window, which was raised a little from the bottom.

"Mister—Roger—" she whispered. "Is it—YOU?"

"Yes," he said, finding a little hand in the darkness. "It's me."

The hand was cold, and its fingers clung tightly to his, as if the girl was frightened. Peter, restless with waiting, had come up quietly in the dark, and he heard the low, trembling whisper of Nada's voice at the window. There was something in the note of it, and in the caution of Jolly Roger's reply, that held him stiff and attentive, his ears wide-open for approaching sound. For several minutes he stood thus, and then the whispering voices at the window ceased and he heard his master retreating very quietly through the night. When Jolly Roger spoke to him, back under the broken shoulder of the ridge, he did not know that Peter had stood near the window.

McKay stood looking back at the pale glow of light in the cabin.

"Something happened there tonight—something she wouldn't tell me about," he said, speaking half to Peter and half to himself. "I could FEEL it. I wish I could have seen her face."

He set out over the plain; and then, as if remembering that he must explain the matter to Peter, he said:

"She can't get out tonight, Pied-Bot, but she'll come to us in the jackpines tomorrow afternoon. We'll have to wait"

He tried to say the thing cheerfully, but between this night and tomorrow afternoon seemed an interminable time, now that he was determined to make a clean breast of his affairs to Nada, and leave the country. Most of that night he walked in the coolness of the moonlit plain, and for a long time he sat amid the flower- scented shadows of the trysting-place in the heart of the jackpine clump, where Nada had a hidden place all her own. It was here that Peter discovered something which Jolly Roger could not see in the deep shadows, a bundle warm and soft and sweet with the presence of Nada herself. It was hidden under a clump of young banksians, very carefully hidden, and tucked about with grass and evergreen boughs. When McKay left the jackpines he wondered why it was that Peter showed no inclination to follow him until he was urged.

They did not return to the Stew-Kettle until dawn, and most of that day Jolly Roger spent in sleep between the two big rocks. It was late afternoon when they made their last meal. In this farewell hour McKay climbed up close to the pinnacle, where he smoked his pipe and measured the shadows of the declining sun until it was time to leave for the jackpines.

Retracing his steps to the hiding place under Gog and Magog he looked for Peter. But Peter's sand-wallow was empty, and Peter was gone.

CHAPTER VII

PETER was on his way to the mystery of the bundle he had found in the jackpines.

At the foot of the ridge, where the green plain fought with the blighting edge of the Stew-Kettle, he stood for many minutes before he started eastward. With keen eyes gleaming behind his mop of scraggly face-bristles he critically surveyed both land and air, and then, with the slight limp in his gait which would always remain as a mark of Jed Hawkins' brutality, he trotted deliberately in the direction of the whiskey-runner's cabin home.

A bitter memory of Jed Hawkins flattened his ears when he came near the rock-cluttered coulee in which he had fought for Nada, and had suffered his broken bones, and today—even as he obeyed the instinctive caution to stop and listen—Jed Hawkins himself came out of the mouth of the coulee, bearing a brown jug in one hand and a thick cudgel in the other. His one wicked eye gleamed in the waning sun. His lean and scraggly face was alight with a sinister exultation as he paused for a moment close to the rock behind which Peter was hidden, and Peter's fangs lay bare and his body trembled while the man stood there. Then he moved on, and Peter did not stir, but waited until the jug and the cudgel and the man were out of sight.

Low under his breath he was snarling when he went on. Hatred, for a moment, had flamed hot in his soul. Then he turned, and buried himself in a clump of balsams that reached out into the plain, and a few moments later came to the edge of a tiny meadow in the heart of them, where a warbler was bursting its throat in evening-song.

Around the edge of the meadow Peter circled, his feet deep in buttercups and red fire-flowers, and crushing softly ripe strawberries that grew in scarlet profusion in the open, until he came to a screen of young jackpines, and through these he quietly and apologetically nosed his way. Then he stood wagging his tail, with Nada sitting on the grass half a dozen steps from him, wiping the strawberry stain from her finger-tips. And the stain was on her red lips, and a bit of it against the flush of her cheek, as she gave a little cry of gladness and greeting to Peter. Her eyes flashed beyond him, and every drop of blood in her slim, beautiful little body seemed to be throbbing with an excitement new to Peter as she looked for Jolly Roger.

Peter went to her, and dropped down, with his head in her lap, and looking up through his bushy eye-brows he saw a livid bruise just under the ripples of her brown hair, where there had been no mark yesterday, or the day before. Nada's hands drew him closer, until he was half in her lap, and she bent her face down to him, so that her thick, shining hair fell all about him. Peter loved her hair, almost as much as Jolly Roger loved it, and he closed his eyes and drew a deep breath of content as the smothering sweetness of it shut out the sunlight from him.

"Peter," she whispered, "I'm almost scared to have him come today. I've promised him. You remember—I promised to tell him if Jed Hawkins struck me again. And he has! He made that mark, and if Jolly Roger knows it he'll kill him. I've got to lie—lie—"

Peter wriggled, to show his interest, and his hard tail thumped the ground. For a space Nada said nothing more, and he could hear and feel the beating of her heart close down against him. Then she raised her head, and looked in the direction from which she would first hear Jolly Roger as he came through the young jack-pines. Peter, with his eyes half closed in a vast contentment, did not see or sense the change in her today—that her blue eyes were brighter, her cheeks flushed, and in her body a strange and subdued throbbing that had never been there before. Not even to Peter did she whisper her secret, but waited and listened for Jolly Roger, and when at last she heard him and he came through the screen of jackpines, the color in her cheeks was like the stain of strawberries crimsoning her finger-tips. In an instant, looking down upon her, Jolly Roger saw what Peter had not discovered, and he stopped in his tracks, his heart thumping like a hammer inside him. Never, even in his dreams, had the girl looked lovelier than she did now, and never had her eyes met his eyes as they met them today, and never had her red lips said as much to him, without uttering a word. In the same instant he saw the livid bruise, half hidden under her hair—and then he saw a big bundle behind her, partly screened by a dwarfed banksian. After that his eyes went back to the bruise.

"Jed Hawkins didn't do it," said Nada, knowing what was in his mind. "It was Jed's woman. And you can't kill her!" she added a little defiantly.

Jolly Roger caught the choking throb in her throat, and he knew she was lying. But Nada thrust Peter from her lap, and stood up, and she seemed taller and more like a woman than ever before in her life as she faced Jolly Roger there in the tiny open, with violets and buttercups and red strawberries in the soft grass under their feet. And behind them, and very near, a rival to the warbler in the meadow began singing. But Nada did not hear. The color had rushed hot into her cheeks at first, but now it was fading out as swiftly, and her hands trembled, clasped in front of her. But the blue in her eyes was as steady as the blue in the sky as she looked at Jolly Roger.

"I'm not going back to Jed Hawkins' any more, Mister Roger," she said.

A soft breath of wind lifted the tress of hair from her forehead, revealing more clearly the mark of Jed Hawkins' brutality, and Nada saw gathering in Jolly Roger's eyes that cold, steely glitter which always frightened her when it came. His hands clenched, and when she reached out and touched his arm the flesh of it was as hard as white birch. Even in her fear there was glory in the thought that at a word from her he would kill the man who had struck her. Her fingers crept up his arm, timidly, and the blue in her eyes darkened, and there was a pleading tremble in the curve of her lips as she looked straight at him.

"I'm not going back," she repeated.

Jolly Roger, looking beyond her, saw the significance of the bundle. His eyes met her steady gaze again, and his heart seemed to swell in his chest, and choke him. He tried to let his tense muscles relax. He tried to smile. He struggled to bring up the courage which would make possible the confession he had to make. And Peter, sitting on his haunches in a patch of violets, watched them both, wondering what was going to happen between these two.

"Where are you going?" Jolly Roger asked.

Nada's fingers had crept almost to his shoulder. They were twisting at his flannel shirt nervously, but not for the tenth part of a second did she drop her eyes, and that strange, wonderful something which he saw looking at him so clearly out of her soul brought the truth to Jolly Roger, before she had spoken.

"I'm goin' with you and Peter."

The low cry that came from Jolly Roger was almost a sob as he stepped back from her. He looked away from her—at Peter. But her pale face, her parted red lips, her wide-open, wonderful eyes, her radiant hair stirred by the wind—came between them. She was no longer the little girl—"past seventeen, goin' on eighteen." To Jolly Roger she was all that the world held of glorious womanhood.

"But—you can't!" he cried desperately. "I've come to tell you things, Nada. I'm not fit. I'm not what you think I am. I've been livin' a lie—"

He hesitated, and then lashed himself on to the truth.

"You'll hate me when I tell you, Nada. You think Jed Hawkins is bad. But the law thinks I'm worse. The police want me. They've wanted me for years. That's why I came down here, and hid over in Indian Tom's cabin—near where I first met you. I thought they wouldn't find me away down here, but they did. That's why Peter and I moved over to the big rock-pile at the end of the Ridge. I'm—an outlaw. I've done a lot of bad things—in the eyes of the law, and I'll probably die with a bullet in me, or in jail. I'm sorry, but that don't help. I'd give my life to be able to tell you what's in my heart. But I can't. It wouldn't be square."

He wondered why no change came into the steady blue of her eyes as he went on with the truth. The pallor was gone from her cheeks. Her lips seemed redder, and what he was saying did not seem to startle her, or frighten her.

"Don't you understand, Nada?" he cried. "I'm bad. The police want me. I'm a fugitive—always running away, always hiding—an outlaw—"

She nodded.

"I know it, Mister Roger," she said quietly. "I heard you tell Peter that a long time ago. And Mister Cassidy was at our place the day after you and Peter ran away from Indian Tom's cabin, and I showed him the way to Father John's, and he told me a lot about you, and he told Father John a lot more, and it made me awful proud of you, Mister Roger—and I want to go with you and Peter!"

"Proud!" gasped Jolly Roger. "Proud, of ME—"

She nodded again.

"Mister Cassidy—the policeman—he used just the word you used a minute ago. He said you was square, even when you robbed other people. He said he had to get you in jail if he could, but he hoped he never would. He said he'd like to have a man like you for a brother. And Peter loves you. And I—"

The color came into her white face.

"I'm goin' with you and Peter," she finished.

Something came to relieve the tenseness of the moment for Jolly Roger. Peter, nosing in a thick patch of bunch-grass, put out a huge snowshoe rabbit, and the two crashed in a startling avalanche through the young jackpines, Peter's still puppyish voice yelling in a high staccato as he pursued. Jolly Roger turned from Nada, and stared where they had gone. But he was seeing nothing. He knew the hour of his mightiest fight had come. In the reckless years of his adventuring he had more than once faced death. He had starved. He had frozen. He had run the deadliest gantlets of the elements, of beast, and of man. Yet was the strife in him now the greatest of all his life. His heart thumped. His brain was swirling in a vague and chaotic struggle for the mastery of things, and as he fought with himself—his unseeing eyes fixed on the spot where Peter and the snowshoe rabbit had disappeared—he heard Nada's voice behind him, saying again that she was going with him and Peter. In those seconds he felt himself giving way, and the determined action he had built up for himself began to crumble like sand. He had made his confession and in spite of it this young girl he worshipped—sweeter and purer than the flowers of the forest—was urging herself upon him! And his soul cried out for him to turn about, and open his arms to her, and gather her into them for as long as God saw fit to give him freedom and life.

But still he fought against that mighty urge, dragging reason and right back fragment by fragment, while Nada stood behind him, her wide-open, childishly beautiful eyes beginning to comprehend the struggle that was disrupting the heart of this man who was an outlaw—and her god among men. And when Jolly Roger turned, his face had aged to the grayness of stone, and his eyes were dull, and there was a terribly dead note in his voice.

"You can't go with us," he said. "You can't. It's wrong—all wrong. I couldn't take care of you in jail, and some day—that's where I'll be."

More than once when she had spoken of Jed Hawkins he had seen the swift flash of lightning come into the violet of her eyes. And it came now, and her little hands grew tight at her sides, and bright spots burned in her cheeks.

"You won't!" she cried. "I won't let you go to jail. I'll fight for you—if you'll let me go with you and Peter!"

She came a step nearer.

"And if I stay here Jed Hawkins is goin' to sell me to a tie- cutter over on the railroad. That's what it is—sellin' me. I ain't—I mean I haven't—told you before, because I was afraid of what you'd do. But it's goin' to happen, unless you let me go with you and Peter. Oh, Mister Roger—Mister Jolly Roger—"

Her fingers crept up his arms. They reached his shoulders, and her blue eyes, and her red lips, and the woman's soul in her girl-body were so close to him he could feel their sweetness and thrill, and then he saw a slow-gathering mist, and tears—

"I'll go wherever you go," she was whispering, "And we'll hide where they won't ever find us, and I'll be happy, so happy, Mister Roger—and if you won't take me I want to die. Oh—"

She was crying, with her head on his breast, and her slim, half bare arms around his neck, and Jolly Roger listened like a miser to the choking words that came with her sobs. And where there had been tumult and indecision in his heart there came suddenly the clearness of sunshine and joy, and with it the happiness of a new and mighty possession as his arms closed about her, and he turned her face up, so that for the first time he kissed the soft red lips that for some inscrutable reason the God of all things had given into his keeping this day.

And then, holding her close, with her arms still tighter about his neck, he cried softly,

"I'm goin' to take you, little girl. You're goin' with Peter and me, for ever—and ever. And we'll go—tonight!"

When Peter came back, just in the last sunset glow of the evening, he found his master alone in the bit of jackpine opening, and Nada was swiftly crossing the larger meadow that lay between them and the break in Cragg's Ridge, beyond which was Jed Hawkins' cabin. It was not the same Jolly Roger whom he had left half an hour before. It was not the man of the hiding-place in the rock-pile. Jolly Roger McKay, standing there in the last soft glow of the day, was no longer the fugitive and the outcast. He stood with silent lips, yet his soul was crying out its gratitude to all that God of Life which breathed its sweetness of summer evening about him. He was the First Possessor of the earth. In that hour, that moment, he would not have sold his place for all the happiness of all the remaining people in the world. He cried out aloud, and Peter, squatted at his feet with his red tongue lolling out, listened to him.

"She is mine, mine, mine," he was saying, and he repeated that word over and over, until Peter quirked his ears, and wondered what it meant. And then, seeing Peter, Jolly Roger laughed softly, and bent over him, with a look of awe and wonderment mingling with the happiness in his face.

"She's mine—ours," he cried boyishly. "God A'mighty took a hand, Pied-Bot, and she's going with us! We're going tonight, when the moon comes up. And Peter—Peter—we're going straight to the Missioner's, and he'll marry us, and then we'll hit for a place where no one in the world will ever find us. The law may want us, Pied-Bot, but God—this God all around—is good to us. And we'll try and pay Him back. We will, Peter!"

He straightened himself, and faced the west. Then he picked up the bundle Nada had brought, and dived through the jackpines, with Peter at his heels. Swiftly they moved through the shadowing dusk of the plain, and came at last to the Stew-Kettle, and to their hiding-place under the shoulders of Gog and Magog. There was still a faint twilight in the tunnel, and in this twilight Jolly Roger McKay packed his possessions; and then, with fingers that trembled as if they were committing a sacrilege, he drew Nada's few treasures from her bundle and placed them tenderly with his own. And all the time Peter heard him saying things under his breath, so softly that it was like the whispered drone of song.

In darkness they went down through the rocks to the plain, and half an hour later they came to the break in the Ridge, and went through it, and stopped in the black shadow of a great rock, with Jed Hawkins' cabin half a rifle-shot away. Here Nada was to come to them with the first rising of the moon.

It was very still all about, and Peter sensed a significance in the silence, and lay very quietly watching the light in the cabin, and the shadowy form of his master. Also he knew that somewhere in the distance a storm was gathering. The breath of it was in the air, though the sky was clear of cloud overhead, except for the haze of a gray and ghostly mist that lay between them and the yellow stars. Jolly Roger counted the seconds between then and moonrise. It seemed hours before the golden rim of it rose in the east. Shadows grew swiftly after that. Grotesque things took shape. The rock-caps of the ridge began to light up, like timid signal-fires. Black spruce and balsam and cedar glistened as if bathed in enamel. And the moon came on, and mellow floods of light played in the valleys and plains, and danced over the forest-tops, and in voice-less and soundless miracle called upon all living things to look upon the glory of God. In his soul Jolly Roger McKay felt the urge and the call of that voiceless Master Power, and through his lips came an unconscious whisper of prayer—of gratitude.

And he watched the light in Jed Hawkins' cabin, and strained his ears to hear a sound of footsteps coming through the moonlight.

But there was no change. The light did not move. A door did not open or close. There was no sound, except the growing whisper of the wind, the call of a night bird, and the howl of the old gray wolf that always cried out to the moon from the tangled depths of Indian Tom's swamp.

A thrill of nervousness swept through Jolly Roger. He waited half an hour, three-quarters, an hour—after the moon had risen. And Nada did not come. The nervousness grew in him, and he moved out into the moon-glow, and slowly and watchfully followed the edge of the rock-shadows until he came to the fringe of cedars and spruce behind the cabin. Peter, careful not to snap a twig under his paws, followed closely. They came to the cabin, and there—very distinctly—Jolly Roger McKay heard the low moaning of a voice.

He edged his way to the window, and looked in.

Crouched beside a chair in the middle of the floor was Jed Hawkins's woman. She was moaning, and her thin body was rocking back and forth, and with her hands clasped at her bony breast she was staring at the open door. With a shock Jolly Roger saw that except for the strangely crying old woman the cabin was empty. Sudden fear chilled his blood—a fear that scarcely took form before he was at the door, and in the cabin. The woman's eyes were red and wild as she stared at him, and she stopped her moaning, and her hands unclasped. Jolly Roger went nearer and bent over her and shivered at the half-mad terror he saw in her face.

"Where is Nada?" he demanded. "Tell me—where is she?"

"Gone, gone, gone," crooned the woman, clutching her hands at her breast again. "Jed has taken her—taken her to Mooney's shack, over near the railroad. Oh, my God!—I tried to keep her, but I couldn't. He dragged her away, and tonight he's sellin' her to Mooney—the devil—the black brute—the tie-cutter—"

She choked, and began rocking herself back and forth, and the moaning came again from her thin lips. Fiercely McKay gripped her by the shoulder.

"Mooney's shack—where?" he cried. "Quick! Tell me!"

"A thousand—a thousand—he's givin' a thousand dollars to git her in the shack—alone," she cried in a dull, sing-song voice. "The road out there leads straight to it. Near the railroad. A mile. Two miles. I tried to keep him from doin' it, but I couldn't—I couldn't—"

Jolly Roger heard no more. He was out of the door, and running across the open, with Peter racing close behind him. They struck the road, and Jolly Roger swung into it, and continued to run until the breath was out of his lungs. And all that time the things Nada had told him about Jed Hawkins and the tie-cutter were rushing madly through his brain. An hour or two ago, when the words had come from her lips in the jackpine thicket, he had believed that Nada was frightened, that a distorted fear possessed her, that such a thing as she had half confessed to him was too monstrous to happen. And now he cried out aloud, a groaning, terrible cry as he went on. Hawkins and Nada had reached Mooney's shack long before this, a shack buried deep in the wilderness, a shack from which no cries could be heard—

Peter, trotting behind, whined at what he heard in Jolly Roger McKay's panting voice. And the moon shone on them as they staggered and ran, and here and there dark clouds were racing past the face of it, and the slumberous whisper of storm grew nearer in the air. And then came the time when one of the dark clouds rode under the moon and the two ran on in darkness. The cloud passed, and the moon flooded the road again with light—and suddenly Jolly Roger stopped in his tracks, and his heart almost broke in the strain of that moment.

Ahead of them, staggering toward them, sobbing as she came, was Nada. Jolly Roger's blazing eyes saw everything in that vivid light of the moon. Her hair was tangled and twisted about her shoulders and over her breast. One arm was bare where the sleeve had been torn away, and her girlish breast gleamed white where her waist had been stripped half from her body. And then she saw Jolly Roger in the trail, with wide-open, reaching arms, and with a cry such as Peter had never heard come from her lips before she ran into them, and held up her face to him in the yellow moon-light. In her eyes— great, tearless, burning pools—he saw the tragedy and yet it was only that, and not horror, not despair, NOT the other thing. His arms closed crushingly about her. Her slim body seemed to become a part of him. Her hot lips reached up and clung to his.

And then,

"Did—he get you—to—Mooney's shack—" He felt her body stiffen against him.

"No," she panted. "I fought—every inch. He dragged me, and hit me, and tore my clothes—but I fought. And up there—in the trail —he turned his back for a moment, when he thought I was done, and I hit him with a club. And he's there, now, on his back—"

She did not finish. Jolly Roger thrust her out from him, arm's length. A cloud under the moon hid his face. But his voice was low, and terrible.

"Nada, go to the Missioner's as fast as you can," he said, fighting to speak coolly. "Take Peter—and go. You will make it before the storm breaks. I am going back to have a few words with Jed Hawkins—alone. Then I will join you, and the Missioner will marry us—"

The cloud was gone, and he saw joy and radiance in her face. Fear had disappeared. Her eyes were luminous with the golden glow of the night. Her red lips were parted, entreating him with the lure of their purity and love, and for a moment he held her close in his arms again, kissing her as he might have kissed an angel, while her little hands stroked his face, and she laughed softly and strangely in her happiness—the wonder of a woman's soul rising swiftly out of the sweetness of her girlhood.

And then Jolly Roger set her firmly in the direction she was to go.

"Hurry, little girl," he said. "Hurry—before the storm breaks!"

She went, calling Peter softly, and Jolly Roger strode down the trail, not once looking back, and bent only upon the vengeance he would this night wreak upon the two lowest brutes in creation. Never before had he felt the desire to kill. But he felt that desire now. Before the night was much older he would do unto Hawkins and Mooney as Hawkins had done unto Peter. He would leave them alive, but broken and crippled and forever punished.

And then he stumbled over something in another darkening of the moon. He stopped, and the light came again, and he looked down into the upturned face of Jed Hawkins. It was a distorted and twisted face, and its one eye was closed. The body did not move. And close to the head was the club which Nada had used.

Jolly Roger laughed grimly. Fate was kind to him in making a half of his work so easy. But he wanted Hawkins to rouse himself first. Roughly he stirred him with the toe of his boot.

"Wake up, you fiend," he said. "I'm going to break your bones, your arms, your legs, just as you broke Peter—and that poor old woman back in the cabin. Wake up!"

Jed Hawkins made no stir. He was strangely limp. For many seconds Jolly Roger stood looking down at him, his eyes growing wider, more staring. Darkness came again. It was an inky blackness this time, like a blotter over the world. Low thunder came out of the west. The tree-tops whispered in a frightened sort of way. And Jolly Roger could hear his heart beating. He dropped upon his knees, and his hands moved over Jed Hawkins. For a space not even Peter could have heard his movement or his breath.

In the ebon darkness he rose to his feet, and the night— lifelessly still for a moment—heard the one choking word that came from his lips.

"Dead!"

And there he stood, the heat of his rage changing to an icy chill, his heart dragging within him like a chunk of lead, his breath choking in his throat. Jed Hawkins was dead! He was growing stiff there in the black trail. He had ceased to breathe. He had ceased to be a part of life. And the wind, rising a little with the coming of storm, seemed to whisper and chortle over the horrible thing, and the lone wolf in Indian Tom's swamp howled weirdly, as if he smelled death.

Jolly Roger McKay's finger-nails dug into the flesh of his palms. If he had killed the human viper at his feet, if his own hands had meted out his punishment, he would not have felt the clammy terror that wrapped itself about him in the darkness. But he had come too late. It was Nada who had killed Jed Hawkins. Nada, with her woman's soul just born in all its glory, had taken the life of her foster-father. And Canadian law knew no excuse for killing.

The chill crept to his finger-tips, and unconsciously, in a childish sort of way, he sobbed between his clenched teeth. The thunder was rolling nearer, and it was like a threatening voice, a deep-toned booming of a thing inevitable and terrible. He felt the air shivering about him, and suddenly something moved softly against his foot, and he heard a questioning whine. It was Peter— come back to him in this hour when he needed a living thing to give him courage. With a groan he dropped on his knees again, and clutched his hands about Peter.

"My God," he breathed huskily. "Peter, she's killed him. And she mustn't know. We mustn't let anyone know—"

And there he stopped, and Peter felt him growing rigid as stone, and for many moments Jolly Roger's body seemed as lifeless as that of the man who lay with up-turned face in the trail. Then he fumbled in a pocket and found a pencil and an old envelope. And on the envelope, with the darkness so thick he could not see his hand, he scribbled, "I killed Jed Hawkins," and after that he signed his name firmly and fully—"Jolly Roger McKay."

Then he tucked the envelope under Jed Hawkins' body, where the rain could not get at it. And after that, to make the evidence complete, he covered the dead man's face with his coat.

"We've got to do it, Peter," he said, and there was a new note in his voice as he stood up on his feet again. "We've got to do it— for her. We'll—tell her we caught Jed Hawkins in the trail and killed him."

Caution, cleverness, his old mental skill returned to him. He dragged the bootlegger's body to a new spot, turned it face down, threw the club away, and kicked up the earth with his boots to give signs of a struggle.

The note in his voice was triumph—triumph in spite of its heartbreak—as he turned back over the trail after he had finished, and spoke to Peter.

"We may have done some things we oughtn't to, Pied-Bot," he said, "but to-night I sort o' think we've tried to make—restitution. And if they hang us, which they probably will some time, I sort o' think it'll make us happy to know we've done it—for her. Eh, Pied-Bot?"

And the moon sailed out for a space, and shone on the dead whiteness of Jolly Roger's face. And on the lips of that face was a strange, cold smile, a smile of mastery, of exaltation, and the eyes were looking straight ahead—the eyes of a man who had made his sacrifice for a thing more precious to him than his God.

Only now and then did the moon gleam through the slow-moving masses of black cloud when he came to the edge of the Indian settlement clearing three miles away, where stood the cabin of the Missioner. The storm had not broken, but seemed holding back its forces for one mighty onslaught upon the world. The thunder was repressed, and the lightning held in leash, with escaping flashes of it occasionally betraying the impending ambuscades of the sky.

The clearing itself was a blot of stygian darkness, with a yellow patch of light in the center of it—the window of the Missioner's cabin. And Jolly Roger stood looking at it for a space, as a carven thing of rock might have stared. His heart was dead. His soul crushed. His dream broken. There remained only his brain, his mind made up, his worship for the girl—a love that had changed from a thing of joy to a fire of agony within him. Straight ahead he looked, knowing there was only one thing for him to do. And only one. There was no alternative. No hope. No change of fortune that even the power of God might bring about. What lay ahead of him was inevitable.

After all, there is something unspeakable in the might and glory of dying for one's country—or for a great love. And Jolly Roger McKay felt that strength as he strode through the blackness, and knocked at the door, and went in to face Nada and the little old gray-haired Missioner in the lampglow.

Swift as one of the flashes of lightning in the sky the anxiety and fear had gone out of Nada's face, and in an instant it was flooded with the joy of his coming. She did not mark the strange change in him, but went to him as she had gone to him in the trail, and Jolly Roger's arms closed about her, but gently this time, and very tenderly, as he might have held a little child he was afraid of hurting. Then she felt the chill of his lips as she pressed her own to them. Startled, she looked up into his eyes. And as he had done in the trail, so now Jolly Roger stood her away from him, and faced the Missioner. In a cold, hard voice he told what had happened to Nada that evening, and of the barbarous effort Jed Hawkins had made to sell her to Mooney. Then, from a pocket inside his shirt, he drew out a small, flat leather wallet, and thrust it in the little Missioner's hand.

"There's close to a thousand dollars in that," he said. "It's mine. And I'm giving it to you—for Nada. I want you to keep her, and care for her, and mebby some day—"

With both her hands Nada clutched his arm. Her eyes had widened. Swift pallor had driven the color from her face, and a broken cry was in her voice.

"I'm goin' with you," she protested. "I'm goin' with you—and Peter!"

"You can't—now," he said. "I've got to go alone, Nada. I went back—and I killed Jed Hawkins."

Over the roof of the cabin rolled a crash of thunder. As the explosion of it rocked the floor under their feet, Jolly Roger pointed to a door, and said,

"Father, if you will leave us alone—just a minute—"

White-faced, clutching the wallet, the little gray Missioner nodded, and went to the door, and as he opened it and entered into the darkness of the other room he saw Jolly Roger McKay open wide his arms, and the girl go into them. After that the storm broke. The rain descended in a deluge upon the cabin roof. The black night was filled with the rumble and roar and the hissing lightning-flare of pent-up elements suddenly freed of bondage. And in the darkness and tumult the Missioner stood, a little gray man of tragedy, of deeply buried secrets, a man of prayer and of faith in God—his heart whispering for guidance and mercy as he waited. The minutes passed. Five. Ten. And then there came a louder roaring of the storm, shut off quickly, and the little Missioner knew that a door was opened—and closed.

He lifted the latch, and looked out again into the lampglow. Huddled at the side of a chair on the floor, her arms and face buried in the lustrous, disheveled mass of her shining hair—lay Nada, and close beside her was Peter. He went to her. Tenderly he knelt down beside her. His thin arm went about her, and as the storm raved and shrieked above them he tried to comfort her—and spoke of God.

And through that storm, his head bowed, his heart gone, went Jolly Roger McKay—heading north.

CHAPTER VIII

PETER, thrust back from the door through which through which his master had gone, listened vainly for the sound of returning footsteps in the beat of rain and the crash of thunder outside. A strange thing had burned itself into his soul, a thing that made his flesh quiver and set hot fires running in his blood. As a dog sometimes senses the stealthy approach of death, so he began to sense the tragedy of this night that had brought with it not only a chaos of blackness and storm, but an anguish which roused an answering whimper in his throat as he turned toward Nada.

She was crumpled with her head in her arms, where she had flung herself with Jolly Roger's last kiss of worship on her lips, and she was sobbing like a child with its heart broken. And beside her knelt the old gray Missioner, man of God in the deep forest, who stroked her hair with his thin hand, whispering courage and consolation to her, with the wind and rain beating overhead and the windows rattling to the accompaniment of ghostly voices that shrieked and wailed in the tree-tops outside.

Peter trembled at the sobbing, but his heart and his desire were with the man who had gone. In his unreasoning little soul it was Jed Hawkins who was rattling the windows with his unseen hands and who was pounding at the door with the wind, and who was filling the black night with its menace and fear. He hated this man, who lay back in the trail with his lifeless face turned up to the deluge that poured out of the sky. And he was afraid of the man, even as he hated him, and he believed that Nada was afraid of him, and that because of her fear she was crying there in the middle of the floor, with Father John patting her shoulder and stroking her hair, and saying things to her which he could not understand. He wanted to go to her. He wanted to feel himself close against her, as Nada had held him so often in those hours when she had unburdened her grief and her unhappiness to him. But even stronger than this desire was the one to follow his master.

He went to the door, and thrust his nose against the crack at the bottom of it. He felt the fierceness of the wind fighting to break in, and the broken mist of it filled his nostrils. But there came no scent of Jolly Roger McKay. For a moment he struggled at the crack with his paws. Then he flopped himself down, his heart beating fast, and fixed his eyes inquiringly on Nada and the Missioner.

His four and a half months of life in the big wilderness, and his weeks of constant comradeship with Jolly Roger, had developed in him a brain that was older than his body. No process of reasoning could impinge upon him the fact that his master was an outlaw, but with the swift experiences of tragedy and hiding and never-ceasing caution had come instinctive processes which told him almost as much as reason. He knew something was wrong tonight. It was in the air. He breathed it. It thrilled in the crash of thunder, in the lightning fire, in the mighty hands of the wind rocking the cabin and straining at the windows. And vaguely the knowledge gripped him that the dead man back in the trail was responsible for it all, and that because of this something that had happened his mistress was crying and his master was gone. And he believed he should also have gone with Jolly Roger into the blackness and mystery of the storm, to fight with him against the one creature in all the world he hated—the dead man who lay back in the thickness of gloom between the forest walls.

And the Missioner was saying to Nada, in a quiet, calm voice out of which the tragedies of years had burned all excitement and passion:

"God will forgive him, my child. In His mercy He will forgive Roger McKay, because he killed Jed Hawkins to save YOU. But man will not forgive. The law has been hunting him because he is an outlaw, and to outlawry he has added what the law will call murder. But God will not look at it in that way. He will look into the heart of the man, the man who sacrificed himself—"

And then, fiercely, Nada struck up the Missioner's comforting hand, and Peter saw her young face white as star-dust in the lampglow.

"I don't care what God thinks," she cried passionately. "God didn't do right today. Mister Roger told me everything, that he was an outlaw, an' I oughtn't to marry him. But I didn't care. I loved him. I could hide with him. An' we were coming to have you marry us tonight when God let Jed Hawkins drag me away, to sell me to a man over on the railroad—an' it was God who let Mister Roger go back and kill him. I tell you He didn't do right! He didn't—he didn't—because Mister Roger brought me the first happiness I ever knew, an' I loved him, an' he loved me—an' God was wicked to let him kill Jed Hawkins—"

Her voice cried out, a woman's soul broken in a girl's body, and Peter whimpered and watched the Missioner as he raised Nada to her feet and went with her into his bedroom, where a few minutes before he had lighted a lamp. And Peter crept in quietly after them, and when the Missioner had gone and closed the door, leaving them alone in their tragedy, Nada seemed to see him for the first time and slowly she reached out her arms.

"Peter!" she whispered. "Peter—Peter—"

In the minutes that followed, Peter could feel her heart beating. Clutched against her breast he looked up at the white, beautiful face, the trembling throat, the wide-open blue eyes staring at the one black window between them and the outside night. A lull had come in the storm. It was quiet and ominous stillness, and the ticking of a clock, old and gray like the Missioner himself, filled the room. And Nada, seated on the edge of Father John's bed, no longer looked like the young girl of "seventeen goin' on eighteen." That afternoon, in the hidden jackpine open, with its sweet-scented jasmines, its violets and its crimson strawberries under their feet, the soul of a woman had taken possession of her body. In that hour the first happiness of her life had come to her. She had heard Jolly Roger McKay tell her those things which she already knew—that he was an outlaw, and that he was hiding down on the near-edge of civilization because the Royal Mounted were after him farther north—and that he was not fit to love her, and that it was a crime to let her love him. It was then the soul of the woman had come to her in all its triumph. She had made her choice, definitely and decisively, without hesitation and without fear. And now, as she stared unseeingly at the window against which the rain was beating, the woman in her girlish body rose in her mightier than in the hour of her happiness, fighting to find a way—crying out for the man she loved.

Her mind swept back in a single flash through all the years she had lived, through her years of unhappiness and torment as the foster-girl of Jed Hawkins and his broken, beaten wife; through summers and winters that had seemed ages to her, eternities of desolation, of heartache, of loneliness, with the big wilderness her one friend on earth. As the window rattled in a fresh blast of storm, she thought of the day months ago when she had accidentally stumbled upon the hiding-place of Roger McKay. Since that day he had been her God, and she had lived in a paradise. He had been father, mother, brother, and at last—what she most yearned for—a lover to her. And this day, when for the first time he had held her in his arms, when the happiness of all the earth had reached out to them, God had put it into Jed Hawkins' heart to destroy her—and Jolly Roger had killed him!

With a sharp little cry she sprang to her feet, so suddenly that Peter fell with a thump to the floor. He looked up at her, puzzled, his jaws half agape. She was breathing quickly. Her slender body was quivering. Suddenly Peter saw the fire in her eyes and the flame that was rushing into her white cheeks. Then she turned to him, and panted in a wild little whisper, so low that the Missioner could not hear:

"Peter, I was wrong. God wasn't wicked to let Mister Roger kill Jed Hawkins. He oughta been killed. An' God meant him to be killed. Peter—Peter—we don't care if he's an outlaw! We're goin' with him. We're goin'—goin'—"

She sprang to the window, and Peter was at her heels as she strained at it with all her strength, and he could hear her sobbing:

"We're goin' with him, Peter. We're goin'—if we die for it!"

An inch at a time she pried the window up. The storm beat in. A gust of wind blew out the light, but in the last flare of it Nada saw a knife in an Eskimo sheath hanging on the wall. She groped for it, and clutched it in her hand as she climbed through the window and dropped to the soggy ground beneath. In a single leap Peter followed her. Blackness swallowed them as they turned toward the trail leading north—the only trail which Jolly Roger could travel on a night like this. They heard the voice of the Missioner calling from the window behind them. Then a crash of thunder set the earth rolling under their feet, and the lull in the storm came to an end. The sky split open with the vivid fire of lightning. The trees wailed and whined, the rain fell again in a smothering deluge, and through it Nada ran, gripping the knife as her one defense against the demons of darkness—and always close at her side ran Peter.

He could not see her in that pitchy blackness, except when the lightning flash-es came. Then she was like a ghostly wraith, with drenched clothes clinging to her until she seemed scarcely dressed, her wet hair streaming and her wide, staring eyes looking straight ahead. After the lightning flashes, when the world was darkest, he could hear the stumbling tread of her feet and the panting of her breath, and now and then the swish of brush as it struck across her face and breast. The rain had washed away the scent of his master's feet but he knew they were following Jolly Roger, and that the girl was running to overtake him. In him was the desire to rush ahead, to travel faster through the night, but Nada's stumbling feet and her panting breath and the strange white pictures he saw of her when the sky split open with fire held him back. Something told him that Nada must reach Jolly Roger. And he was afraid she would stop. He wanted to bark to give her encouragement, as he had often barked in their playful races in the green plain-lands on the farther side of Cragg's Ridge. But the rain choked him. It beat down upon him with the weight of heavy hands, it slushed up into his face from pools in the trail and drove the breath from him when he attempted to open his jaws. So he ran close—so close that at times Nada felt the touch of his body against her.

In these first minutes of her fight to overtake the man she loved Nada heard but one voice—a voice crying out from her heart and brain and soul, a voice rising above the tumult of thunder and wind, urging her on, whipping the strength from her frail body in pitiless exhortation. Jolly Roger was less than half an hour ahead of her. And she must overtake him—quickly—before the forests swallowed him, before he was gone from her life forever.

The wall of blackness against which she ran did not frighten her. When the brush tore at her face and hair she swung free of it, and stumbled on. Twice she ran blindly into broken trees that lay across her path, and dragged her bruised body through their twisted tops, moaning to Peter and clutching tightly to the sheathed knife in her hand. And the wild spirits that possessed the night seemed to gather about her, and over her, exulting in the helplessness of their victim, shrieking in weird and savage joy at the discovery of this human plaything struggling against their might. Never had Peter heard thunder as he heard it now. It rocked the earth under his feet. It filled the world with a ceaseless rumble, and the lightning came like flashes from swift- loading guns, and with it all a terrific assault of wind and rain that at last drove Nada down in a crumpled heap, panting for breath, with hands groping out wildly for him.

Peter came to them, sodden and shivering. His warm tongue found the palm of her hand, and for a space Nada hugged him close to her, while she bowed her head until her drenched curls became a part of the mud and water of the trail. Peter could hear her sobbing for breath. And then suddenly, there came a change. The thunder was sweeping eastward. The lightning was going with it. The wind died out in wailing sobs among the treetops, and the rain fell straight down. Swiftly as its fury had come, the July storm was passing. And Nada staggered to her feet again and went on.

Her mind began to react with the lessening of the storm, dragging itself out quickly from under the oppression of fear and shock. She began to reason, and with that reason the beginning of faith and confidence gave her new strength. She knew that Jolly Roger would take this trail, for it was the one trail leading from the Missioner's cabin through the thick forest country north. And in half an hour he would not travel far. The thrilling thought came to her that possibly he had sought shelter in the lee of a big tree trunk during the fury of the storm. If he had done that he would be near, very near. She paused in the trail and gathered her breath, and cried out his name. Three times she called it, and only the low whine in Peter's throat came in answer. Twice again during the next ten minutes she cried out as loudly as she could into the darkness. And still no answer came back to her through the gloom ahead.

The trail had dipped, and she felt the deepening slush of swamp- mire under her feet. She sank in it to her shoe-tops, and stumbled into pools knee-deep, and Peter wallowed in it to his belly. A quarter of an hour they fought through it to the rising ground beyond. And by that time the last of the black storm clouds had passed overhead. The rain had ceased. The rumble of thunder came more faintly. There was no lightning, and the tree-tops began to whisper softly, as if rejoicing in the passing of the wind. About them—everywhere—they could hear the run and drip of water, the weeping of the drenched trees, the gurgle of flooded pools, and the trickle of tiny rivulets that splashed about their feet. Through a rift in the breaking clouds overhead came a passing flash of the moon.

"We'll find him now, Peter," moaned the girl. "We'll find him— now. He can't be very far ahead—"

And Peter waited, holding his breath, listening for an answer to the cry that went out for Jolly Roger McKay.

The glory of July midnight, with a round, full moon straight overhead, followed the stress of storm. The world had been lashed and inundated, every tree whipped of its rot and slag, every blade of grass and flower washed clean. Out of the earth rose sweet smells of growing life, the musky fragrance of deep moss and needle-mold, and through the clean air drifted faintly the aroma of cedar and balsam and the subtle tang of unending canopies and glistening tapestries of evergreen breathing into the night. The deep forest seemed to tremble with the presence of an invisible and mysterious life—life that was still, yet wide-awake, breathing, watchful, drinking in the rejuvenating tonic of the air which had so quietly followed thunder and lightning and the roar of wind and rain. And the moon, like a queen who had so ordered these things, looked down in a mighty triumph. Her radiance, without dust or fog or forest-smoke to impede its way, was like the mellow glow of half-day. It streamed through the treetops in paths of gold and silver, throwing dark shadows where it failed to penetrate, and gathering in wide pools where its floods poured through broad rifts in the roofs of the forest. And the trail, leading north, was like a river of shimmering silver, splitting the wilderness from earth to sky.

In this trail, clearly made in the wet soil, were Jolly Roger's foot-prints, and in a wider space, where at some time a trapper had cleared himself a spot for his tepee or shack, Jolly Roger had paused to rest after his fight through the storm—and had then continued on his way. And into this clearing, three hours after they left the Missioner's cabin, came Nada and Peter.

They came slowly, the girl a slim wraith in the moon-light; in the open they stood for a moment, and Peter's heart weighed heavily within him as his mistress cried out once more for Jolly Roger. Her voice rose only in a sob, and ended in a sob. The last of her strength was gone. Her little figure swayed, and her face was white and haggard, and in her drawn lips and staring eyes was the agony of despair. She had lost, and she knew that she had lost as she crumpled down in the trail, crying out sobbingly to the footprints which led so clearly ahead of her.

"Peter, I can't go on," she moaned. "I can't—go on—"

Her hands clutched at her breast. Peter saw the glint of the moonlight on the ivory sheath of the Eskimo knife, and he saw her white face turned up to the sky—and also that her lips were moving, but he did not hear his name come from them, or any other sound. He whined, and foot by foot began to nose along the trail on the scent left by Jolly Roger. It was very clear to his nostrils, and it thrilled him. He looked back, and again he whined his encouragement to the girl.

"Peter!" she called. "Peter!"

He returned to her. She had drawn the knife out of its scabbard, and the cold steel glistened in her hand. Her eyes were shining, and she reached out and clutched Peter close up against her, so that he could hear the choke and throb of her heart.

"Oh, Peter, Peter," she panted. "If you could only talk! If you could run and catch Mister Roger, an' tell him I'm here, an' that he must come back—"

She hugged him closer. He sensed the sudden thrill that leapt through her body.

"Peter," she whispered, "will you do it?"

For a few moments she did not seem to breathe. Then he heard a quick little cry, a sob of inspiration and hope, and her arms came from about him, and he saw the knife flashing in the yellow moonlight.

He did not understand, but he knew that he must watch her carefully. She had bent her head, and her hair, nearly dry, glowed softly in the face of the moon. Her hands were fumbling in the disheveled curls, and Peter saw the knife flash back and forth, and heard the cut of it, and then he saw that in her hand she held a thick brown tress of hair that she had severed from her head. He was puzzled. And Nada dropped the knife, and his curiosity increased when she tore a great piece out of her tattered dress, and carefully wrapped the tress of hair in it. Then she drew him to her again, and tied the knotted fold of dress securely about his neck; after that she tore other strips from her dress, and wound them about his neck until he felt muffled and half smothered.

And all the time she was talking to him in a half sobbing, excited little voice, and the blood in Peter's body ran swifter, and the strange thrill in him was greater. When she had finished she rose to her feet, and stood there swaying back and forth, like one of the spruce-top shadows, while she pointed up the moonlit trail.

"Go, Peter!" she cried softly. "Quick! Follow him, Peter—catch him—bring him back! Mister Roger—Jolly Roger—go, Peter! Go—go —go—"

It was strange to Peter. But he was beginning to understand. He sniffed in Jolly Roger's footprints, and then he looked up quickly, and saw that it had pleased the girl. She was urging him on. He sniffed from one footprint to another, and Nada clapped her hands and cried out that he was right—for him to hurry—hurry—

Impulse, thought, swiftly growing knowledge of something to be done thrilled in his brain. Nada wanted him to go. She wanted him to go to Jolly Roger. And she had put something around his neck which she wanted him to take with him. He whined eagerly, a bit excitedly. Then he began to trot. Instinctively it was his test. She did not call him back. He flattened his ears, listening for her command to return, but it did not come. And then the thrill in him leapt over all other things. He was right. He was not abandoning Nada. He was not running away. She WANTED him to go!

The night swallowed him. He became a part of the yellow floods of its moonlight, a part of its shifting shadows, a part of its stillness, its mystery, its promise of impending things. He knew that grim and terrible happenings had come with the storm, and he still sensed the nearness of tragedy in this night-world through which he was passing. He did not go swiftly, yet he went three times as fast as the girl and he had traveled together. He was cautious and watchful, and at intervals he stopped and listened, and swallowed hard to keep the whine of eagerness out of his throat. Now that he was alone every instinct in him was keyed to the pulse and beat of life about him. He knew the Night People of the deep forests were awake. Softly padded, clawed, sharp-beaked and feathered—the prowlers of darkness were on the move. With the stillness of shadows they were stealing through the moonlit corridors of the wilderness, or hovering gray-winged and ghostly in the ambuscades of the treetops, eager to waylay and kill, hungering for the flesh and blood of creatures weaker than themselves. Peter knew. Both heritage and experience warned him. And he watched the shadows, and sniffed the air, and kept his fangs half bared and ready as he followed the trail of McKay.

He was not stirred by the impulse of adventure alone. Without the finesse of what man might charitably call reason in a beast, he had sensed a responsibility. It was present in the closely drawn strips of faded cloth about his neck. It was, in a way, a part of the girl herself, a part of her flesh and blood, a part of her spirit—something vital to her and dependent upon him. He was ready to guard it with every instinct of caution and every ounce of courage there was in him. And to protect it meant to fight. That was the first law of his breed, the primal warning which came to him through the red blood of many generations of wilderness fore-fathers. So he listened, and he watched, and his blood pounded hot in his veins as he followed the footprints in the trail. A bit of brush, swinging suddenly free from where it had been prisoned by the storm, drew a snarl from him as he faced the sound with the quickness of a cat. A gray streak, passing swiftly over the trail ahead of him, stirred a low growl in his throat. It was a lynx, and for a space Peter paused, and then sped soft-footed past the moon-lit spot where the stiletto-clawed menace of the woods had passed.

Now that he was alone, and no longer accompanied by a human presence whose footsteps and scent held the wild things aloof and still, Peter felt nearer and nearer to him the beat and stir of life. Powerful beaks, instead of remaining closed and without sound, snapped and hissed at him as the big gray owls watched his pass-ing. He heard the rustling of brush, soft as the stir of a woman's dress, where living things were secretly moving, and he heard the louder crash of clumsy and piggish feet, and caught the strong scent of a porcupine as it waddled to its midnight lunch of poplar bark. Then the trail ended, and Jolly Roger's scent led into the pathless forest, with its shifting streams and pools of moonlight, its shadows and black pits of darkness. And here—now— Peter began his trespass into the strongholds of the People of the Night. He heard a wolf howl, a cry filled with loneliness, yet with a shivering death-note in it; he caught the musky, skunkish odor of a fox that was stalking prey in the face of a whispering breath of wind; once, in a moment of dead stillness, he listened to the snap of teeth and the crackle of bones in one of the dark pits, where a fisher-cat—with eyes that gleamed like coals of fire—was devouring the warm and bleeding carcass of a mother partridge. And beaks snapped at him more menacingly as he went on, and gray shapes floated over his head, and now and then he heard the cries of dying things—the agonized squeak of a wood-mouse, the cry of a day-bird torn from its sleeping place by a sinuous, beady-eyed creature of fur and claw, the noisy screaming of a rabbit swooped upon and pierced to the vitals by one of the gray- feathered pirates of the air. And then, squarely in the center of a great pool of moonlight, Peter came upon a monster. It was a bear, a huge mother bear, with two butter-fat cubs wrestling and rolling in the moon glow. Peter had never seen a bear. But the mother, who raised her brown nose suddenly from the cool mold out of which she had been digging lily-bulbs, had seen dogs. She had seen many dogs, and she had heard their howl, and she knew that always they traveled with man. She gave a deep, chesty sniff, and close after that sniff a WHOOF that startled the cubs like the lashing end of a whip. They rolled to her, and with two cuffs of the mother's huge paws they were headed in the right direction, and all three crashed off into darkness.

In spite of his swelling heart Peter let out a little yip. It was a great satisfaction, just at a moment when his nerves were getting unsteady, to discover that a monster like this one in the moonlight was anxious to run away from him. And Peter went on, a bit of pride and jauntiness in his step, his bony tail a little higher.

A mile farther on, in another yellow pool of the moon, lay the partly devoured carcass of a fawn. A wolf had killed it, and had fed, and now two giant owls were rending and tearing in the flesh and bowels of what the wolf had left. They were Gargantuans of their kind, one a male, the other a female. Their talons warm in blood, their beaks red, their slow brains drunk with a ravenous greed, they rose on their great wings in sullen rage when Peter came suddenly upon them. He had ceased to be afraid of owls. There was something shivery in the gritting of their beaks, especially in the dark places, but they had never attacked him, and had always kept out of his reach. So their presence in a black spruce top directly over the dead fawn did not hold him back now. He sniffed at the fresh, sweet meat, and hunger all at once possessed him. Where the wolf had stripped open a tender flank he began to eat, and as he ate he growled, so that warning of his possessorship reached the spruce top.

In answer to it came a stir of wings, and the male owl launched himself out into the moon glow. The female followed. For a few moments they floated like gray ghosts over Peter, silent as the night shadows. Then, with the suddenness and speed of a bolt from a catapult, the giant male shot out of a silvery mist of gloom and struck Peter. The two rolled over the carcass of the fawn, and for a space Peter was dazed by the thundering beat of powerful wings, and the hammering of the owl's beak at the back of his neck. The male had missed his claw-hold, and driven by rage and ferocity, fought to impale his victim from the ground, without launching himself into the air again. Swiftly he struck, again and again, while his wings beat like clubs. Suddenly his talons sank into the cloth wrapped about Peter's neck. Terror and shock gave way to a fighting madness inside Peter now. He struck up, and buried his fangs in a mass of feathers so thick he could not feel the flesh. He tore at the padded breast, snarling and beating with his feet, and then, as the stiletto-points of the owl's talons sank through the cloth into his neck, his jaws closed on one of the huge bird's legs. His teeth sank deep, there was a snapping and grinding of tendon and bone, and a hissing squawk of pain and fear came from above him as the owl made a mighty effort to launch himself free. As the five-foot pinions beat the air Peter was lifted from the ground. But the owl's talons were hopelessly entangled in the cloth, and the two fell in a heap again. Peter scarcely sensed what happened after that, except that he was struggling against death. He closed his eyes, and the leg between his jaws was broken and twisted into pulp. The wings beat about him in a deafening thunder, and the owl's beak tore at his flesh, until the pool of moonlight in which they fought was red with blood. At last something gave way. There was a ghastly cry that was like the cry of neither bird nor beast, a weak flutter of wings, and Gargantua of the Air staggered up into the treetops and fell with a crash among the thick boughs of the spruce.

Peter raised himself weakly, the severed leg of the owl dropping from his jaws. He was half blinded. Every muscle in his body seemed to be torn and bleeding, yet in his discomfort the thrilling conviction came to him that he had won. He tensed himself for another attack, hugging the ground closely as he watched and waited, but no attack came. He could hear the flutter and wheeze of his maimed adversary, and slowly he drew himself back—still facing the scene of battle—until in a farther patch of gloom he turned once more to his business of following the trail of Jolly Roger McKay.

There was no mark of bravado in his advance now. If he had possessed an overgrowing confidence, Gargantua's attack had set it back, and he stole like a shifty fox through the night. Driven into his brain was the knowledge that all things were not afraid of him, for even the snapping beaks and floating gray shapes to which he had paid but little attention had now become a deadly menace. His egoism had suffered a jolt, a healthful reaction from its too swift ascendency. He sensed the narrowness of his escape without the mental action of reasoning it out, and his injuries were secondary to the oppressive horror of the uncanny combat out of which he had come alive. Yet this horror was not a fear. Heretofore he had recognized the ghostly owl-shapes of night more or less as a curious part of darkness, inspiring neither like nor dislike in him. Now he hated them, and ever after his fangs gleamed white when one of them floated over his head.

He was badly hurt. There were ragged tears in his flank and back, and a last stroke of Gargantua's talons had stabbed his shoulder to the bone. Blood dripped from him, and one of his eyes was closing, so that shapes and shadows were grotesquely dim in the night. Instinct and caution, and the burning pains in his body, urged him to lie down in a thicket and wait for the day. But stronger than these were memory of the girl's urging voice, the vague thrill of the cloth still about his neck, and the freshness of Jolly Roger's trail as it kept straight on through the forest's moonlit corridors and caverns of gloom.

It was in the first graying light of July dawn that Peter dragged himself up the rough side of a ridge and looked down into a narrow strip of plain on the other side. Just as Nada had given up in weakness and despair, so now he was almost ready to quit. He had traveled miles since the owl fight, and his wounds had stiffened, and with every step gave him excruciating pain. His injured eye was entirely closed, and there was a strange, dull ache in the back of his head, where Gargantua had pounded him with his beak. The strip of valley, half hidden in its silvery mist of dawn, seemed a long distance away to Peter, and he dropped on his belly and began to lick his raw shoulder with a feverish tongue. He was sick and tired, and the futility of going farther oppressed him. He looked again down into the strip of plain, and whined.

Then, suddenly, he smelled something that was not the musty fog- mist that hung between the ridges. It was smoke. Peter's heart beat faster, and he pulled himself to his feet, and went in its direction.

Hidden in a little grassy cup between two great boulders that thrust themselves out from the face of the ridge, he found Jolly Roger. First he saw the smouldering embers of a fire that was almost out—and then his master. Jolly Roger was asleep. Storm- beaten and strangely haggard and gray his face was turned to the sky. Peter did not awaken him. There was something in his master's face that quieted the low whimper in his throat. Very gently he crept to him, and lay down. The movement, slight as it was, made the man stir. His hand rose, and then fell limply across Peter's body. But the fingers moved.

Unconsciously, as if guided by the spirit and prayer of the girl waiting far back in the forest, they twined about the cloth around Peter's neck—his message to his master.

And for a long time after that, as the sun rose over a wonderful world, Peter and his master slept.

CHAPTER IX

I T was the restlessness of Peter that roused Jolly Roger. Half awake, and before he opened his eyes, life seized upon him where sleep had cut it off for a time last night. His muscles ached. His neck was stiff. He seemed weighted like a log to the hard earth. Swiftly the experience of the preceding hours rushed upon him, and it was in the first of this wakefulness that he felt the presence of Peter.

He sat up and stared wide-eyed at the dog. The fact that Peter had escaped from the cabin, and had followed him, was not altogether amazing. It was quite the natural thing for a one-man dog to do. But the unexpectedness of it held McKay speechless, and at first a little disappointed. It was as if Peter had deliberately betrayed a trust. During the storm and flight of the night McKay had thought of him as the one connecting link remaining between him and the girl he loved. He had left Peter to fill his place, to guard and watch and keep alive the memory of the man who was gone. For him there had been something of consolation in this giving up of his comradeship to Nada. And Peter had turned traitor.

Even Peter seemed to sense the argument and condemnation that was passing behind McKay's unsmiling eyes. He did not move, but lay squatted on his belly, with his nose straight out on the ground between his forepaws. It was his attitude of self-immolation. His acknowledgment of the other's right to strike with lash or club. Yet in his eyes, bright and steady behind his mop of whiskers, Jolly Roger saw a prayer.

Without a word he held out his arms. It was all Peter needed, and in a moment he was hugged up close against McKay. After all, there was a mighty something that reached from heart to heart of these two, and Jolly Roger said, with a sound that was half laugh and half sob in his throat,

"Pied-Bot, you devil—you little devil—"

His fingers closed in the cloth about Peter's neck, and his heart jumped when he saw what it was—a piece of Nada's dress. Peter, realizing that at last the importance of his mission was understood, waited in eager watchfulness while his master untied the knot. And in another moment, out in the clean and glorious sun that had followed storm, McKay held the shining tress of Nada's hair.

It was a real sob that broke in his throat now, and Peter saw him crush the shining thing to his face, and hold it there, while strange quivers ran through his strong shoulders, and a wetness that was not rain gathered in his eyes.

"God bless her!" he whispered. And then he said, "I wish I was a kid, Peter—a kid. Because—if I ever wanted to cry—IT'S NOW"

In his face, even with the tears and the strange quivering of his lips, Peter saw a radiance that was joy. And McKay stood up, and looked south, back over the trail he had followed through the blackness and storm of night. He was visioning things. He saw Nada in Father John's cabin, urging Peter out into the wild tumult of thunder and lightning with that precious part of her which she knew he would love forever. Her last message to him. Her last promise of love and faith until the end of time.

He guessed only the beginning of the truth. And Peter, denied the power of thought transmission because of an error in the creation of things, ran back a little way over the trail, trying to tell his master that Nada had come with him through the storm, and was back in the deep forest calling for him to return.

But McKay's mind saw nothing beyond the dimly lighted room of the Missioner's cabin.

He pressed his lips to the silken tress of Nada's hair, still damp with the rain; and after that, with the care of a miser he smoothed it out, and tied the end of the tress tightly with a string, and put it away in the soft buckskin wallet which he carried.

There was a new singing in his heart as he gathered sticks with which to build a small fire, for after this he would not travel quite alone.

That day they went on; and day followed day, until August came, and north—still farther north they went into the illimitable wilderness which reached out in the drowsing stillness of the Flying-up-Month—the month when newly fledged things take to their wings, and the deep forests lie asleep.

Days added themselves into weeks, until at last they were in the country of the Reindeer waterways.

To the east was Hudson's Bay; westward lay the black forests and twisting waterways of Upper Saskatchewan; and north—always north —beckoned the lonely plains and unmapped wildernesses of the Athabasca, the Slave and the Great Bear—toward which far country their trail was slowly but surely wending its way.

The woodlands and swamps were now empty of man. Cabin and shack and Indian tepee were lifeless, and waited in the desolation of abandonment. No smoke rose in the tree-tops; no howl of dog came with the early dawn and the setting sun; trap lines were over- growing, and laughter and song and the ring of the trapper's axe were gone, leaving behind a brooding silence that seemed to pulse and thrill like a great heart—the heart of the wild unchained for a space from its human bondage.

It was the vacation time—the midsummer carnival weeks of the wilderness people. Wild things were breeding. Fur was not good. Flesh was unfit to kill. And so they had disappeared, man, woman and child, and their dogs as well, to foregather at the Hudson's Bay Company's posts scattered here and there in the fastnesses of the wilderness lands. A few weeks more and they would return. Cabins would send up their smoke again. Brown-faced children would play about the tepee door. Ten thousand dwellers of the forests, white and half-breed and Indian born, would trickle in twos and threes and family groups back into the age-old trade of a domain that reached from Hudson's Bay to the western mountains and from the Height of Land to the Arctic Sea.

Until then nature was free, and in its freedom ran in riotous silence over the land. These were days when the wolf lay with her young, but did not howl; when the lynx yawned sleepily, and hunted but little—days of breeding, nights of drowsy whisperings, and of big red moons, and of streams rippling softly at lowest ebb while they dreamed of rains and flood-time. And through it all—through the lazy drone of insects, the rustling sighs of the tree-tops and the subdued notes of living things ran a low and tremulous whispering, as if nature had found for itself a new language in this temporary absence of man.

To Jolly Roger this was Life, It breathed for him out of the cool earth. He heard it over him, and under him, and on all sides of him where other ears would have found only a thing vast and oppressive and silent. On what he called these "mother-hood days of the earth" the passing years had built his faith and his creed.

One evening he stopped for camp at the edge of the Burntwood. From his feet reached out the wide river, ankle deep in places, knee deep in others, rippling and singing between sandbars and driftwood where in May and June it had roared with the fury of flood Peter, half asleep after their day's travel through a hot forests watched his master. Since their flight from the edge of civilization far south he had grown heavier and broadened out. The hardship of adventuring and the craft of fighting for food and life had whipped the last of his puppyhood behind him At six months of age he was scarred, and lithe-muscled, and ready for instant action at all times. Through the mop of Airedale whiskers that covered his face his bright eyes were ever alert, and always they watched the back-trail as he wondered why the slim, blue-eyed girl they both loved and missed so much did not come. And vaguely he wondered why it was that his master always went on and on, and never waited for her to catch up with them.

And Jolly Roger was changed. He was not the plump and rosy-faced wilderness freebooter who whistled and sang away down at Cragg's Ridge even when he knew the Law was at his heels. The steadiness of their flight had thinned him, and a graver look had settled in his face. But in his clear eyes was still the love of life—a thing even stronger than the grief which was eating at his heart as their trail reached steadily toward the Barren Lands.

In the sunset glow of this late afternoon Peter's watchful eyes saw his master draw forth their treasure.

It was something he had come to look for, and expect—once, twice, and sometimes half a dozen times between the rising and the setting of the sun. And at night, when they paused in their flight for the day, Jolly Roger never failed to do what he was doing now. Peter drew nearer to where his master was sitting with his back to the big rock, and his eyes glistened. Always he caught the sweet, illusive perfume of the girl when Jolly Roger drew out their preciously guarded package. He un-wrapped it gently now, and in a moment held in his hands the tress of Nada's hair, the last of her they would ever possess or see. And Peter wondered again why they did not go back to where they had left the rest of the girl. Many times, seeing his restlessness and his yearning, Jolly Roger had tried to make him understand. And Peter tried to comprehend. But always in his dreams he was with the girl he loved, following her, playing with her, fighting for her, hearing her voice—feeling the touch of her hand. In his dog soul he wanted her, just as Jolly Roger wanted her with all the yearning and heartbreak of the man. Yet always when he awoke from his dreams they went on again—not south—but north. To Peter this was hopeless mystery, and he possessed no power of reason to solve it. Nor could he speak in words the message which he carried in his heart—that last crying agony of the girl when she had sent him out on the trail of Roger McKay, entreating him to bring back the man she loved and would always love in spite of all the broken and unbroken laws in the world.

That night, as they lay beside the Burntwood, Peter heard his master crying out Nada's name in his sleep.

And the next dawn they went on—still farther north.

In these days and weeks, with the hot inundation of the wilderness about him, McKay fought doggedly against the forces which were struggling to break down the first law of his creed. The law might catch him, and probably would, and when it caught him the law might hang him—and probably would. But it would never KNOW him. There was something grimly and tragically humorous in this. It would never know of the consuming purity of his worship for little children, and old people—and women. It would laugh at the religion he had built up for himself, and it would cackle tauntingly if he dared to say he was not wholly bad. For it believed he was bad, and it believed he had killed Jed Hawkins, and he knew that seven hundred men were anxious to get him, dead or alive.

But was he bad?

He took the matter up one evening, with Peter.

"If I'm bad, mebby it isn't all my fault, Pied-Bot," he said. "Mebby it's this—" and he swept his arms out to the gathering night." I was born in the open, on a night just like this is going to be. My mother, before she died, told me many times how she watched the moon come up that night, and how it seemed to look down on her, and talk to her, like a living thing. And I've loved the moon ever since, and the sun, and everything that's outdoors— and if there's a God I don't believe He ever intended man to make a law that wasn't right according to the plans He laid out. That's where I've got in wrong, Pied-Bot, I haven't always believed in man-made law, and I've settled a lot of things in my own way. And I guess I've loved trees and flowers and sunshine and wind and storm too much. I've just wandered. And I've done things along the way. The thrill of it got into me, Pied-Bot, and—the law wants me!"

Peter heard the subdued humor of the man, a low laugh that held neither fear nor regret.

"It was the Treaty Money first," he went on, leaning very seriously toward Peter, as if he expected an argument. "You see, Yellow Bird was in that particular tribe, Pied-Bot. I remember her as she looked to me when a boy, with her two long, shining black braids and her face that was almost as beautiful to me as my mother's. My mother loved her, and she loved my mother, and I loved Yellow Bird, just as a child loves a fairy. And always Yellow Bird has been my fairy, Peter. I guess child worship is the one thing that lasts through life, always remaining ideal, and never forgotten. Years after my mother's death, when I was a young man, and had been down to Montreal and Ottawa and Quebec, I went back to Yellow Bird's tribe. And it was starving, Pied-Bot. Starving to death!"

Reminiscent tenderness and humor were gone from McKay's voice. It was hard and flinty.

"It was winter," he continued, "the dead of winter. And cold. So cold that even the wolves and foxes had buried themselves in. No fish that autumn, no game in the deep snows, and the Indians were starving. Pied-Bot, my heart went dead when I saw Yellow Bird. There didn't seem to be anything left of her but her eyes and her hair—those two great, shining braids, and eyes that were big and deep and dark, like beautiful pools. Boy, you never saw an Indian —an Indian like Yellow Bird—cry. They don't cry very much. But when that childhood fairy of mine first saw me she just stood there, swaying in her weakness, and the tears filled those big, wide-open eyes and ran down her thin cheeks. She had married Slim Buck. Two of their three children had died within a fortnight. Slim Buck was dying of hunger and exhaustion. And Yellow Bird's heart was broken, and her soul was crying out for God to let her lie down beside Slim Buck and die with him—when I happened along.

"Peter—" Jolly Roger leaned over in the thickening dusk, and his eyes gleamed. "Peter, if there's a God, an' He thinks I did wrong then, let Him strike me dead right here! I'm willin'. I found out what the trouble was. There was a new Indian Agent, a cur. And near the tribe was a Free Trader, another cur. The two got together. The Agent sent up the Treaty Money, and along with it— underground, mind you—he sent a lot of whiskey to the Free Trader. Inside of five days the whiskey got the Treaty Money from the Indians. Then came winter. Everything went bad, When I came— and found out what had happened—eighteen out of sixty had died, and inside of another two weeks half the others would follow. Pied-Bot, away back—somewhere—there must have been a pirate before me—mebby a great-grandfather of mine. I set out, I came back in three days, and I had a sledge-load of grub, and warm things to wear—plenty of them. My God, how those starving things did eat! I went again, and returned in another week, with a still bigger sledge-load. And Yellow Bird was getting beautiful again, and Slim Buck was on his feet, growing strong, and there was happiness—and I think God A'mighty was glad. I kept it up for two months. Then the back-bone of the winter broke. Game came into the country I left them well supplied—and skipped. That was what made me an outlaw, Pied-Bot. That!"

He chuckled, and Peter heard the rubbing of his hands in the gloom.

"Want to know why?" he asked. "Well, you see, I went over to the Free Trader's, and this God the law don't take into account went with me, and we found the skunk alone. First I licked him until he was almost dead. Then, sticking a knife into him about half an inch, I made him write a note saying he was called south suddenly, and authorizing me to take charge in his absence. Then I chained him in a dugout in a place where nobody would find him. And I took charge. Pied-Bot, I sure did! Everybody was on the trap-lines, and I wasn't bothered much by callers. And I fed and clothed my tribe for eight straight weeks, fed 'em until they grew fat, Boy—and Yellow Bird's eyes were bright as stars again. Then I brought Roach—that was his name—back to his empty post, and I lectured him, an' gave him another licking—and left."

McKay rose to his feet. The first stars were peeping out of the velvety darkness of the sky, and Peter heard his master draw in a deep breath—the breath of a man whose lungs rejoice in the glory of life.

After a moment he said,

"And the Royal Mounted have been after me ever since that winter, Peter. And the harder they've chased me the more I've given them reason to chase me. I half killed Beaudin, the Government mail- runner, because he insulted another man's wife when that man—my friend—was away. Then Beaudin, seeing his chance, robbed the mail himself, and the crime was laid to me. Well, I got even, and stuck up a mail-sledge myself—but I guess there was a good reason for it. I've done a lot of things since then, but I've done it all with my naked fists, and I've never put a bullet or a knife into a man except Roach the Free Trader. And the funniest thing of the whole business, Pied-Bot, is this—I didn't kill Jed Hawkins. Some day mebby I'll tell you about what happened on the trail, the thing which you and Nada didn't see. But now—"

For a moment he stood very still, and Peter sensed the sudden thrill that was going through the man as he stood there in darkness. And then, suddenly, Jolly Roger bent over him.

"Peter, there's three women we'll love as long as we live," he whispered. "There's my mother, and she is dead. There's Nada back there, and we'll never see her again—" His voice choked for an instant. "And then—there's Yellow Bird—" he added. "It's five years since I fed the tribe. Mebby they've had more kids! Boy, let's go and see!"

CHAPTER X

NORTH and west, in the direction of Yellow Bird's people, went Jolly Roger and Peter after that night. They traveled slowly and cautiously, and with each day Peter came to understand more clearly there was some reason why they must be constantly on their guard. His master, he noticed, was thrillingly attentive whenever a sound came to their ears—perhaps the cracking of a twig, a mysterious movement of brush, or the tread of a cloven hoof. And instinctively he came to know they were evading Man. He remembered vividly their escape from Cassidy and their quiet hiding for many days in the mass of sun-baked rocks which Jolly Roger had called the Stew-Kettle. The same vigilance seemed to be a part of his master's movements now. He did not laugh, or sing, or whistle, or talk loudly. He built fires so small that at first Peter was absorbed in an almost scientific analysis of them; and instead of shooting game which could have been easily secured he set little snares in the evening, and caught fish in the streams. At night they always slept half a mile or more from the place where they had built their tiny supper-fire. And during these hours of sleep Peter was ready to rouse himself at the slightest sound of movement near them. Scarcely a night passed that his low growl of warning did not bring Jolly Roger out of his slumber, a hand on his gun, and his eyes and ears wide open.

Whether he would have used the gun had the red-coated police suddenly appeared, McKay had not quite assured himself. Day after day the same old fight went on within him. He analyzed his situation from every point of view, and always—no matter how he went about it—eventually found himself face to face with the same definite fact. If the law succeeded in catching Him it would not trouble itself to punish him for stealing back the Treaty Money, or for holding up Government mails, or for any of his other misdemeanors. It would hang him for the murder of Jed Hawkins. And the minions of the law would laugh at the truth, even if he told it—which he never would. More than once his imaginative genius had drawn up a picture of that impossible happening. For it was a truth so inconceivable that he found the absurdity of it a grimly humorous thing. Even Nada believed he had killed her scoundrelly foster-father. Yet it was she—herself—who had killed him! And it was Nada whom the law would hang, if the truth was known—and believed.

Frequently he went back over the scenes of that tragic night at Cragg's Ridge when all the happiness in the world seemed to be offering itself to him—the night when Nada was to go with him to the Missioner's, to become his wife, And then—the dark trail— the disheveled girl staggering to him through the starlight, and her sobbing story of how Jed Hawkins had tried to drag her through the forest to Mooney's cabin, and how—at last—she had saved herself by striking him down with a stick which she had caught up out of the darkness. Would the police believe HIM—an outlaw—if he told the rest of the story?—how he had gone back to give Jed Hawkins the beating of his life, and had found him dead in the trail, where Nada had struck him down? Would they believe him if, in a moment of cowardice, he told them that to protect the girl he loved he had fastened the responsibility of the crime upon himself? No, they would not. He had made the evidence too complete. The world would call him a lying yellow-back if he betrayed what had actually happened on the trail between Cragg's Ridge and Mooney's cabin.

And this, after all, was the one remaining bit of happiness in Jolly Roger's heart, the knowledge that he had made the evidence utterly complete, and that Nada would never know, and the world would never know—the truth. His love for the blue-eyed girl-woman who had given her heart and her soul into his keeping, even when she knew he was an outlaw, was an undying thing, like his love for the mother of years ago. "It will be easy to die for her," he told Peter, and this, in the end, was what he knew he was going to do. Thought of the inevitable did not make him afraid. He was determined to keep his freedom and his life as long as he could, but he was fatalistic enough, and sufficiently acquainted with the Royal Northwest Mounted Police, to know what the ultimate of the thing would be. And yet, with tragedy behind him, and a still grimmer tragedy ahead, the soul of Jolly Roger was not dead or in utter darkness. In it, waking and sleeping, he enshrined the girl who had been willing to give up all other things in the world for him, who had pleaded with him in the last hour of storm down on the edge of civilization that she be given the privilege of accompanying him wherever his fate might lead. That he was an outlaw had not destroyed her faith in him. That he had killed a man—a man unfit to live—had only drawn her arms more closely about him, and had made her more completely a part of him. And a thousand times the maddening thought possessed Jolly Roger—was he wrong, and not right, in refusing to accept the love and companionship which she had begged him to accept, in spite of all that had happened and all that might happen?

Day by day he slowly won for himself, and at last, as they traveled in the direction of Yellow Bird's country, he crushed the final doubt that oppressed him, and knew that he was right. In his selfishness he had not shackled her to an outlaw. He had left her free. Life and hope and other happiness were ahead of her. He had not destroyed her, and this thought would strengthen him and leave something of gladness in his heart, even in that gray dawn when the law would compel him to make his final sacrifice.

It is a strange peace which follows grief, a secret happiness no other soul but one can understand. Out of it excitement and passion have been burned, and it is then the Great God of things comes more closely into the possession of his own. And now, as they went westward and north toward the Wollaston Lake country, this peace possessed Jolly Roger. It mellowed his world. It was half an ache, half a steady and undying pain, but it drew Life nearer to him than he had ever known it before. His love for the sun and the sky, for the trees and flowers and all growing things of the earth was more worship of the divine than a love for physical things, and each day he felt it drawing more closely about him in its comradeship, whispering to him of its might, and of its power to care for him in the darkest hours of stress that might come.

He did not travel fast after he had reached the decision to go to Yellow Bird's people. And he tried to imagine, a great deal of the time, that Nada was with him. He succeeded in a way that bewildered Peter, for quite frequently the man talked to someone who was not there.

The slowness and caution with which they traveled developed Peter's mental faculties with marvelous swiftness. His master, free of egoism and prejudice, had placed him on a plane of intimate equality, and Peter struggled each day to live up a little more to the responsibility of this intimacy and confidence. Instinct, together with human training, taught him woodcraft until in many ways he was more clever than his master. And along with this Jolly Roger slowly but surely impressed upon him the difference between wanton slaughter and necessary killing.

"Everything that's got a breath of life must kill—up to a certain point," Jolly Roger explained to him, repeating the lesson over and over. "And that isn't wrong, Peter. The sin is in killing when you don't have to. See that tree over there, with a vine as big as my wrist winding around it, like a snake? Well, that vine is choking the life out of the tree, and in time the tree will die. But the vine is doing just what God A'mighty meant it to do. It needs a tree to live on. But I'm going to cut the vine, because I think more of the tree than I do the vine. That's MY privilege— following my conscience. And we're eating young partridges tonight, because we had to have something to keep us alive. It's the necessity of the thing that counts, Peter. Think you can understand that?"

It was pretty hard for Peter at first, but he was observant, and his mind worked quickly. The crime of destroying birdlings in their nest, or on the ground, was impressed upon him. He began to understand there was a certain humiliating shame attached to an attack upon a creature weaker than himself, unless there was a reason for it. He looked chiefly to his master for decisions in the matter. Snowshoe rabbits, young and half grown, were very tame in this month of August, and ordinarily he would have destroyed many of them in a day's travel. But unless Jolly Roger gave him a signal, or he was hungry, he would pass a snowshoe unconcernedly. This phase of Peter's development interested Jolly Roger greatly. The outlaw's philosophy had not been punctured by the egotistical "I am the only reasoning being" arguments of narrow-gauged nature scientists. He believed that Peter possessed not only a brain and super-instinct, but also a very positive reasoning power which he was helping to develop. And the process was one that fascinated him. When he was not sleeping, or traveling, or teaching Peter he was usually reading the wonderful little red volumes of history which he had purloined from the mail sledge up near the Barren Lands. He knew their contents nearly by heart. His favorites were the life-stories of Napoleon, Margaret of Anjou, and Peter the Great, and always when he compared his own troubles with the difficulties and tragedies over which these people had triumphed he felt a new courage and inspiration, and faced the world with better cheer. If Nature was his God and Bible, and Nada his Angel, these finger-worn little books written by a man half a century dead were voices out of the past urging him on to his best. Their pages were filled with the vivid lessons of sacrifice, of courage and achievement, of loyalty, honor and dishonor—and of the crashing tragedy which comes always with the last supreme egoism and arrogance of man. He marked the dividing lines, and applied them to himself. And he told Peter of his conclusions. He felt a consuming tenderness for the glorious Margaret of Anjou, and his heart thrilled one day when a voice seemed to whisper to him out of the printed page that Nada was another Margaret—only more wonderful because she was not a princess and a queen.

"The only difference," he explained to Peter, "is that Margaret sacrificed and fought and died for a king, and our Nada is willing to do all that for a poor beggar of an outlaw. Which makes Margaret a second-rater compared with Nada," he added. "For Margaret wanted a kingdom along with her husband, and Nada would take—just you and me. And that's where we're pulling some Peter the Great stuff," he tried to laugh. "We won't let her do it!"

And so they went on, day after day, toward the Wollaston waterways—the country of Yellow Bird and her people.

It was early September when they crossed the Geikie and struck up the western shore of Wollaston Lake. The first golden tints were ripening in the canoe-birch leaves, and the tremulous whisper of autumn was in the rustle of the aspen trees. The poplars were yellowing, the ash were blood red with fruit, and in cool, dank thickets wild currants were glossy black and lusciously ripe. It was the season which Jolly Roger loved most of all, and it was the beginning of Peter's first September. The days were still hot, but at night there was a bracing something in the air that stirred the blood, and Peter found a sharp, new note in the voices of the wild. The wolf howled again in the middle of the night. The loon forgot his love-sickness, and screamed raucous defiance at the moon. The big snowshoes were no longer tame, but wary and alert, and the owls seemed to slink deeper into darkness and watch with more cunning. And Jolly Roger knew the human masters of the wilderness were returning from the Posts to their cabins and trap- lines, and he advanced with still greater caution. And as he went, watching for smoke and listening for sound, he began to reflect upon the many changes which five years might have produced among Yellow Bird's people. Possibly other misfortunes had come, other winters of hunger and pestilence, scattering and destroying the tribe. It might even be that Yellow Bird was dead.

For three days he followed slowly the ragged shore of Wollaston Lake, and foreboding of evil was oppressing him when he came upon the fish-racks of the Indians. They had been abandoned for many days, for black bear tracks fairly inundated the place, and Peter saw two of the bears—fat and unafraid—nosing along the shore where the fish offal had been thrown.

It was the next day, in the hour before sunset, that Jolly Roger and Peter came out on the edge of a shelving beach where Indian children were playing in the white sand. Among these children, playing and laughing with them, was a woman. She was tall and slim, with a skirt of soft buckskin that came only a little below her knees, and two shining black braids which tossed like velvety ropes when she ran. And she was running when they first saw her— running away from them, pursued by the children; and then she twisted suddenly, and came toward them, until with a startled cry she stopped almost within the reach of Jolly Roger's hands. Peter was watching. He saw the half frightened look in her face, then the slow widening of her dark eyes, and the quick intake of her breath. And in that moment Jolly Roger cried out a name.

"Yellow Bird!"

He went to her slowly, wondering if it could be possible the years had touched Yellow Bird so lightly; and Yellow Bird reached out her hands to him, her face flaming up with sudden happiness, and Peter wondered what it was all about as he cautiously eyed the half dozen brown-faced little Indian children who had now gathered quietly about them. In another moment there was an interruption. A girl came through the fringe of willows behind them. It was as if another Yellow Bird had come to puzzle Peter—the same slim, graceful little body, the same shining eyes, and yet she was half a dozen years younger than Nada. For the first time Peter was looking at Sun Cloud, the daughter of Yellow Bird. And in that moment he loved her, just as something gave him confidence and faith in the starry-eyed woman whose hands were in his master's. Then Yellow Bird called, and the girl went to her mother, and Jolly Roger hugged her in his arms and kissed her on the scarlet mouth she turned up to him. Then they hurried along the shore toward the fishing camp, the children racing ahead to tell the news, led by Sun Cloud—with Peter running at her heels.

Never had Peter heard anything from a man's throat like the two yells that came from Slim Buck, Yellow Bird's husband and chief of the tribe, after he had greeted Jolly Roger McKay. It was a note harking back to the old war trails of the Crees, and what followed it that night was most exciting to Peter. Big fires were built of white driftwood, and there was singing and dancing, and a great deal of laughter and eating, and the interminable howling of half a hundred Siwash dogs. Peter did not like the dogs, but he did no fighting because his love for Sun Cloud kept him close to the touch of her little brown hand.

That night, in the glow of the big fire outside of Slim Buck's tepee, Jolly Roger's heart thrilled with a pleasure which it had not known for a long time. He loved to look at Yellow Bird. Five years had not changed her. Her eyes were starry bright. Her teeth were like milk. The color still came and went in her brown cheeks, even as it did in Sun Cloud's. All of which, in this heart of a wilderness, meant that she had been happy and prosperous. And he also loved to look at Sun Cloud, who possessed all of that rare wildflower beauty sometimes given to the northern Crees. And it did him good to look at Slim Buck. He was a splendid mate, and a royal father, and Jolly Roger found himself strangely happy in their happiness. In the eyes of men and women and little children he saw that happiness all about him. For three winters there had been splendid trapping, Slim Buck told him, and this season they had caught and dried enough fish to carry them through the following winter, even if black days should come. His people were rich. They had many warm blankets, and good clothes, and the best of tepees and guns and sledges, and several treasures besides. Two of these Yellow Bird and her husband disclosed to Jolly Roger this first night. One of them was a sewing machine, and the other—a phonograph! And Jolly Roger listened to "Mother Machree" and "The Rosary" that night as he sat by Wollaston Lake with six hundred miles of wilderness between him and Cragg's Ridge.

Later, when the camp slept, Yellow Bird and Slim Buck and Jolly Roger still sat beside the red embers of their fire, and Jolly Roger told of what had happened down at the edge of civilization. It was what his heart needed, and he left out none of the details. Slim Buck was listening, but Jolly Roger knew he was talking straight at Yellow Bird, and that her warm heart was full of understanding. Softly, in that low Cree voice which is the sweetest of all voices, she asked him many questions about Nada, and gently her slim fingers caressed the tress of Nada's hair which he let her take in her hands. And after a long time, she said.

"I have given her a name. She is Oo-Mee, the Pigeon."

Slim Buck started at the strange note in her voice.

"The Pigeon," he repeated,

"Yes, Oo-Mee, the Pigeon," Yellow Bird nodded. She was not looking at them. In the firelight her eyes were glowing pools. Her body had grown a little tense. Without asking Jolly Roger's permission she placed the tress of Nada's hair in her bosom. "Oo-Mee, the Pigeon," she said again, looking far away. "That is her name, because the Pigeon flies fast and straight and true. Over forests and lakes and worlds the Pigeon flies. It is tireless. It is swift. It always—flies home."

Slim Buck rose quietly to his feet.

"Come," he whispered, looking at Jolly Roger,

Yellow Bird did not look at them or speak to them, and Slim Buck— with his hand on Jolly Roger's arm—pulled him gently away. In his eyes was a little something of fear, and yet along with it a sublime faith.

"Her spirit will be with Oo-Mee, the Pigeon, tonight," he said in a voice struck with awe. "It will go to this place which you have described, and it will live in the body of the girl, and through Yellow Bird it will tell you tomorrow what has happened, and what is going to happen."

In the edge of the shore-willows Jolly Roger stood for a time watching Yellow Bird as she sat under the stars, motionless as a figure graven out of stone. He felt a curious tingling at his heart, something stirring uneasily in his breast, and he stood alone even after Slim Buck had stretched himself out in the soft sand to sleep. He was not superstitious. Yet it was equally a part of his philosophy and his creed to believe in the overwhelming power of the mind. "If you have faith enough, and think hard enough, you can think anything until it comes true," he had told himself more than once. And he knew Yellow Bird possessed that illimitable faith, and that behind her divination lay generations and centuries of an unbreakable certainty in the power of mind over matter. He realized his own limitations, but a mysterious voice in the still night seemed whispering to him that in the crude wisdom of Yellow Bird's brain lay the secret to strange achievement, and that on this night her mind might perform for him what he, in his greater wisdom, would call a miracle. He had seen things like that happen. And he sat down in the sand, sleepless, and with Peter at his feet waited for Yellow Bird to stir.

He could see the dull shimmer of starlight in her hair, but the rest of her was a shadow that gave no sign of life. The camp was asleep. Even the dogs were buried in their wallows of sand, and the last red spark of the fires had died out. The hour passed, and another hour followed, and the lids of Jolly Roger's eyes grew heavier as the fading stars seemed to be sinking deeper into infinity. At last he slept, with his back leaning against a sand- dune the children had made. He dreamed, and was flying through the air with Yellow Bird. She was traveling swift and straight, like an arrow, and he had difficulty in keeping up with her, and at last he cried out for her to wait—that he could go no farther. The cry roused him. He opened his eyes, and found cool, gray dawn in the sky. Peter, alert, was muzzling his hand. Slim Buck lay in the sand, still asleep. There was no stir in the camp. And then, with a sudden catch in his breath, he looked toward Yellow Bird's tepee.

Yellow Bird still sat in the sand. Through the hours of fading starlight and coming dawn she had not moved. Slowly McKay rose to his feet. When he came to her, making no sound, she looked up. The shimmer of glistening dew was in her hair. Her long lashes were wet with it. Her face was very pale, and her eyes so large and dark that for a moment they startled him. She was tired. Exhaustion was in her slim, limp body.

A sigh came from her lips, and her shoulders swayed a little.

"Sit down, Neekewa," she whispered, drawing the ropes of her hair about her as if she were cold.

Then she drew a slim hand over her eyes, and shivered.

"It is well, Neekewa," she spoke softly. "I have gone through the clouds to where lives Oo-Mee, the Pigeon. I found her crying in a trail. I whispered to her and happiness came, and that happiness is going to live—for Neekewa and The Pigeon. It cannot die. It cannot be killed. The Red Coated men of the Great White Father will never destroy it. You will live. She will live. You will meet again—in happiness. And happiness will follow ever after. That much I learned, Neekewa. In happiness—you will meet again."

"Where? When?" whispered Jolly Roger, his heart beating with sudden swiftness.

Again Yellow Bird passed her hand over her eyes, and as she held it there for a moment she bowed her head until Jolly Roger could see only her dew-wet hair and she said,

"In the Country Beyond, Neekewa."

Her eyes were looking at him again, big, dark and filled with mystery.

"And where is this country, Yellow Bird?" he asked, a strange chill driving the warmth out of his heart. "You mean—up there?" And he pointed to the gray sky above them.

"No, it is happiness to come in life, not in death," said Yellow Bird slowly. "It is not beyond the stars. It is—"

He waited, leaning toward her.

"In the Country Beyond," she repeated with a tired little droop of her head. "And where that is I do not know, Neekewa. I could not pass beyond the great white cloud that shut me out. But it is— somewhere, I will find it. And then I will tell you—and The Pigeon."

She stood up, and swayed in the gray light, like one worn out by hard travel. Then she passed into the tepee, and Jolly Roger heard her fall on her blanket-bed.

And still stranger whisperings filled his heart as he faced the east, where the first red blush of day drove back the star-mists of dawn. He heard a step in the soft sand, and Slim Buck stood beside him. And he asked.

"Did you ever hear of the Country Beyond?" Slim Buck shook his head, and both looked in silence toward the rising sun.

Peter was glad when the camp roused itself out of sleep with waking voices, and laughter, and the building of fires. He waited eagerly for Sun Cloud. At last she came out of Yellow Bird's tepee, rubbing her eyes in the face of the glow in the east, and then her white teeth flashed a smile of welcome at him. Together they ran down to the edge of the lake, and Peter wagged his tail while Sun Cloud went out knee-deep and scrubbed her pretty face with handfuls of the cool water. It was a happy day for him. He was different from the Indian dogs, and Sun Cloud and her playmates made much of him. But never, even in their most exciting play, did he entirely lose track of his master.

Jolly Roger, to an extent, forgot Peter. He tried to deaden within him the impulses which Yellow Bird's conjuring had roused. He tried to see in them a menace and a danger, and he repeated to himself the folly of placing credence in Yellow Bird's "medicine." But his efforts were futile, and he was honest enough to admit it. The uneasiness was in his breast. A new hope was rising up. And with that hope were fear and suspense, for deep in him was growing stronger the conviction that what Yellow Bird would tell him would be true. He noted the calm and dignified stiffness with which Slim Buck greeted the day. The young chief passed quietly among his people. A word traveled in whispers, voices and footsteps were muffled and before the sun was an hour high there was no tepee standing but one on that white strip of beach. And the one tepee was Yellow Bird's,

Not until the camp was gone, leaving her alone, did Yellow Bird come out into the day. She saw the food placed at her tepee door. She saw the empty places where the homes of her people had stood, and in the wet sand of the beach the marks of their missing canoes. Then she turned her pale face and tired eyes to the sun, and unbraided her hair so that it streamed glistening all about her and covered the white sand when she sat down again in front of the smoke-darkened canvas that had become her conjurer's house.

Two miles up the beach Slim Buck's people made another camp. But Slim Buck and Jolly Roger remained in the cover of a wooded headland only half a mile from Yellow Bird. They saw her when she came out. They watched for an hour after she sat down in the sand. And then Slim Buck grunted, and with a gesture of his hands said they would go. Jolly Roger protested. It was not safe for Yellow Bird to remain entirely beyond their protection. There were bears prowling about. And human beasts occasionally found their way through the wilderness. But Slim Buck's face was like a bronze carving in its faith and pride.

"Yellow Bird only goes with the good spirits," he assured Jolly Roger. "She does not do witchcraft with the bad. And no harm can come while the good spirits are with her. It is thus she has brought us happiness and prosperity since the days of the famine, Neekewa!"

He spoke these words in Cree, and McKay answered him in Cree as they turned in the direction of the camp. Half way, Sun Cloud came to meet them, with Peter at her side. She put a brown little hand in Jolly Roger's. It was quite new and pleasant to be kissed as Jolly Roger had kissed her, and she held up her mouth to him again. Then she ran ahead, with Peter yipping foolishly and happily at her moccasined heels.

And Jolly Roger said,

"I wish I was your brother, Slim Buck, and Nada was Yellow Bird's sister—and that I had many like her," and his eyes followed Sun Cloud with hungry yearning.

And as he said these words, Yellow Bird sat with bowed head and closed eyes, with the soft tress of Nada's hair in her hands. It was the physical union between them, and all that day, and the night that followed, Yellow Bird held it in her hand or against her breast as she struggled to send out the soul that was in her on its mission to Oo-Mee the Pigeon. In darkness she buried the food that was left her, and stamped on it with her feet. The sacrifice of her body had begun, and for two days thereafter Jolly Roger and Slim Buck saw no movement of life about the lone tepee in the sand.

But the third morning they saw the smoke of a little greenwood fire rising straight up from in front of it.

Slim Buck drew in a deep breath. It was the signal fire.

"She knows," he said, pointing for Jolly Roger to go. "She is calling you!"

The tenseness was gone from the bronze muscles of his face. He was lonely without Yellow Bird, and the signal fire meant she would be with him again soon. Jolly Roger walked swiftly over the white beach. Again he tried to tell himself what folly it all was, and that he was answering the signal-fire only to humor Yellow Bird and Slim Buck. But words, even spoken half aloud, did not quiet the eager beating of his heart.

Not until he was very near did Yellow Bird come out of the tepee. And it was then Jolly Roger stopped short, a gasp on his lips. She was changed. Her radiant hair was still down, polished smooth; but her face was whiter than he had ever seen it, and drawn and pinched almost as in the days of the famine. For two days and two nights she had taken no food, and for two days and two nights she had not slept. But there was triumph in her big, wide-open eyes, and Jolly Roger felt something strange rising up in his breast.

Yellow Bird held out her hands toward him.

"We have been together, The Pigeon and I," she said. "We have slept in each other's arms, and the warmth of her head has lain against my breast. I have learned the secrets, Neekewa—all but one. The spirits will not tell me where lies the Country Beyond. But it is not up there—beyond the stars. It is not in death, but in life you will find it. That they have told me. And you must not go back to where The Pigeon lives, for you will find black desolation there—but always you must keep on and on, seeking for the Country Beyond. You will find it. And there also you will find The Pigeon—and happiness. You cannot fail, Neekewa, yet my heart stings me that I cannot tell you where that strange country is. But when I came to it gold and silver clouds shut it in, and I could see nothing, and yet out of it came the singing of birds and the promise of sweet voices that it shall be found—if you seek faithfully, Neekewa. I am glad."

Each word that she spoke in her soft and tremulous Cree was a new message of hope in the empty heart of Jolly Roger McKay. The world might laugh. Men might tap their heads and smile. His own voice might argue and taunt. But deep in his heart he believed.

Something of the radiance of the new day came into his face, even as it was returning into Yellow Bird's. He looked about him—east, west, north and south—upon the sunlit glory of water and earth, and suddenly he reached out his arms.

"I'll find it, Yellow Bird," he cried. "I'll find this place you call the Country Beyond! And when I do—"

He turned and took one of Yellow Bird's slim hands in both his own.

"And when I do, we'll come back to you, Yellow Bird," he said.

And like a cavalier of old he touched his lips gently to the palm of Yellow Bird's little brown hand.

CHAPTER XI

DAYS of new hope and gladness followed in the camp of Yellow Bird and Slim Buck. It was as if McKay, after a long absence, had come back to his own people. The tenderness of mother and sister lay warm in Yellow Bird's breast. Slim Buck loved him as a brother. The wrinkled faces of the old softened when he came near and spoke to them; little children followed him, and at dusk and dawn Sun Cloud held up her mouth to be kissed. For the first time in years McKay felt as if he had found home. The northland Indian Summer held the world in its drowsy arms, and the sun-filled days and the starry nights seemed overflowing with the promise of all time. Each day he put off his going until tomorrow, and each day Slim Buck urged him to remain with them always.

But in Yellow Bird's eyes was a strange, quiet mystery, and she did not urge. Each day and night she was watching—and waiting.

And at last that for which she watched and waited came to pass.

It was night, a dark, still night with a creeping restlessness in it. This restlessness was like the ghostly pulse of a great living body, still for a time, then moving, hiding, whispering between the clouds in the sky and the deeper shadowed earth below. A night of uneasiness, of unseen forces chained and stifled, of impending doubt and oppressive lifelessness.

There was no wind, yet under the stars gray masses of cloud sped as if in flight.

There was no breeze in the treetops, yet they whispered and sighed.

In the strange spell of this midnight, heavy with its unrest, the wilderness lay half asleep, half awake, with the mysterious stillness of death enshrouding it.

At the edge of the white sands of Wollaston, whose broad water was like oil to-night, stood the tepees of Yellow Bird's people. Smoke- blackened and seasoned by wind and rain they were dark blotches sentineling the shore of the big lake. Behind them, beyond the willows, were the Indian dogs. From them came an occasional whine, a deep sigh, the snapping of a jaw, and in the gloom their bodies moved restlessly. In the tepees was the spell of this same unrest. Sleep was never quite sure of itself. Men, women and little children twisted and rolled, or lay awake, and weird and distorted shapes and fancies came in dreams.

In her tepee Yellow Bird lay with her eyes wide open, staring at the gray blur of the smoke hole above. Her husband was asleep. Sun Cloud, tossing on her blankets, had flung one of her long braids so that it lay across her mother's breast. Yellow Bird's slim fingers played with its silken strands as she looked straight up into nothingness. Wide awake, she was thinking—thinking as Slim Buck—would never be able to think, back to the days when a white woman had been her goddess, and when a little white boy—the woman's son—had called Yellow Bird "my fairy."

In the gloom, with foreboding eating at her heart, Yellow Bird's red lips parted in a smile as those days came back to her, for they were pleasing days to think about. But after that the years sped swiftly in her mind until the day when the little boy—a man grown—came to save her tribe, and her own life, and the life of Sun Cloud, and of Slim Buck her husband. Since then prosperity and happiness had been her lot. The spirits had been good. They had not let her grow old, but had kept her still beautiful. And Sun Cloud, her little daughter, was beautiful, and Slim Buck was more than ever her god among men, and her people were happy. And all this she owed to the man who was sleeping under the gloom of the sky outside, the hunted man, the outlaw, "the little boy grown up"—Jolly Roger McKay.

As she listened, and stared up at the smoke hole, strange spirits were whispering to her, and Yellow Bird's blood ran a little faster and her eyes grew bigger and brighter in the darkness. They seemed to be accusing her. They told her it was because of her that Roger McKay had come in that winter of starvation and death, and had robbed and almost killed, that she and Slim Buck and little Sun Cloud might live. That was the beginning, and the thrill of it had got into the blood of Neekewa, her "little white brother grown up." And now he was out there, alone with his dog in the night—and the red-coated avengers of the law were hunting him. They wanted him for many things, but chiefly for the killing of a man.

Yellow Bird sat up, her little hands clenched about the thick braid of Sun Cloud's hair. She had conjured with the spirits and had let the soul go out of her body that she might learn the future for Neekewa, her white brother. And they had told her that Roger McKay had done right to think of killing.

Their voices had whispered to her that he would not suffer more than he had already suffered—and that in the Country Beyond he would find Nada the white girl, and happiness, and peace. Yellow Bird did not disbelieve. Her faith was illimitable. The spirits would not lie. But the unrest of the night was eating at her heart. She tried to lift herself to the whisperings above the tepee top. But they were unintelligible, like many voices mingling, and with them came a dull fear into her soul.

She put out a hand, as if to rouse Slim Buck. Then she drew it back, and placed Sun Cloud's braid away from her. She rose to her feet so quietly that even in their restlessness they did not fully awake. Through the tepee door she went, and stood up straight in the night, as if now she might hear more clearly, and understand.

For a space she breathed in the oppressive something that was in the air, and her eyes went east and west for sign of storm. But there was no threat of storm. The clouds were drifting slowly and softly, with starlight breaking through their rifts, and there was no moan of thunder or wail of wind far away. Her heart, for a little, seemed to stop its beating, and her hands clasped tightly at her breast. She began to understand, and a strange thrill crept into her. The spirits had put a great burden upon the night so that it might drive sleep from her eyes. They were warning her. They were telling her of danger, approaching swiftly, almost impending. And it was peril for the white man who was sleeping somewhere near.

Swiftly she began seeking for him, her naked little brown feet making no sound in the soft white sands of Wollaston.

And as she sought, the clouds thinned out above, and the stars shone through more clearly, as if to make easier for her the quest in the gloom.

Where he had made his bed of blankets in the sand, close beside a flat mass of water-washed sandstone, Jolly Roger lay half asleep. Peter was wide awake. His eyes gleamed brightly and watchfully. His lank and bony body was tense and alert. He did not whine or snap his jaws, though he heard the Indian dogs occasionally doing so. The comradeship of a fugitive, ever on the watch for his fellow men, had made him silent and velvet-footed, and had sharpened his senses to the keenness of knives. He, too, felt the impelling force of an approaching menace in this night of stillness and mystery, and he watched closely the restless movements of his master's body, and listened with burning eyes to the name which he had spoken three times in the last five minutes of his sleep.

It was Nada's name, and as Jolly Roger cried it out softly in the old way, as if Nada was standing before them, he reached out, and his hands struck the sand-stone rock. His eyes opened, and slowly he sat up. The sky had cleared of clouds, and there was starlight, and in that starlight Jolly Roger saw a figure standing near him in the sand. At first he thought it was Sun Cloud, for Peter stood with his head raised to her. Then he saw it was Yellow Bird, with her beautiful eyes looking at him steadily and strangely as he awakened.

He got upon his feet and went to her, and took one of her hands. It was cold. He felt the shiver that ran through her slim body, and suddenly her eyes swept from him out into the night.

"Listen, Neekewa!"

Her fingers tightened in his hand. For a space he could hear the beating of her heart.

"Twice I have heard it," she whispered then. "Neekewa, you must go!"

"Heard what?" he asked.

She shook her head.

"Something—I don't know what. But it tells me there is danger. And I saw danger over the tepee top, and I have heard whisperings of it all about me. It is com-ing. It is coming slowly and cautiously. It is very near. Hark, Neekewa! Was that not a sound out on the water?"

"I think it was the wing of a duck, Yellow Bird."

"And THAT!" she cried swiftly, her fingers tightening still more. "That sound—as if wood strikes on wood!"

"The croak of a loon far up the shore, Yellow Bird."

She drew her hand away.

"Neekewa, listen to me," she importuned him in Cree. "The spirits have made this night heavy with warning. I could not sleep. Sun Cloud twitches and moans. Slim Buck whispers to himself. You were crying out the name of Nada—Oo-Mee the Pigeon—when I came to you. I know. It is danger. It is very near. And it is danger for you."

"And only a short time ago you were confident happiness and peace were coming to me, Yellow Bird," reminded Jolly Roger. "The spirits, you said, promised the law should never get me, and I would find Nada again in that strange place you called the Country Beyond. Have the spirits changed their message, because the night is heavy?"

Yellow Bird's eyes were staring into darkness.

"No, they have not changed," she whispered. "They have spoken the truth. They want to tell me more, but for some reason it is impossible. They have tried to tell me where lies this place they call the Country Beyond—where you will again find Oo-Mee the Pigeon. But a cloud always comes between. And they are trying to tell me what the danger is off there—in the darkness." Suddenly she caught his arm. "Nee-kewa, DID YOU HEAR?"

"A fish leaping in the still water, Yellow Bird."

He heard a low whimper in Peter's throat, and looking down he saw Peter's muzzle pointing toward the thick cloud of gloom over the lake.

"What is it, Pied-Bot?" he asked.

Peter whimpered again.

Jolly Roger touched the cold hand that rested on his arm.

"Go back to your bed, Yellow Bird. There is only one danger for me—the red-coated police. And they do not travel in the dark hours of a night like this."

"They are coming," she replied. "I cannot hear or see, but they are coming!"

Her fingers tightened.

"And they are near," she cried softly.

"You are nervous, Yellow Bird," he said, thinking of the two days and three nights of her conjuring, when she had neither slept nor taken food, that she might more successfully commune with the spirits. "There is no danger. The night is a hard one for sleep. It has frightened you."

"It has warned me," she persisted, standing as motionless as a statue at his side. "Neekewa, the spirits do not forget. They have not forgotten that winter when you came, and my people were dying of famine and sickness—when I dreaded to see little Sun Cloud close her eyes even in sleep, fearing she would never open them again. They have not forgotten how all that winter you robbed the white people over on the Des Chenes, that we might live. If they remember those things, and lie, I would not be afraid to curse them. But they do not lie."

Jolly Roger McKay did not answer. Deep down in him that strange something was at work again, compelling him to believe Yellow Bird. She did not look at him, but in her low Cree voice, soft as the mellow notes of a bird, she was saying:

"You will be going very soon, Neekewa, and I shall not see you again for a long time. Do not forget what I have told you. And you must believe. Somewhere there is this place called the Country Beyond. The spirits have said so. And it is there you will find your Oo-Mee the Pigeon—and happiness. But if you go back to the place where you left The Pigeon when you fled from the red-coated men of the law, you will find only blackness and desolation. Believe, and you shall be guided. If you disbelieve—"

She stopped.

"You heard that, Neekewa? It was not the wing of a duck, nor was it the croak of a loon far up the shore, or a fish leaping in the still water. IT WAS A PADDLE!"

In the star-gloom Jolly Roger McKay bowed his head, and listened.

"Yes, a paddle," he said, and his voice sounded strange to him. "Probably it is one of your people returning to camp, Yellow Bird."

She turned toward him, and stood very near. Her hands reached out to him. Her hair and eyes were filled with the velvety glow of the stars, and for an instant he saw the tremble of her parted lips.

"Goodby, Neekewa," she whispered.

And then, without letting her hands touch him, she was gone. Swiftly she ran to Slim Buck's tepee, and entered, and very soon she came out again with Slim Buck beside her. Jolly Roger did not move, but watched as Yellow Bird and her husband went down to the edge of the lake, and stood there, waiting for the strange canoe to pass—or come in. It was approaching. Slowly it came up, an indistinct shadow at first, but growing clearer, until at last he could see the silhouette of it against the star-silvered water beyond. There were two people in it. Before the canoe reached the shore Slim Buck stood out knee-deep in the water and hailed it.

A voice answered. And at the sound of that voice McKay dropped like a shot beside Peter, and Peter's lips curled up, and he snarled. His master's hand warned him, and together they slipped back into the shadows, and from under a piece of canvas Jolly Roger dragged forth his pack, and quietly strapped it over his shoulders while he waited and listened.

And then, as he heard the voice again, he grinned, and chuckled softly.

"It's Cassidy, Pied-Bot! We can't lose that redheaded fox, can we?"

A good humored deviltry lay in his eyes, and Peter—looking up— thought for a moment his master was laughing. Then Jolly Roger made a megaphone of his hands, and called very clearly out into the night.

"Ho, Cassidy! Is that you, Cassidy?"

Peter's heart was choking him as he listened. He sensed a terrific danger. There was no sound at the edge of the lake. There was no sound anywhere. For a few moments a death-like stillness followed Jolly Roger's words.

Then a voice came in answer, each word cutting the gloom with the decisive clearness of a bullet coming from a gun.

"Yes, this is Cassidy—Corporal Terence Cassidy, of 'M' Division, Royal Northwest Mounted Police. Is that you, McKay?"

"Yes, it's me," replied Jolly Roger. "Does the wager still hold, Cassidy?"

"It holds."

There was a shadowy movement on the beach. The voice came again.

"Watch yourself, McKay. If I see you I shall fire!"

With drawn gun Cassidy rushed toward the spot where Jolly Roger and Peter had stood. It was empty now, except for the bit of old canvas. Cassidy's Indian came up and stood behind him, and for many minutes they listened for the crackling of brush. Slim Buck joined them, and last came Yellow Bird, her dark eyes glowing like pools of fire in their excitement. Cassidy looked at her, marveling at her beauty, and suspicious of something that was in her face. He went back to the beach. There he caught himself short, astonishment bringing a sharp exclamation from his lips.

His canoe and outfit were gone!

Out of the star-gloom behind him floated a soft ripple of laughter as Yellow Bird ran to her tepee.

And from the mist of water—far out—came a voice, the voice of Jolly Roger McKay.

"Goodby, Cassidy!"

With it mingled the defiant bark of a dog.

In her tepee, a moment later, Yellow Bird drew Sun Cloud's glossy head close against her warm breast, and turned her radiant face up thankfully to the smoke hole in the tepee top, through which the spirits had whispered their warning to her. Indistinctly, and still farther away, her straining ears heard again the cry,

"Goodby, Cassidy!"

CHAPTER XII

IN Cassidy's canoe, driving himself with steady strokes deeper into the mystery of the starlit waters of Wollaston, Jolly Roger felt the night suddenly filled with an exhilarating tonic. Its deadness was gone. Its weight had lifted. A ripple broke the star gleams where an increasing breeze touched the surface of the lake. And the thrill of adventure stirred in his blood. He laughed as he put his skill and strength in the sweep of his paddle, and for a time the thought that he was an outlaw, and in losing Nada had lost everything in life worth righting for, was not so oppressive. It was the old, joyous laugh, stirred by his sense of humor, and the trick he had played on Cassidy. He could imagine Cassidy back on the shore, his temper redder than his hair as he cursed and tore up the sand in his search for another canoe.

"We're inseparable," Jolly Roger explained to Peter. "Wherever I go, Cassidy is sure to follow. You see, it's this way. A long time ago someone gave Cassidy what they call an assignment, and in that assignment it says 'go get Jolly Roger McKay, dead or alive'—or something to that effect. And Cassidy has been on the job ever since. But he can't quite catch up with me, Pied-Bot. I'm always a little ahead."

And yet, even as he laughed, there was in Jolly Roger's heart a yearning to which he had never given voice. Half a dozen times he might have killed Cassidy, and an equal number of times Cassidy might have killed him. But neither had taken advantage of the opportunity to destroy. They had played the long and thrilling game like men, and because of the fairness and sportsmanship of the man who hunted him Jolly Roger thought of Cassidy as he might have thought of a brother, and more than once he yearned to go to him, and hold out his hand in friendship.

Yet he knew Corporal Cassidy was the deadliest menace the earth held for him, a menace that had followed him like a shadow through months and years— across the Barren Lands, along the rim of the Arctic, down the Mackenzie, and back again—a menace that never tired, and was never far behind in that ten thousand miles of wilderness they had covered. Together in the bloodstirring game of One against One they had faced the deadliest perils of the northland. They had gone hungry, and cold, and more than once a thousand miles of nothingness lay behind them, and death seemed preferable to anything that might lie ahead. Yet in that aloneness, when companionship was more precious than anything else on earth, neither had cried quits. The game had gone on, Cassidy after his man—and Jolly Roger McKay fighting for his freedom.

As he headed his canoe north and east, Jolly Roger thought again of the wager made weeks ago down at Cragg's Ridge, when he had turned the tables on Cassidy and when Cassidy had made a solemn oath to resign from the service if he failed to get his man in their next encounter. He knew Cassidy would keep his word, and something told him that tonight the last act in this tragedy of two had begun. He chuckled again as he pictured the probable course of events on shore. Cassidy, backed by the law, was demanding another canoe and a necessary outfit of Slim Buck. Slim Buck, falling back on his tribal dignity, was killing all possible time in making the preparations. When pursuit was resumed Jolly Roger would have at least a mile the start of the red-headed nemesis who hung to his trail. And Wollaston Lake, sixty miles from end to end, and half as wide, offered plenty of room in which to find safety.

The rising of the wind, which came from the south and west, was pleasing to Jolly Roger, and he put less caution and more force into the sweep of his paddle. For two hours he kept steadily eastward, and then swung a little north, guiding himself by the stars. With the breaking of dawn he made out the thickly wooded shore on the opposite side of the lake from Slim Buck's camp, and before the sun was half an hour high he had drawn up his canoe at the tip of a headland which gave him a splendid view of the lake in all directions.

From this point, comfortably encamped in the cool shadows of a thick clump of spruce, Jolly Roger and Peter watched all that day for a sign of their enemy. As far as the eye could reach no movement of human life appeared on the quiet surface of Wollaston. Not until that hazy hour between sunset and dusk did he build a fire and cook a meal from the supplies in Cassidy's pack, for he knew smoke could be discerned much farther than a canoe. Yet even as he observed this caution he was confident there was no longer any danger in returning to Yellow Bird and her people.

"You see, Pied-Bot," he said, discussing the matter with Peter, while he smoked a pipeful of tobacco in the early evening, "Cassidy thinks we're on our way north, as fast as we can go. He'll hit for the upper end of the Lake and the Black River waterway, and keep right on into the Porcupine country. It's a big country up there, and we've always taken plenty of space for our travels. Shall we go back to Yellow Bird, Peter? And Sun Cloud?"

Peter tried to answer, and thumped his tail, but even as he asked the questions there was a doubt growing in Jolly Roger's mind. He wanted to go back, and as darkness gathered about him he was urged by a great loneliness. Only Yellow Bird grieved with him in his loss of Nada, and understood how empty life had become for him. She had, in a way, become a part of Nada; her presence raised him out of despair, her voice gave him hope, her unconquerable spirit —fighting for his happiness—inspired him until he saw light where there had been only darkness. The impelling desire to return to her brought him to his feet and down to the pebbly shore of the lake, where the water rippled softly in the thickening gloom. But a still more powerful force held him back, and he went to his blankets, spread over a thick couch of balsam boughs. For hours his eyes were wide open and sleepless.

He no longer thought of Cassidy, but of Yellow Bird. Doubt—a charitable inclination to half believe— gave way in him to a conviction which he could not fight down. More than once in his years of wilderness life strange facts had compelled him to give some credence to the power of the Indian conjurer. Belief in the mastery of the mind was part of his faith in nature. It had come to him from his mother, who had lived and died in the strength of her creed.

"Think hard, and with faith, if you want anything to come true," she had told him. And this was also Yellow Bird's creed. Was it possible she had told him the truth? Had her mind actually communed with the mind of Nada? Had she, through the sheer force of her illimitable faith, projected her subconscious self into the future that she might show him the way? His eyes were staring, his ears unhearing, as he thought of the proof which Yellow Bird had given to him. A few hours ago she had brought him warning of impending danger. There had been no hesitation and no doubt. She had come to him unequivocal and sure. Without seeing, without hearing, she knew Cassidy was stealing upon him through the night.

In the darkness Jolly Roger sat up, his heart beating fast. Without effort, and with no thought of the necessity of proof, Yellow Bird had given him a test of her power. It had been a spontaneous and unstaged thing, a woman's heart reaching out for him—as she had promised that it would. And yet, even as the simplicity and truth of it pressed upon him, doubt followed with its questions. If, after this, Yellow Bird had told him to return to Nada as swiftly as he could, he would have believed, and this night would have seen him on his way. But she had warned him against this, predicting desolation and grief if he returned. She had urged him to go on, somewhere, anywhere, seeking for an illusion and an unreality which the spirits had named, to her as the Country Beyond. And when he reached this Country Beyond, wherever it might be, he would possess Nada again, and happiness for all time. After all, there was something archaically crude in what he was trying to believe, when he came to analyze it. Yellow Bird possessed her powers, but they were definitely limited. And to believe beyond those limitations, to ride upon the wings of superstition and imagination, was sheer savagery.

Jolly Roger stretched himself upon his blankets again, repeating this final argument to himself. But as the night drew closer about him, and his eyes closed, and sleep came, there was a lightness in his heart which he had not known for many days. He dreamed, and his dream was of Nada. He was with her again and it seemed, in this dream, that Yellow Bird was always watching them, and they could not quite get away from her. They ran through the jackpine openings where the strawberries and blue violets grew, and he always ran behind Nada, so he could see her brown curls flying about her.

But they never could rid themselves of Yellow Bird, no matter how fast they ran or where they tried to hide. From somewhere Yellow Bird's dark eyes would look out at them, and finally, laughing at his own discomfiture, he drew Nada down beside him in a little fen, white and yellow and blue with wildflowers, and boldly took her head in his arms and kissed her—with Yellow Bird looking at them from behind a banksian clump twenty feet away. So real was the kiss, and so real the warm pressure of Nada's slim arms about his neck that he awoke with a glad cry—and sat up to find the dawn had come.

For a few moments he sat stupidly, looking about him as if not quite believing the unreality of it all. Then with Peter he went down to the edge of the lake.

All that day Peter sensed a quiet change in his master. Jolly Roger did not talk. He did not whistle or laugh, but moved quietly when he moved at all, with a set, strange look in his face. He was making his last big fight against the desire to return to Cragg's Ridge. Yellow Bird's predictions, and her warning, had no influence with him now. He was thinking of Nada alone. She was back there, waiting for him, praying for his return, ready and happy to become a fugitive with him—to accept her chances of life or death, of happiness or grief, in his company. A dozen times the determination to return for her almost won. But each time came the other picture—a vision of ceaseless flight, of hiding, of hunger and cold and never ending hardship, and at the last, inevitable as the dawning of another day—prison, and possibly the hangman.

Not until late that afternoon did Peter see the old Jolly Roger in the face of his master. And Jolly Roger said:

"We've made up our mind, Pied-Bot. We can't go back. We'll hit north and spend the winter along the edge of the Barren Lands. It's the biggest country I know of, and if Cassidy comes—"

He shrugged his shoulders grimly.

In half an hour they had started, with the sun beginning to sink in the west.

For two days Jolly Roger and Peter paddled their way slowly up the eastern shore of Wollaston. That he had correctly analyzed the mental arguments which would guide Cassidy in his pursuit Jolly Roger had little doubt. He would keep to the west shore, and up through the Hatchet Lake and Black River waterways, as his quarry had never failed to hit straight for the farther north in time of peril. Meanwhile Jolly Roger had decided to make his way without haste up the east shore of Wollaston, and paddle north and east through the Du Brochet and Thiewiaza River waterways. If these courses were followed, each hour would add to the distance between them, and when the way was safe they would head straight for the Barren Lands.

Peter, and only Peter, sensed the glory of that third afternoon when they paddled slowly ashore close to the shimmering stream of spring water that was called Limping Moose Creek. The sun was still two hours high in the west. There was no wind, and Wollaston was like a mirror; yet in the still air was the clean, cool tang of early autumn, and shoreward the world reached out in ridges and billows of tinted forests, with a September haze pulsing softly over them, fleecy as the misty shower of a lady's powder puff. It was destined to be a memorable afternoon for Peter, a going down of the sun that he would never forget as long as he lived.

Yet there was no warning of the thing impending, and his eyes saw only the mystery and wonder of the big world, and his ears heard only the drowsing murmur of it, and his nose caught only the sweet scents of cedars and balsams and of flowering and ripening things. Straight ahead, beyond the white shore line, was a low ridge, and this ridge—where it was not purple and black with the evergreen—was red with the crimson blotches of mountain-ash berries, and patches of fire flowers that glowed like flame in the setting sun.

From out of this paradise, as they drew near to it, came softly the voice and song of birds and the chatter of red squirrels. A big jay was screeching over it all, and between the first ridge and the second—which rose still higher beyond it—a cloud of crows were circling excitedly over a mother black bear and her half grown cubs as they feasted on the red ash berries. But Peter could not smell the bears, nor hear them, and the distant crows were of less interest than the wonder and mystery of the shore close at hand.

He turned from his place in the bow of the canoe, and looked at his master. There was little of inspiration in Jolly Roger's face or eyes. The glory of the world ahead gave him no promise, as it gave promise to Peter. Beyond what he could see there lay, for him, a vast emptiness, a chaos of loneliness, an eternity of shattered hopes and broken dreams. Love of life was gone out of him. He saw no beauty. The sun had changed. The sky was different. The bigness of his wilderness no longer thrilled him, but oppressed him.

Peter sensed sharply the change in his master without knowing the reason for it. Just as the world had changed for Jolly Roger, so Jolly Roger had changed for Peter.

They landed on a beach of sand, soft as a velvet carpet. Peter jumped out. A long-legged sandpiper and her mate ran down the shore ahead of him. He perked up his angular ears, and then his nose caught a fresh scent under his feet where a porcupine had left his trail. And he heard more clearly the raucous tumult of the jay and the musical chattering of the red squirrels.

All these things were satisfactory to Peter. They were life, and life thrilled him, just as it had thrilled his master a few days ago. He adventured a little distance up to the edge of the green willows and the young birch and the crimson masses of fire flowers that fringed the beginning of the forest. It had rained recently here, and the scents were fresh and sweet.

He found a wild currant bush, glistening with its juscious black berries, and began nibbling at them. A gopher, coming to his supper bush, gave a little squeak of annoyance, and Peter saw the bright eyes of the midget glaring at him from under a big fern leaf. Peter wagged his tail, for the savagery of his existence was qualified by that mellowing sense of humor which had always been a part of his master. He yipped softly, in a companionable sort of way.

And then there smote upon his ears a sound which hardened every muscle in his body.

"Throw up your hands, McKay!"

He turned his head. Close to him stood a man. In an instant he had recognized him. It was the man whose scent he had first discovered down at Cragg's Ridge, the man from whom his master was always running away, the man whose voice he had heard again at Yellow Bird's Camp a few nights ago— Corporal Terence Cassidy, of the Royal Northwest Mounted Police.

Twenty paces away stood McKay. His dunnage was on his back, his paddle in his hand. And Cassidy, smiling grimly, a dangerous humor in his eyes, was leveling an automatic at his breast. It was, in that instant, a tableau which no man could ever forget. Cassidy was bareheaded, and the sun burned hotly in his red hair. And his face was red, and in the pale blue of his Irish eyes was a fierce joy of achievement. At last, after months and years, the thrilling game of One against One was at an end. Cassidy had made the last move, and he was winner.

For half a minute after the command to throw up his hands McKay did not move. And Cassidy did not repeat the command, for he sensed the shock that had fallen upon his adversary, and was charitable enough to give him time. And then, with something like a deep sigh from between his lips, Jolly Roger's body sagged.

The dunnage dropped from his shoulder to the sand. The paddle slipped from his hand. Slowly he raised his arms above his head, and Cassidy laughed softly.

A few days ago McKay would have grinned back, coolly, good humoredly, appreciative of the other's craftsmanship even in the hour of his defeat. But today there was another soul within him.

His eyes no longer saw the old Cassidy, brave and loyal to his duty, a chivalrous enemy, the man he had yearned to love as brother loves brother, even in the hours of sharpest pursuit. In Cassidy he saw now the hangman himself. The whole world had turned against him, and in this hour of his greatest despair and hopelessness a bitter fate had turned up Cassidy to deal him the finishing blow.

A swift rage burned in him, even as he raised his hands. It swept through his brain in a blinding inundation. He did not think of the law, or of death, or of freedom. It was the unfairness of the thing that filled his soul with the blackness of one last terrible desire for vengeance. Cassidy's gun, leveled at his breast, meant nothing. A thousand guns leveled at his breast would have meant nothing. A choking sound came from his lips, and like a shot his right hand went to his revolver holster.

In that last second or two Cassidy had foreseen the impending thing, and with the movement of the other's hand he cried out:

"Stop! For God's sake stop—or I shall fire!"

Even into the soul of Peter there came in that moment the electrical thrill of something terrific about to happen, of impending death, of tragedy close at hand. Once, a long time ago, Peter had felt another moment such as this—when he had buried his fangs in Jed Hawkins' leg to save Nada.

In that fraction of a second which carried Peter through space, Corporal Cassidy's finger was pressing the trigger of his automatic, for McKay's gun was half out of its holster. He was aiming at the other's shoulder, somewhere not to kill.

The shock of Peter's assault came simultaneously with the explosion of his gun, and McKay heard the hissing spit of the bullet past his ear. His arm darted out. And as Peter buried his teeth deeper into Cassidy's leg, he heard a second shot, and knew that it came from his master. There was no third. Cassidy drooped, and something like a little laugh came from him—only it was not a laugh. His body sagged, and then crumpled down, so that the weight of him fell upon Peter.

For many seconds after that Jolly Roger stood with his gun in his hand, not a muscle of his body moving, and with something like stupor in his staring eyes. Peter struggled out from under Cassidy, and looked inquisitively from his master to the man who lay sprawled out like a great spider upon the sand. It was then that life seemed to come back into Jolly Roger's body. His gun fell, as if it was the last thing in the world to count for anything now, and with a choking cry he ran to Cassidy and dropped upon his knees beside him.

"Cassidy—Cassidy—" he cried. "Good God, I didn't mean to do it! Cassidy, old pal—"

The agony in his voice stilled the growl in Peter's throat. McKay saw nothing for a space, as he raised Cassidy's head and shoulders, and brushed back the mop of red hair. Everything was a blur before his eyes. He had killed Cassidy. He knew it. He had shot to kill, and not once in a hundred times did he miss his mark. At last he was what the law wanted him to be—a murderer. And his victim was Cassidy—the man who had played him fairly and squarely from beginning to end, the man who had never taken a mean advantage of him, and who had died there in the white sand because he had not shot to kill. With sobbing breath he cried out his grief, and then, looking down, he saw the miracle in Cassidy's face. The Irishman's eyes were wide open, and there was pain, and also a grin, about his mouth.

"I'm glad you're sorry," he said. "I'd hate to have a bad opinion of you, McKay. But—you're a rotten shot!"

His body sagged heavily, and the grin slowly left his lips, and a moan came from between them. He struggled and spoke.

"It may be—you'll want help, McKay. If you do—there's a cabin half a mile up the creek. Saw the smoke—heard axe—I don't blame you. You're a good sport—pretty quick—but—rotten shot! Oh, Lord—such—rotten—shot—"

And he tried vainly to grin up into Jolly Roger's face as he became a lifeless weight in the other's arms.

Jolly Roger was sobbing. He was sobbing, in a strange, hard man- fashion, as he tore open Cassidy's shirt and saw the red wound that went clean through Cassidy's right breast just under the shoulder. And Peter still heard that strange sound coming from his lips, a moaning as if for breath, as his master ran and brought up water, and worked over the fallen man. And then he got under Cassidy, and rose up with him on his shoulders, and staggered off with him toward the creek. There he found a path, a narrow foot trail, and not once did he stop with his burden until he came into a little clearing, out of which Cassidy had seen the smoke rising. In this clearing was a cabin, and from the cabin came an old man to meet him—an old man and a girl.

At first something shot up into Peter's throat, for he thought it was Nada who came behind the grizzled and white-headed man. There was the same lithe slimness in her body, the same brown glint in her hair, and the same—but he saw then that it was not Nada. She was older. She was a bit taller. And her face was white when she saw the bleeding burden on Jolly Roger's back.

"I shot him," panted McKay. "God knows I didn't mean to! I'm afraid—"

He did not finish giving voice to the fear that Cassidy was dead— or dying, and for a moment he saw only the big staring eyes of the girl as the gray-bearded man helped him with his burden. Not until the Irishman was on a cot in the cabin did he discover how childishly weak he had become and what a terrific struggle he had made with the weight on his shoulders. He sank into a chair, while the old trapper worked over Cassidy.

He heard the girl call him grandfather. She was no longer frightened, and she moved like a swift bird about the cabin, getting water and bandages and pillows, and the sight of fresh blood and of Cassidy's dead-white face brought a glow of tenderness into her eyes. McKay, sitting dumbly, saw that her hands were doing twice the work his own could have accomplished, and not until he heard a low moan from the wounded man did he come to her side.

"The bullet went through clean as a whistle," the old man said. "Lucky you don't use soft nosed bullets, friend."

A deep sigh came from Cassidy's lips. His eyelids fluttered, and then slowly his eyes opened. The girl was bending over him, and Cassidy saw only her face, and the brown sheen of her hair.

"He'll live?" Jolly Roger said tremulously.

The older man remained mute. It was Cassidy, turning his head a little, who answered weakly.

"Don't worry, McKay. I'll—live."

Jolly Roger bent over the cot, between Cassidy and the girl. Gently he took one of the wounded man's hands in both his own.

"I'm sorry, old man," he whispered. "You won, fair and square. And I won't go far away. I'll be waiting for you when you get on your feet. I promise that. I'll wait."

A wan smile came over Cassidy's lips, and then he moaned again, and his eyes closed. The girl thrust Jolly Roger back.

"No—you better not go far, an' you better wait," she said, and there was an unspoken thing in the dark glow of her eyes that made him think of Nada on that day when she told him how Jed Hawkins had struck her in the cabin at Cragg's Ridge.

That night Jolly Roger made his camp close to the mouth of the Limping Moose. And for three days thereafter his trail led only between this camp and the cabin of old Robert Baron and his granddaughter, Giselle. All this time Cassidy was telling things in a fever. He talked a great deal about Jolly Roger. And the girl, nursing him night and day, with scarcely a wink of sleep between, came to believe they had been great comrades, and had been inseparable for a long time. Even then she would not let McKay take her place at Cassidy's side. The third day she started him off for a post sixty miles away to get a fresh supply of bandages and medicines.

It was evening, three days later, when Jolly Roger and Peter returned. The windows of the cabin were brightly lighted, and McKay came up to one of these windows and looked in. Cassidy was bolstered up in his cot. He was very much alive, and on the floor at his side, sitting on a bear rug, was the girl. A lump rose in Jolly Roger's throat. Quietly he placed the bundle which he had brought from the post close up against the door, and knocked. When Giselle opened it he had disappeared into darkness, with Peter at his heels.

The next morning he found old Robert and said to him:

"I'm restless, and I'm going to move a little. I'll be back in two weeks. Tell Cassidy that, will you?"

Ten minutes later he was paddling up the shore of Wollaston, and for a week thereafter he haunted the creeks and inlets, always on the move. Peter saw him growing thinner each day. There was less and less of cheer in his voice, seldom a smile on his lips, and never did his laugh ring out as of old. Peter tried to understand, and Jolly Roger talked to him, but not in the old happy way.

"We might have finished him, an' got rid of him for good," he said to Peter one chilly night beside their campfire. "But we couldn't, just like we couldn't have brought Nada up here with us. And we're going back. I'm going to keep that promise. We're going back, Peter, if we hang for it!"

And Jolly Roger's jaw would set grimly as he measured the time between.

The tenth day came and he set out for the mouth of the Canoe River. On the afternoon of the twelfth he paddled slowly into Limping Moose Creek. Without any reason he looked at his watch when he started for old Robert's cabin. It was four o'clock. He was two days ahead of his promise, and there was a bit of satisfaction in that. There was an odd thumping at his heart. He had faith in Cassidy, a belief that the Irishman would call their affair a draw, and tell him to take another chance in the big open. He was the sort of man to live up to the letter of a wager, when it was honestly made. But, if he didn't—

Jolly Roger paused long enough to take the cartridges from his gun. There would be no more shooting'—on his part.

The mellow autumn sun was flooding the open door of the cabin when he came up. He heard laughter. It was Giselle. She was talking, too. And then he heard a man's voice—and from far off to his right came the chopping of an axe. Old Robert was at work. Giselle and Cassidy were at home.

He stepped up to the door, coughing to give notice of his approach. And then, suddenly, he stopped, staring thunderstruck at what was happening within.

Terence Cassidy was sitting in a big chair. The girl was behind him. Her white arms were around his neck, her face was bent down, her lips were kissing him.

In an instant Cassidy's eyes had caught him.

"Come in," he cried, so suddenly and so loudly that it startled the girl. "McKay, come in!"

Jolly Roger entered, and the girl stood up straight behind Cassidy's chair, her cheeks aflame and her eyes filled with the glow of the sunset. And Terence Cassidy was grinning in that old triumphant way as he leaned forward in his chair, gripping the arms of it with both hands.

"McKay, you've lost," he cried. "I'm the winner!"

In the same moment he took the girl's hand and drew her from behind his chair.

"Giselle, do as you said you were going to do. Prove to him that I've won."

Slowly she came to Jolly Roger. Her cheeks were like the red of the sunset. Her eyes were flaming. Her lips were parted. And dumbly he waited, and wondered, until she stood close to him. Then, swiftly, her arms were around his neck, and she kissed him. In an instant she was back on her knees at the wounded man's side, her burning face hidden against him, and Cassidy was laughing, and holding out both hands to McKay.

"McKay, Roger McKay, I want you to meet Mrs. Terence Cassidy, my wife," he said. And the girl raised her face, so that her shining eyes were on Jolly Roger.

Still dumbly he stood where he was.

"The Missioner from Du Brochet was here yesterday, and married us," he heard Cassidy saying. "And we've written out my resignation together, old man. We've both won. I thank God you put that bullet into me down on the shore, for it's brought me paradise. And here's my hand on it, McKay—forever and ever!"

Half an hour later, when McKay stumbled out into the forest trail again, his eyes were blinded by tears and his heart choked by a new hope as big as the world itself. Yellow Bird was right, and God must have been with her that night when her soul went to commune with Nada's. For Yellow Bird had proved herself again. And now he believed her.

He believed in the world again. He believed in love and happiness and the glory of life, and as he went down the narrow trail to his canoe, with Peter close behind him, his heart was crying out Nada's name and Yellow Bird's promise that sometime—somewhere— they two would find happiness together, as Giselle and Terence Cassidy had found it.

And Peter heard the chopping of the distant axe, and the song of birds, and the chattering of squirrels—but thrilling his soul most of all was the voice of his master, the old voice, the glad voice, the voice he had first learned to love at Cragg's Ridge in the days of blue violets and red strawberries, when Nada had filled his world.

CHAPTER XIII

MCKAY still had his mind on a certain stretch of timber that reached out into the Barren Lands, hundreds of miles farther north. In this hiding place, three years before, he had built himself a cabin, and had caught foxes during half the long winter. Not only the cabin, but the foxes, were drawing him. Necessity was close upon his heels. What little money he possessed after leaving Cragg's Ridge was exhausted, his supplies were gone, and his boots and clothes were patched with deer hide.

In the Snowbird Lake country, a week after he left Cassidy in his paradise at Wollaston, he fell in with good fortune. Two trappers had come in from Churchill. One of them was sick, and the other needed help in the building of their winter cabin. McKay remained with them for ten days, and when he continued his journey northward his pack was stuffed with supplies, and he wore new boots and more comfortable clothes.

It was the middle of October when he found his old cabin, a thousand miles from Cragg's Ridge. It was as he had left it three years ago. No one had opened its door since then. The little box stove was waiting for a fire. Behind it was a pile of wood. On the table were the old tin dishes, and hanging from babiche cords fastened to the roof timbers, out of reach of mice and ermine, were blankets and clothing and other possessions he had left behind him in that winter break-up of what seemed like ages ago to him. He raised a small section in the floor, and there were his traps, thickly coated with caribou grease. For half an hour before he built a fire he sought eagerly for the things he had concealed here and there. He found oil, and a tin lamp, and candles, and as darkness of the first night gathered outside a roaring fire sent sparks up the chimney, and the little cabin's one window glowed with light, and the battered old coffee pot bubbled and steamed again, as if rejoicing at his return.

With the breaking of another day he immediately began preparations for the season's trapping. In two days' hunting he killed three caribou, his winter meat. Then he cut wood, and made his strychnine poison baits, and marked out his trap-lines.

The first of November brought the chill whisperings of an early winter through the Northland. Farther south autumn was dying, or dead. The last of the red ash berries hung shriveled and frost- bitten on naked twigs, freezing nights were nipping the face of the earth, the voices of the wilderness were filled with a new note and the winds held warning for every man and beast between Hudson's Bay and the Great Slave and from the Height of Land to the Arctic Sea. Seven years before there had come such a winter, and the land had not forgotten it—a winter sudden and swift, deadly in its unexpectedness, terrific in its cold, bringing with it such famine and death as the Northland had not known for two generations.

But this year there was premonition. Omen of it came with the first wailing night winds that bore the smell of icebergs from over the black forests north and west. The moon came up red, and it went down red, and the sun came up red in the morning. The loon's call died a month ahead of its time. The wild geese drove steadily south when they should have been feeding from the Kogatuk to Baffin's Bay, and the beaver built his walls thick, and anchored his alders and his willows deep so that he would not starve when the ice grew heavy. East, west, north and south, in forest and swamp, in the trapper's cabin and the wolf's hiding- place, was warning of it. Gray rabbits turned white. Moose and caribou began to herd. The foxes yipped shrilly in the night, and a new hunger and a new thrill sent the wolves hunting in packs, while the gray geese streaked southward under the red moon overhead.

Through this November, and all of December, Jolly Roger and Peter were busy from two hours before dawn of each day until late at night. The foxes were plentiful, and McKay was compelled to shorten his lines and put out fewer baits, and on the tenth of December he set out for a fur-trading post ninety miles south with two hundred and forty skins. He had made a toboggan, and a harness for Peter, and pulling together they made the trip in three days, and on the fourth started for the cabin again with supplies and something over a thousand dollars in cash.

Through the weeks of increasing storm and cold that followed, McKay continued to trap, and early in February he made another trip to the fur post.

It was on their return that they were caught in the Black Storm. It will be a long time before the northland will forget that storm. It was a storm in which the Sarcees died to a man, woman and child over on the Dubawnt waterways, and when trees froze solid and split open with the sharp explosions of high-power guns. In it, all furred and feathered life and all hoof and horn along the edge of the Barren Lands from Aberdeen Lake to the Coppermine was swallowed up. It was in this storm that streams froze solid, and the man who was cautious fastened a babiche rope about his waist when he went forth from his cabin for wood or water, so that his wife might help to pull and guide him back through that blinding avalanche of wind and freezing fury that held a twisted and broken world in its grip.

In the country west of Artillery Lake and south of the Theolon River, Jolly Roger and Peter were compelled to "dig in." They were in a country where the biggest stick of wood that thrust itself up out of the snow was no bigger than McKay's thumb; a country of green grass and succulent moss on which the caribou fed in season, but a hell on earth when arctic storm howled and screamed across it in winter.

Piled up against a mass of rock Jolly Roger found a huge snow drift. This drift was as long as a church and half as high, with its outer shell blistered and battered to the hardness of rock by wind and sleet. Through this shell he cut a small door with his knife, and after that dug out the soft snow from within until he had a room half as big as his cabin, and so snug and warm after a little with the body heat of himself and Peter that he could throw off the thick coat which he wore.

To Peter, in the first night of this storm, it seemed as though all the people in the world were shrieking and wailing and sobbing in the blackness outside. Jolly Roger sat smoking his pipe at intervals in the gloom, though there was little pleasure in smoking a pipe in darkness. The storm did not oppress him, but filled him with an odd sense of security and comfort. The wind shrieked and lashed itself about his snow-dune, but it could not get at him. Its mightiest efforts to destroy only beat more snow upon him, and made him safer and warmer. In a way, there was something of humor as well as tragedy in its wild frenzy, and Peter heard him laugh softly in the darkness. More and more frequently he had heard that laugh since those warm days of autumn when they had last met the red-headed man, Terence Cassidy, of the Royal Northwest Mounted Police, and his master had shot him on the white shore of Wollaston.

"You see," said McKay, caressing Peter's hairy neck in the gloom. "Everything is turning out right for us, and I'm beginning to believe more and more what Yellow Bird told us, and that in the end we're going to be happy—somewhere—with Nada. What do you think, Pied-Bot? Shall we take a chance, and go back to Cragg's Ridge in the spring?"

Peter wriggled himself in answer, as a wild shriek of wind wailed over the huge snow-dune.

Jolly Roger's fingers tightened at Peter's neck.

"Well, we're going," he said, as though he was telling Peter something new. "I'm believing Yellow Bird, Pied-Bot. I'm believing her—now. What she told us was more than fortune-telling. It wasn't just Indian sorcery. When she shut herself up and starved for those three days and nights in her little conjurer's house, just for you and me—SOMETHING HAPPENED. Didn't it? Wouldn't you say something happened?"

Peter swallowed and his teeth clicked as he gave evidence of understanding.

"She told us a lot of truth," went on Jolly Roger, with deep faith in his voice "And we must believe, Pied-Bot. She told us Cassidy was coming after us, and he came. She said the spirits promised her the law would never get us, and we thought it looked bad when Cassidy had us covered with his gun on the shore at Wollaston. But something more than luck was with us, and we shot him. Then we brought him back to life and lugged him to a cabin, and the little stranger girl took him, and nursed him, and Cassidy fell in love with her—and married her. So Yellow Bird was right again, Pied- Bot. We've got to believe her. And she says everything is coming out right for us, and that we are going back to Nada, and be happy—"

Jolly Roger's pipe-bowl glowed in the blackness.

"I'm going to light the alcohol lamp," he said. "We can't sleep. And I want a good smoke. It isn't fun when you can't see the smoke. Too bad God forgot to make you so you could use a pipe, Peter. You don't know what you are missing—in times like these."

He fumbled in his pack and found the alcohol lamp, which was fresh filled and screwed tight. Peter heard him working for a moment in the darkness. Then he struck a match, and the yellow flare of it lighted up his face. In his joy Peter whined. It was good to see his master. And then, in another moment, the little lamp was filling their white-walled refuge with a mellow glow. Jolly Roger's eyes, coming suddenly out of darkness, were wide and staring. His face was covered with a scrub beard. But there was something of cheer about him even in this night of terror outside, and when he had driven his snowshoe into the snow wall, and had placed the lamp on it, he grinned companionably at Peter.

Then, with a deep breath of satisfaction, he puffed out clouds of smoke from his pipe, and stood up to look about their room.

"Not so bad, is it?" he asked. "We could have a big house here if we wanted to dig out rooms—eh, Peter? Parlors, and bed-rooms, and a library—and not a police-man within a million miles of us. That's the nice part of it, PIED-BOT—none of the Royal Mounties to trouble us. They would never think of looking for us in the heart of a big snow-dune out in this God-forsaken barren, would they?"

The thought was a pleasing one to Jolly Roger. He spread out his blankets on the snow floor, and sat down on them, facing Peter.

"We've got 'em beat," he said, a chuckling note of pride in his voice. "The world is small when it comes to hiding, Pied-Bot, but all the people in it couldn't find us here—not in a million years. If we could only find a place as safe as this—where a girl could live—and had Nada with us—"

Many times during the past few weeks Peter had seen the light that flamed up now in his master's eyes. That, and the strange thrill in Jolly Roger's voice, stirred him more than the words to which he listened, and tried to understand.

"And we're GOING to," finished McKay, almost fiercely, his hands clenching as he leaned toward Peter. "We have made a big mistake, Pied-Bot, and it has taken us a long time to see it. It will be hard for us to leave our north country, but that is what we must do. Maybe Yellow Bird's good spirits meant that when they said we would find happiness with Nada in a place called The Country Beyond. There are a lot of 'Countries Beyond,' Peter, and as soon as the spring break-up comes and we can travel without leaving trails behind us we will go back to Cragg's Ridge and get

Nada, and hit for some place where the law won't expect to find us. There's China, for instance. A lot of yellow people. But what do we care for color as long as we have her with us? I say—"

Suddenly he stopped. And Peter's body grew tense. Both faced the round hole, half filled with softly packed snow, which McKay had cut as a door into the heart of the big drift. They had grown accustomed to the tumult of the storm. Its strange wailings and the shrieking voices which at times seemed borne in the moaning sweep of it no longer sent shivers of apprehension through Peter. But in that moment when both turned to listen there came a sound which was not like the other sounds they had heard. It was a voice—not one of the phantom voices of the screaming wind, but a voice so real and so near that for a beat or two even Jolly Roger McKay's heart stood still. It was as if a man, standing just beyond their snow barricade, had shouted a name. But there came no second call. The wind lulled, so that for a space there was stillness outside.

Jolly Roger laughed a little uneasily.

"Good thing we don't believe in ghosts, Peter, or we would swear it was a Loup-Garou smelling us through the wall!" He thumbed the tobacco down in his pine, and nodded. "Then—there is South America," he said. "They have everything down there—the biggest rivers in the world, the biggest mountains, and so much room that even a Loup-Garou couldn't hunt us out. She will love it, Pied- Bot. But if it happens she likes Africa better, or Australia, or the South Sea—Now, what the devil was that?"

Peter had jumped as if stung, and for a moment Jolly Roger sat tense as a carven Indian. Then he rose to his feet, a look of perplexity and doubt in his eyes.

"What was it, Peter? Can the wind shoot a gun—like THAT?"

Peter was sniffing at the loosely blocked door of their snow-room. A whimper rose in his throat. He looked up at Jolly Roger, his eyes glowing fiercely through the mass of Airedale whiskers that covered his face. He wanted to dig. He wanted to plunge out into the howling darkness. Slowly McKay beat the ash out of his pipe and placed the pipe in his pocket.

"We'll take a look," he said, something repressive in his voice. "But it isn't reasonable, Peter. It is the wind. There couldn't be a man out there, and it wasn't a rifle we heard. It is the wind— with the devil himself behind it!"

With a few sweeps of his hands and arms he scooped out the loose snow from the hole. The opening was on the sheltered side of the drift, and only the whirling eddies of the storm swept about him as he thrust out his head and shoulders. But over him it was rushing like an avalanche. He could hear nothing but the moaning advance of it. And he could see nothing. He held out his hand before his face, and blackness swallowed it.

"We have been chased so much that we're what you might call super- sensitive," he said, pulling himself back and nodding at Peter in the gray light of the alcohol lamp. "Guess we'd better turn in, boy. This is a good place to sleep—plenty of fresh air, no mosquitoes or black flies, and the police so far away that we will soon forget how they look. If you say so we will have a nip of cold tea and a bite—"

He did not finish. For a moment the wind had lessened in fury, as if gathering a deeper breath. And what he heard drew a cry from him this time, and a sharper whine from Peter. Out of the blackness of the night had come a woman's voice! In that first instant of shock and amazement he would have staked his life that what he heard was not a mad outcry of the night or an illusion of his brain. It was clear—distinct—a woman's voice coming from out on the Barren, rising above the storm in an agony of appeal, and dying out quickly until it became a part of the moaning wind. And then, with equal force, came the absurdity of it to McKay. A woman! He swallowed the lump that had risen in his throat, and tried to laugh. A WOMAN—out in that storm—a thousand miles from nowhere! It was inconceivable.

The laugh which he forced from his lips was husky and unreal, and there was a smothering grip of something at his heart. In the ghostly light of the alcohol lamp his eyes were wide open and staring.

He looked at Peter. The dog stood stiff-legged before the hole. His body was trembling.

"Peter!"

With a responsive wag of his tail Peter turned his bristling face up to his master. Many times Jolly Roger had seen that unfailing warning in his comrade's eyes. THERE WAS SOME ONE OUTSIDE—or Peter's brain, like his own, was twisted and fooled by the storm!

Against his reasoning—in the face of the absurdity of it—Jolly Roger was urged into action. He changed the snowshoe and replaced the alcohol lamp so that the glow of light could be seen more clearly from the Barren. Then he went to the hole and crawled through. Peter followed him.

As if infuriated by their audacity, the storm lashed itself over the top of the dune. They could hear the hissing whine of fine hard snow tearing above their heads like volleys of shot, and the force of the wind reached them even in their shelter, bringing with it the flinty sting of the snow-dust. Beyond them the black barren was filled with a dismal moaning. Looking up, and yet seeing nothing in the darkness, Peter understood where the weird shriekings and ghostly cries came from. It was the wind whipping itself up the side and over the top of the dune.

Jolly Roger listened, hearing only the convulsive sweep of that mighty force over a thousand miles of barren. And then came again one of those brief intervals when the storm seemed to rest for a moment, and its moaning grew less and less, until it was like the sound of giant chariot wheels receding swiftly over the face of the earth. Then came the silence—a few seconds of it—while in the north gathered swiftly the whispering rumble of a still greater force.

And in this silence came once more a cry—a cry which Jolly Roger McKay could no longer disbelieve, and close upon the cry the report of a rifle. Again he could have sworn the voice was a woman's voice. As nearly as he could judge it came from dead ahead, out of the chaos of blackness, and in that direction he shouted an answer. Then he ran out into the darkness, followed by Peter. Another avalanche of wind gathered at their heels, driving them on like the crest of a flood. In the first force of it Jolly Roger stumbled and fell to his knees, and in that moment he saw very faintly the glow of his light at the opening in the snow dune. A realization of his deadly peril if he lost sight of the light flashed upon him. Again and again he called into the night. After that, bowing his head in the fury of the storm, he plunged on deeper into darkness.

A sudden wild thought seized upon his soul and thrilled him into forgetfulness of the light and the snow-dune and his own safety. In the heart of this mad world he had heard a voice. He no longer doubted it. And the voice was a woman's voice! Could it be Nada? Was it possible she had followed him after his flight, determined to find him, and share his fate? His heart pounded. Who else, of all the women in the world, could be following his trail across the Barrens—a thousand miles from civilization? He began to shout her name. "Nada—Nada—Nada!" And hidden in the gloom at his side Peter barked.

Storm and darkness swallowed them. The last faint gleam of the alcohol lamp died out. Jolly Roger did not look back. Blindly he stumbled ahead, counting his footsteps as he went, and shouting Nada's name. Twice he thought he heard a reply, and each time the will-o'-the-wisp voice seemed to be still farther ahead of him. Then, with a fiercer blast of the wind beating upon his back, he stumbled and fell forward upon his face. His hand reached out and touched the thing that had tripped him. It was not snow. His naked fingers clutched in something soft and furry. It was a man's coat. He could feel buttons, a belt, and the sudden thrill of a bearded face.

He stood up. The wind was wailing off over the Barren again, leaving an instant of stillness about him. And he shouted:

"Nada—Nada—Nada!"

An answer came so quickly that it startled him, not one voice, but two—three—and one of them the shrill agonized cry of a woman. They came toward him as he continued to shout, until a few feet away he could make out a gray blur moving through the gloom. He went to it, staggering under the weight of the man he had found in the snow. The blur was made up of two men dragging a sledge, and behind the sledge was a third figure, moaning in the darkness.

"I found some one in the snow," Jolly Roger shouted. "Here he is— "

He dropped his burden, and the last of his words were twisted by a fresh blast of the storm. But the figure behind the sledge had heard, and Jolly Roger saw her indistinctly at his feet, shielding the man he had found with her arms and body, and crying out a name which he could not understand in that howling of the wind. But a thing like cold steel sank into his heart, and he knew it was not Nada he had found this night on the Barren. He placed the unconscious man on the sledge, believing he was dead. The girl was crying out something to him, unintelligible in the storm, and one of the men shouted in a thick throaty voice which he could not understand. Jolly Roger felt the weight of him as he staggered in the wind, fighting to keep his feet, and he knew he was ready to drop down in the snow and die.

"It's only a step," he shouted. "Can you make it?"

His words reached the ears of the others. The girl swayed through the darkness and gripped his arm. The two men began to tug at the sledge, and Jolly Roger seized the rope between them, wondering why there were no dogs, and faced the driving of the storm. It seemed an interminable time before he saw the faint glow of the alcohol lamp. The last fifty feet was like struggling against an irresistible hail from machine-guns. Then came the shelter of the dune.

One at a time McKay helped to drag them through the hole which he used for a door. For a space his vision was blurred, and he saw through the hazy film of storm-blindness the gray faces and heavily coated forms of those he had rescued. The man he had found in the snow he placed on his blankets, and the girl fell down upon her knees beside him. It was then Jolly Roger began to see more clearly. And in that same instant came a shock as unexpected as the smash of dynamite under his feet.

The girl had thrown back her parkee, and was sobbing over the man on the blankets, and calling him father. She was not like Nada. Her hair was in thick, dark coils, and she was older. She was not pretty—now. Her face was twisted by the brutal beating of the storm, and her eyes were nearly closed. But it was the man Jolly Roger stared at, while his heart choked inside him. He was grizzled and gray-bearded, with military mustaches and a bald head. He was not dead. His eyes were open, and his blue lips were struggling to speak to the girl whose blindness kept her from seeing that he was alive. And the coat which he wore was the regulation service garment of the Royal Northwest Mounted Police!

Slowly McKay turned, wiping the film of snow-sweat from his eyes, and stared at the other two. One of them had sunk down with his back to the snow wall. He was a much younger man, possibly not over thirty, and his face was ghastly. The third lay where he had fallen from exhaustion after crawling through the hole. Both wore service coats, with holsters at their sides.

The man against the snow-wall was making an effort to rise. He sagged back, and grinned up apologetically at McKay.

"Dam' fine of you, old man," he mumbled between blistered lips. "I'm Por-ter—'N' Division—taking Superintendent Tavish to Fort Churchill—Tavish and his daughter. Made a hell of a mess of it, haven't I?"

He struggled to his knees.

"There's brandy in our kit. It might help—over there," and he nodded toward the girl and the gray-bearded man on the blankets.

CHAPTER XIV

JOLLY Roger did not answer, but crawled through the hole and found the sledge in the outer darkness. He heard Peter coming after him, and he saw Porter's bloodless face in the illumination of the alcohol lamp, where he waited to help him with the dunnage. In those seconds he fought to get a grip on himself. A quarter of an hour ago he had laughed at the thought of the law. Never had it seemed to be so far away from him, and never had he been more utterly isolated from the world. His mind was still a bit dazed by the thing that had happened. The police had not trailed him. They had not ferreted him out, nor had they stumbled upon him by accident. It was he who had gone out into the night and deliberately dragged them in! Of all the trickery fate had played upon him this was the least to be expected.

His mind began to work more swiftly as in darkness he cut the babiche cordage that bound the patrol dunnage to the sledge. "N" Division, he told himself, was away over in the Athabasca country. He had never heard of Porter, nor of Superintendent Tavish, and inasmuch as the outfit was evidently a special escort to Fort Churchill it was very likely that Porter and his companions would not be thinking of outlaws, and especially of Jolly Roger McKay. This was his one chance. To attempt an escape through the blizzard was not only a desperate hazard. It was death.

There were only two packs on the sledge, and these he passed through the hole to Porter. A few moments later he was holding a flask of liquor to the lips of the gray-bearded man, while the girl looked at him with eyes that were widening as the snow-sting left them. Tavish gulped, and his mittened hand closed on the girl's arm.

"I'm all right, Jo," he mumbled. "All right—"

His eyes met McKay's, and then took in the snow walls of the dug- out. They were deep, piercing eyes, overhung by shaggy brows. Jolly Roger felt the intentness of their gaze as he gave the girl a swallow of the brandy, and then passed the flask to Porter.

"You have saved our lives," said Tavish, in a voice that was clearer. "I don't just understand how it happened. I remember stumbling in the darkness, and being unable to rise. I was behind the sledge. Porter and Breault were dragging it, and Josephine, my daughter, was sheltered under the blankets. After that—"

He paused, and Jolly Roger explained how it all had come about. He pointed to Peter. It was the dog, he said. Peter had insisted there was someone outside, and they had taken a chance by going in search of them. He was John Cummings, a fox trapper, and the storm had caught him fifty miles from his cabin. He was traveling without a dog-sledge, and had only a pack-outfit.

Breault, the third man, had regained his wind, and was listening to him. One look at his dark, thin face told McKay that he was the wilderness man of the three. He was staring at Jolly Roger in a strange sort of way. And then, as if catching him- self, he nodded, and began rubbing his frosted face with handfuls of snow.

Porter had thrown off his heavy coat, and was unpacking one of the dunnage sacks. He and the girl seemed to have suffered less than the other two. Jo, the girl, was looking at him. And then her eyes turned to Jolly Roger. They were large, fine eyes, wide open and clear now. There was something of splendid strength about her as she smiled at McKay. She was not of the hysterical sort. He could see that.

"If we could have some hot soup," she suggested. "May we?"

There was gratitude in her eyes, which she made no attempt to express in words. Jolly Roger liked her. And Peter crept up behind her, and watched her as she followed Breault's example, and rubbed the cheeks of the bearded man with snow.

"There's an alcohol stove in the other pack," said Breault, with his hard, narrow eyes fixed steadily on Jolly Roger's face. "By the way, what did you say your name was?"

"Cummings—John Cummings."

Breault made no answer. During the next half hour Jolly Roger felt stealing over him a growing sense of uneasiness. They drank soup and ate bannock. It grew warm, and the girl threw off the heavy fur garment that enveloped her. Color returned into her cheeks. Her eyes were bright, and in her voice was a tremble of happiness at finding warmth and life where she had expected death. Porter's friendliness was almost brotherly. He explained what had happened. Two rascally Chippewyans had deserted them, stealing off into darkness and storm with both dog teams and one of their sledges. After that they had fought on, seeking for a drift into which they might dig a refuge. But the Barren was as smooth as a table. They had shouted, and Miss Tavish had screamed—not because they expected to find assistance—but on account of Tavish falling in the storm, and losing himself. It was quite a joke, Porter thought, that Superintendent Tavish, one of the iron men of the service, should have given up the ghost so easily.

Tavish smiled grimly. They were all in good humor, and happy, with the possible exception of Breault. Not once did he laugh or smile. Yet Jolly Roger noted that each time he spoke the others were specially attentive. There was something repressive and mysterious about the man, and the girl would cut herself short in the middle of a laugh if he happened to speak, and the softness of her mouth would harden in an instant. He understood the significance of her gladness, and of Porter's, for twice he saw their hands come together, and their fingers entwine. And in their eyes was something which they could not hide when they looked at each other. But Breault puzzled him. He did not know that Breault was the best man-hunter in "N" Division, which reached from Athabasca Landing to the Arctic Ocean, or that up and down the two thousand- mile stretch of the Three River Country he was known as Shingoos, the Ferret.

The girl fell asleep first that night, with her cheek on her father's shoulder. Breault, the Ferret, rolled himself in a blanket, and breathed deeply. Porter still smoked his pipe, and looked wistfully at the pale face of Josephine Tavish. He smiled a bit proudly at McKay.

"She's mine," he whispered. "We're going to be married."

Jolly Roger wanted to reach over and grip his hand.

He nodded, a little lump coming in his throat.

"I know how you feel," he said. "When I heard her calling out there—it made me think—of a girl down south."

"Down south?" queried Porter. "Why down south—if you care for her—and you up here?"

McKay shrugged his shoulders. He had said too much. Neither he nor Porter knew that Breault's eyes were half open, and that he was listening.

Jolly Roger held up a hand, as if something in the wailing of the storm had caught his attention.

"We'll have two or three days of this. Better turn in, Porter. I'm going to dig out another room—for Miss Tavish. I'm afraid she'll need the convenience of a private room before we're able to move. It's an easy job—and passes the time away."

"I'll help," offered Porter.

For an hour they worked, using McKay's snowshoes as shovels. During that hour Breault did not close his eyes. A curious smile curled his thin lips as he watched Jolly Roger. And when at last Porter turned in, and slept, the Ferret sat up, and stretched himself. McKay had finished his room, and was beginning a tunnel which would lead as a back door out of the drift, when Breault came in and picked up the snowshoe which Porter had used.

"I'll take my turn," he said. "I'm a bit nervous, and not at all sleepy, Cummings." He began digging into the snow. "Been long in this country?" he asked.

"Three winters. It's a good red fox country, with now and then a silver and a black."

Breault grunted.

"You must have met Cassidy, then," he said casually, without looking at Mc-Kay. "Corporal Terence Cassidy. This is his country."

Jolly Roger did not look up from his work of digging.

"Yes, I know him. Met him last winter. Red headed. A nice chap. I like him. You know him?"

"Entered the service together," said Breault. "But he's unlucky. For two or three years he has been on the trail of a man named McKay. Jolly Roger, they call him—Jolly Roger McKay. Ever hear of him?"

Jolly Roger nodded.

"Cassidy told me about him when he was at my cabin. From what I've heard I—rather like him."

"Who—Cassidy, or Jolly Roger?"

"Both."

For the first time the Ferret leveled his eyes at his companion. They were mystifying eyes, never appearing to open fully, but remaining half closed as if to conceal whatever thought might lie behind them. McKay felt their penetration. It was like a cold chill entering into him, warning him of a menace deadlier than the storm.

"Haven't any idea where one might come upon this Jolly Roger, have you?"

"No."

"You see, he thinks he killed a man down south. Well, he didn't. The man lived. If you happen to see him at any time give him that information, will you?"

Jolly Roger thrust his head and shoulders into the growing tunnel.

"Yes, I will."

He knew Breault was lying. And also knew that back of the narrow slits of Breault's eyes was the cunning of a fox.

"You might also tell him the law has a mind to forgive him for sticking up that free trader's post a few years ago."

Jolly Roger turned with his snowshoe piled high with a load of snow.

"I'll tell him that, too," he said, chuckling at the obviousness of the other's trap. "What do you think my cabin is, Breault—a Rest for Homeless Outlaws?"

Breault grinned. It was an odd sort of grin, and Jolly Roger caught it over his shoulder. When he returned from dumping his load, Breault said:

"You see, we know this Jolly Roger fellow is spending the winter somewhere up here. And Cassidy says there is a girl down south—"

Jolly Roger's face was hidden in the tunnel.

"—who would like to see him," finished Breault.

When McKay turned toward him the Ferret was carelessly lighting his pipe.

"I remember—Cassidy told me about this girl," said Jolly Roger. "He said—some day—he would trap this—this man—through the girl. So if I happen to meet Jolly Roger McKay, and send him back to the girl, it will help out the law. Is that it, Breault? And is there any reward tacked to it? Anything in it for me?"

Breault was looking at him in the pale light of the alcohol lamp, puffing out tobacco smoke, and with that odd twist of a smile about his thin lips.

"Listen to the storm," he said. "I think it's getting worse— Cummings!"

Suddenly he held out a hand to Peter, who sat near the lamp, his bright eyes fixed watchfully on the stranger.

"Nice dog you have, Cummings. Come here, Peter! Peter—Peter—"

Tight ringers seemed to grip at McKay's throat. He had not spoken Peter's name since the rescue of Breault.

"Peter—Peter—"

The Ferret was smiling affably. But Peter did not move. He made no response to the outstretched hand. His eyes were steady and challenging. In that moment McKay wanted to hug him up in his arms.

The Ferret laughed.

"He's a good dog, a very good dog, Cummings. I like a one-man dog, and I also like a one-dog man. That's what Jolly Roger McKay is, if you ever happen to meet him. Travels with one dog. An Airedale, with whiskers on him like a Mormon. And his name is Peter. Funny name for a dog, isn't it?"

He faced the outer room, stretching his long arms above his head.

"I'm going to try sleep again, Cummings. Goodnight! And—Mother of Heaven!—listen to the wind."

"Yes, it's a bad night," said McKay.

He looked at Peter when Breault was gone, and his heart was beating fast. He could hear the wind, too. It was sweeping over the Barren more fiercely than before, and the sound of it brought a steely glitter into his eyes. This time he could not run away from the law. Flight meant death. And Breault knew it. He was in a trap—a trap built by himself. That is, if Breault had guessed the truth, and he believed he had. There was only one way out—and that meant fight.

He went into the outer room for his pack and a blanket. He did not look at Breault, but he knew the man's narrow eyes were following him. He left the alcohol lamp burning, but in his own room, after he had spread out his bed, he extinguished the light. Then, very quietly, he dug a hole through the snow partition between the two rooms. He waited for ten minutes before he thrust a finger-tip through the last thin crust of snow. With his eye close to the aperture he could see Breault. The Ferret was sitting up, and leaning toward Porter, who was sleeping an arm's length away. He reached over, and touched him on the shoulder.

Jolly Roger widened the snow-slit another inch, straining his ears to hear. He could see Tavish and the girl asleep. In another moment Porter was sitting up, with the Ferret's hand gripping his arm warningly. Breault motioned toward the inner room, and Porter was silent. Then Breault bent over and began to whisper. Jolly Roger could hear only the indistinct monotone of his voice. But he could see very clearly the change that came into Porter's face. His eyes widened, and he stared toward the inner room, making a movement as if to rouse Tavish and the girl.

The Ferret stopped him.

"Don't get excited. Let them sleep."

McKay heard that much—and no more. For some time after that the two men sat close together, conversing in whispers. There was an exultant satisfaction in Porter's clean-cut face, as well as in Breault's. Jolly Roger watched them until Breault extinguished the second lamp. Then he lightly plugged the hole in the partition with snow, and reached out in the darkness until his hand found Peter.

"They think they've got us, boy," he whispered, "They think they've got us!"

Very quietly they lay for an hour. McKay did not sleep, and Peter was wide awake. At the end of that hour Jolly Roger crept on his hands and knees to the doorway and listened. One after another he picked out the steady breathing of the sleepers. Then he began feeling his way around the wall of his room until he came to a place where the snow was very soft.

"An air-drift," he whispered to Peter, close at his shoulder. "We'll fool 'em, boy. And we'll fight—if we have to."

He began worming his head and shoulders and body into the air- drift like a gimlet. A foot at a time he burrowed himself through, heaving his body up and down and sideways to pack the light snow, leaving a round tunnel two feet in diameter behind him. Within an hour he had come to the outer crust on the windward side of the big snow-dune. He did not break through this crust, which was as tough as crystal-glass, but lay quietly for a time and listened to the sweep of the wind outside. It was warm, and very comfortable, and he had half-dozed off before he caught himself back into wakefulness and returned to his room. The mouth of his tunnel he packed with snow. After that he wound the blanket about him and gave himself up calmly to sleep.

Only Peter lay awake after that. And it was Peter who roused Jolly Roger in what would have been the early dawn outside the snow- dune. McKay felt his restless movement, and opened his eyes. A faint light was illumining his room, and he sat up. In the outer room the alcohol lamp was burning again. He could hear movement, and voices that were very low and indistinct. Carefully he dug out once more the little hole in the snow wall, and widened the slit.

Breault and Tavish were asleep, but Porter was sitting up, and close beside him sat the girl. Her coiled hair was loosened, and fallen over her shoulders. There was no sign of drowsiness in her wide-open eyes as they stared at the door between the two rooms. McKay could see her hand clasping Porter's arm. Porter was talking, with his face so close to her bent head that his lips touched her hair, and though Jolly Roger could understand no word that was spoken he knew Porter was whispering the exciting secret of his identity to Josephine Tavish. He could see, for a moment, a shadow of protest in her face, he could hear the quick, sibilant whisper of her voice, and Porter cautioned her with a finger at her lips, and made a gesture toward the sleeping Tavish. Then his fingers closed about her uncoiled hair as he drew her to him. McKay watched the long kiss between them. The girl drew away quickly then, and Porter tucked the blanket about her when she lay down beside her father. After that he stretched out again beside Breault.

Jolly Roger guessed what had happened. The girl had awakened, a bit nervous, and had roused Porter and asked him to relight the alcohol lamp. And Porter had taken advantage of the opportunity to tell her of the interesting discovery which Breault had made—and to kiss her. McKay stroked Peter's scrawny neck, and listened. He could no longer hear the storm, and he wondered if the fury of it was spent.

Every few minutes he looked through the slit in the snow wall. The last time, half an hour after Porter had returned to his blanket, Josephine Tavish was sitting up. She was very wide awake. McKay watched her as she rose slowly to her knees, and then to her feet. She bent over Porter and Breault to make sure they were asleep, and then came straight toward the door of his room.

He lay back on his blanket, with the fingers of one hand gripped closely about Peter.

"Be quiet, boy," he whispered. "Be quiet."

He could see the shutting out of light at his door as the girl stood there, listening for his breathing. He breathed heavily, and before he closed his eyes he saw Josephine Tavish coming toward him. In a moment she was bending over him. He could feel the soft caress of her loose hair on his face and hands. Then she knelt quietly down beside him, stroking Peter with her hand, and shook him lightly by the shoulder.

"Jolly Roger!" she whispered. "Jolly Roger McKay!"

He opened his eyes, looking up at the white face in the gloom.

"Yes," he replied softly. "What is it, Miss Tavish?"

He could hear the choking breath in her throat as her fingers tightened at his shoulder. She bent her face still nearer to him, until her hair cluttered his throat and breast.

"You are—awake?"

"Yes."

"Then—listen to me. If you are Jolly Roger McKay you must get away—somewhere. You must go before Breault awakens in the morning. I think the storm is over—there is no wind—and if you are here when day comes—"

Her fingers loosened. Jolly Roger reached out and somewhere in the darkness he found her hand. It clasped his own—firm, warm, thrilling.

"I thank you for what you have done," she whispered. "But the law —and Breault—they have no mercy!"

She was gone, swiftly and silently, and McKay looked through the slit in the wall until she was with her father again.

In the gloom he drew Peter close to him.

"We're up against it again, Pied-Bot," he confided under his breath. "We've got to take another chance."

He worked without sound, and in a quarter of an hour his pack was ready, and the entrance to his tunnel dug out. He went into the outer room then, where Josephine Tavish was awake. Jolly Roger pantomimed his desire as she sat up. He wanted something from one of the packs. She nodded. On his knees he fumbled in the dunnage, and when he rose to his feet, facing the girl, her eyes opened wide at what he held in his hand—a small packet of old newspapers her father was taking to the factor at Fort Churchill. She saw the hungry, apologetic look in his eyes, and her woman's heart understood. She smiled gently at him, and her lips formed an unvoiced whisper of gratitude as he turned to go. At the door he looked back. He thought she was beautiful then, with her shining hair and eyes, and her lips parted, and her hands half reaching out to him, as if in that moment of parting she was giving him courage and faith. Suddenly she pressed the palms of her fingers to her mouth and sent the kiss of benediction to him through the twilight glow of the snow-room.

A moment later, crawling through his tunnel with Peter close behind him, there was an exultant singing in Jolly Roger's heart. Again he was fleeing from the law, but always, as Yellow Bird had predicted in her sorcery, there were happiness and hope in his going. And always there was someone to urge him on, and to take a pride in him, like Josephine Tavish.

He broke through the dune-crust at the end of his tunnel and crawled out into the thick, gray dawn of a barren-land day. The sky was heavy overhead, and the wind had died out. It was the beginning of the brief lull which came in the second day of the Great Storm.

McKay laughed softly as he sensed the odds against them.

"We'll be having the storm at our heels again before long, Pied- Bot," he said. "We'd better make for the timber a dozen miles south."

He struck out, circling the dune, so that he was traveling straight away from the first hole he had cut through the shell of the drift. From that door, made by the outlaw who had saved them, Josephine Tavish watched the shadowy forms of man and dog until they were lost in the gray-white chaos of a frozen world.

CHAPTER XV

THROUGH the blizzard Jolly Roger made his way a score of miles southward from the big dune on the Barren. For a day and a night he made his camp in the scrub timber which edged the vast treeless tundras reaching to the Arctic. He believed he was safe, for the unceasing wind and the blasts of shot-like snow filled his tracks a few moments after they were made. He struck a straight line for his cabin after that first day and night in the scrub timber. The storm was still a thing of terrific force out on the barren, but in the timber he was fairly well sheltered. He was convinced the police patrol would find his cabin very soon after the storm had worn itself out. Porter and Tavish did not trouble him. But from Breault he knew there was no getting away. Breault would nose out his cabin. And for that reason he was determined to reach it first.

The second night he did not sleep. His mind was a wild thing—wild as a Loup-Garou seeking out its ghostly trails; it passed beyond his mastery, keeping sleep away from him though he was dead tired. It carried him back over all the steps of his outlawry, visioning for him the score of times he had escaped, as he was narrowly escaping now; and it pictured for him, like a creature of inquisition, the tightening net ahead of him, the final futility of all his effort. And at last, as if moved by pity to ease his suffering a little, it brought him back vividly to the green valley, the flowers and the blue skies of Cragg's Ridge—and Nada.

It was like a dream. At times he could scarcely assure himself that he had actually lived those weeks and months of happiness down on the edge of civilization; it seemed impossible that Nada had come like an Angel into his life down there, and that she had loved him, even when he confessed himself a fugitive from the law and had entreated him to take her with him. He closed his eyes and that last roaring night of storm at Cragg's Ridge was about him again. He was in the little old Missioner's cabin, with thunder and lightning rending earth and sky outside and Nada was in his arms, her lips against his, the piteous heartbreak of despair in her eyes. Then he saw her—a moment later—a crumpled heap down beside the chair, the disheveled glory of her hair hiding her white face from him as he hesitated for a single instant before opening the door and plunging out into the night.

With a cry he sprang up, dashing the vision from him, and threw fresh fuel on the fire. And he cried out the same old thought to Peter.

"It would have been murder for us to bring her, Pied-Bot. It would have been murder!"

He looked about him at the swirling chaos outside the rim of light made by his fire and listened to the moaning of the wind over the treetops. Beyond the circle of light the dry snow, which crunched like sand under his feet, was lost in ghostly gloom. It was forty degrees below zero. And he was glad, even with this sickness of despair in his heart, that she was not a fugitive with him tonight.

Yet he built up a little make-believe world for himself as he sat with a blanket hugged close about him, staring into the fire. In a hundred different ways he saw her face, a will-o-the-wisp thing amid the flames; an illusive, very girlish, almost childish face— yet always with the light of a woman's soul shining in it. That was the miracle which startled him at last. It seemed as if the fiction he built up in his despair transformed itself subtly into fact and that her soul had come to him from out of the southland and was speaking to him with eyes which never changed or faltered in their adoration, their faith and their courage. She seemed to come to him, to creep into his arms under the folds of the blanket and he sensed the soft crush of her hair, the touch of her lips, the warm encircling of her arms about his neck. Closer to him pressed the mystery, until the beating of her heart was a living pulse against him; and then—suddenly, as an irresistible impulse closed his arms to hold the spirit to him, his eyes were drawn to the heart of the fire, and he saw there for an instant, wide-eyed and speaking to him, the face of Yellow Bird the Indian sorceress. The flames crept up the long braids of her hair, her lips moved, and then she was gone—but slowly, like a ghost slipping upward into the mist of smoke and night.

Peter heard his master's cry. And after that Jolly Roger rose up and threw off the blanket and walked back and forth until his feet trod a path in the snow. He told himself it was madness to believe, and yet he believed. Faith fought itself back into that dark citadel of his heart from which for a time it had been driven. New courage lighted up again the black chaos of his soul. And at last he fell down on his knees and gripped Peter's shaggy head between his two hands.

"Pied-Bot, she said everything would come out right in the end," he cried, a new note in his voice. "That's what Yellow Bird told us, wasn't it? Mebby they would have burned her as a witch a long time ago because she's a sorceress, and says she can send her soul out of her body and see what we can't see. BUT WE BELIEVE!" His voice choked up, and he laughed. "They were both here tonight," he added. "Nada—and Yellow Bird. And I believe—I believe—I know what it means!"

He stood up again, and Peter saw the old smile on his master's lips as Jolly Roger looked up into the swirling black canopy of the spruce-tops. And the wailing of the storm seemed no longer to hold menace and taunt, but in it he heard the whisper of fierce, strong voices urging upon him the conviction that had already swept indecision from his heart.

And then he said, holding out his arms as if encompassing something which he could not see.

"Peter, we're going back to Nada!"

Dawn was a scarcely perceptible thing when it came. Darkness seemed to fade a little, that was all. Frosty shapes took form in the gloom, and the spruce-tops became tangible in an abyss of sepulchral shadow overhead.

Through this beginning of the barren-land day Jolly Roger set out in the direction of his cabin and in his blood was that new singing thing of fire and warmth that more than made up for the hours of sleep he had lost during the night. The storm was dying out, he thought, and it was growing warmer; yet the wind whistled and raved in the open spaces and his thermometer registered the fortieth and a fraction degree below zero. The air he breathed was softer, he fancied, yet it was still heavy with the stinging shot of blizzard; and where yesterday he had seen only the smothering chaos of twisted spruce and piled up snow, there was now—as the pale day broadened—his old wonderland of savage beauty, awaiting only a flash of sunlight to transform it into the pure glory of a thing indescribable. But the sun did not come and Jolly Roger did not miss it over-much for his heart was full of Nada, and a-thrill with the inspiration of his home-going.

"That's what it means, GOING HOME" he said to Peter, who nosed close in the path of his snowshoes. "There's a thousand miles between us and Cragg's Ridge, a thousand miles of snow and ice— and hell, mebby. But we'll make it!"

He was sure of himself now. It was as if he had come up from out of the shadow of a great sickness. He had been unwise. He had not reasoned as a man should reason. The hangman might be waiting for him at Cragg's Ridge, down on the rim of civilization, but that same grim executioner was also pursuing close at his heels. He would always be pursuing in the form of a Breault, a Cassidy, a Tavish, or a Somebody Else of the Royal Northwest Mounted Police. It would be that way until the end came. And when the end did come, when they finally got him, the blow would be easier at Cragg's Ridge than up here on the edge of the Barren Land.

And again there was hope, a wild, almost unbelievable hope that with Nada he might find that place which Yellow Bird, the sorceress, had promised for them—that mystery-place of safety and of happiness which she had called The Country Beyond, where "all would end well." He had not the faith of Yellow Bird's people; he was not superstitious enough to believe fully in her sorcery, except that he seized upon it as a drowning man might grip at a floating sea-weed. Yet was the under-current of hope so persistent that at times it was near faith. Up to this hour Yellow Bird's sorcery had brought him nothing but the truth. For him she had conjured the spirits of her people, and these spirits, speaking through Yellow Bird's lips, had saved him from Cassidy at the fishing camp and had performed the miracle on the shore of Wollaston and had predicted the salvation that had come to him out on the Barren. And so—was it not conceivable that the other would also come true?

But these visions came to him only in flashes. As he traveled through the hours the one vital desire of his being was to bring himself physically into the presence of Nada, to feel the wild joy of her in his arms once more, the crush of her lips to his, the caress of her hands in their old sweet way at his face—and to hear her voice, the girl's voice with the woman's soul behind it, crying out its undying love, as he had last heard it that night in the Missioner's cabin many months ago. After this had happened, then—if fate decreed it so—all other things might end. Breault, the Ferret, might come. Or Porter. Or that Somebody Else who was always on his trail.

If the game finished thus, he would be satisfied.

When he stopped to make a pot of black tea and warm a snack to eat Jolly Roger tried to explain this new meaning of life to Peter.

"The big thing we must do is to get there—safely," he said, already beginning to make plans in the back of his head. And then he went on, building up his fabric of new hope before Peter, while he crunched his luncheon of toasted bannock and fat bacon. There was something joyous and definite in his voice which entered into Peter's blood and body. There was even a note of excitement in it, and Peter's whiskers bristled with fresh courage and his eyes gleamed and his tail thumped the snow comprehendingly. It was like having a master come back to him from the dead.

And Jolly Roger even laughed, softly, under his breath.

"This is February," he said. "We ought to make it late in March. I mean Cragg's Ridge, Pied-Bot."

After that they went on, traveling hard to reach their cabin before the darkness of night, which would drop upon them like a thick blanket at four o'clock. In these last hours there pressed even more heavily upon Jolly Roger that growing realization of the vastness and emptiness of the world. It was as if blindness had dropped from his eyes and he saw the naked truth at last. Out of this world everything had emptied itself until it held only Nada. Only she counted. Only she held out her arms to him, entreating him to keep for her that life in his body which meant so little in all other ways. He thought of one of the little worn books which he carried in his shoulder-pack—Jeanne D'Arc. As she had fought, with the guidance of God, so he believed the blue-eyed girl down at Cragg's Ridge was fighting for him, and had sent her spirit out in quest of him. And he was going back to her. GOING!

The last word, as it came from his lips, meant that nothing would stop them. He almost shouted it. And Peter answered.

In spite of their effort, darkness closed in on them. With the first dusk of this night there came sudden lulls in which the blizzard seemed to have exhausted itself. Jolly Roger read the signs. By tomorrow there would be no storm and Breault the Ferret would be on the trail again, along with Porter and Tavish.

It was his old craft, his old cunning, that urged him to go on. Strangely, he prayed for the blizzard not to give up the ghost. Something must be accomplished before its fury was spent; and he was glad when after each lull he heard again the moaning and screeching of it over the open spaces, and the slashing together of spruce tops where there was cover. In a chaos of gloom they came to the low ridge which reached across an open sweep of tundra to the finger of shelter where the cabin was built. An hour later they were at its door. Jolly Roger opened it and staggered in. For a space he stood leaning against the wall while his lungs drank in the warmer air. The intake of his breath made a whistling sound and he was surprised to find himself so near exhaustion. He heard the thud of Peter's body as it collapsed to the floor.

"Tired, Pied-Bot?"

It was difficult for his storm-beaten lips to speak the words.

Peter thumped his tail. The rat-tap-tap of it came in one of those lulls of the storm which Jolly Roger had begun to dread.

"I hope it keeps up another two hours," he said, wetting his lips to take the stiffness out of them. "If it doesn't—"

He was thinking of Breault as he drew off his mittens and fumbled for a match. It was Breault he feared. The Ferret would find his cabin and his trail if the storm died out too soon.

He lighted the tin lamp on his table and after that, assured that wastefulness would cost him nothing now, he set two bear-drip candles going, one at each end of the cabin. The illumination filled the single room. There was little for it to reveal—the table he had made, a chair, a battered little sheet-iron stove, and the humped up blanket in his bunk, under which he had stored the remainder of his possessions. Back of the stove was a pile of dry wood, and in another five minutes the roar of flames in the chimney mingled with a fresh bluster of the wind outside.

Defying the exhaustion of limbs and body, Jolly Roger kept steadily at work. He threw off his heavier garments as the freezing atmosphere of the room became warmer, and prepared for a feast.

"We'll call it Christmas, and have everything we've got, Pied-Bot. We'll cook a quart of prunes instead of six. No use stinting ourselves—tonight!"

Even Peter was amazed at the prodigality of his master. An hour later they ate, and McKay drank a quart of hot coffee before he was done. Half of his fatigue was gone and he sat back for a few minutes to finish off with the luxury of his pipe.

Peter, gorged with caribou meat, stretched himself out to sleep. But his eyes did not close. His master puzzled him. For after a little Jolly Roger put on his heavy coat and parkee and pocketed his pipe. After that he slipped the straps of his pack over head and shoulders and then, even more to Peter's bewilderment, emptied a quart bottle of kerosene over the pile of dry wood behind the hot stove. To this he touched a lighted match. His next movement drew from Peter a startled yelp. With a single thrust of his foot he sent the stove crashing into the middle of the floor.

Half an hour later, when Peter and Jolly Roger looked back from the crest of the ridge, a red pillar of flame lighted up the gloomy chaos of the unpeopled world they were leaving behind them. The wind was driving fiercely from the Barren and with it came stinging volleys of the fine drift-snow. In the teeth of it Roger McKay stared back.

"It's a good fire," he mumbled in his hood. "Half an hour and it will be out. There'll be nothing for Breault to find if this wind keeps up another two hours—nothing but drift-snow, with no sign of trail or cabin."

He struck out, leaving the shelter of the ridge. Straight south he went, keeping always in the open spaces where the wind-swept drift covered his snowshoe trail almost as soon as it was made. Darkness did not trouble him now. The open barren was ahead, miles of it, while only a little to the westward was the shelter of timber. Twice he blundered to the edge of this timber, but quickly set his course again in the open, with the wind always quartering at his back. He could only guess how long he kept on. The time came when he began to count the swing of his snow-shoes, measuring off half a mile, or a mile, and then beginning over again until at last the achievement of five hundred steps seemed to take an immeasurable length of time and great effort. Like the ache of a tooth came the first warning of snowshoe cramp in his legs. In the black night he grinned. He knew what it meant—a warning as deadly as swimmer's cramp in deep water. If he continued much longer he would be crawling on his hands and knees.

Quickly he turned in the direction of the timber. He had traveled three hours, he thought, since abandoning his cabin to the flames. Another half hour, with the caution of slower, shorter steps, brought him to the timber. Luck was with him and he cried aloud to Peter as he felt himself in the darkness of a dense cover of spruce and balsam. He freed himself from his entangled snowshoes and went on deeper into the shelter. It became warmer and they could feel no longer a breath of the wind.

He unloaded his pack and drew from it a jackpine torch, dried in his cabin and heavy with pitch. Shortly the flare of this torch lighted up their refuge for a dozen paces about them. In the illumination of it, moving it from place to place, he gathered dry fire wood and with his axe cut down green spruce for the smouldering back-fire that would last until morning. By the time the torch had consumed itself the fire was burning, and where Jolly Roger had scraped away the snow from the thick carpet of spruce needles underfoot he piled a thick mass of balsam boughs, and in the center of the bed he buried himself, wrapped warmly in his blankets, and with Peter snuggled close at his side.

Through dark hours the green spruce fire burned slowly and steadily. For a long time there was wailing of wind out in the open. But at last it died away, and utter stillness filled the world. No life moved in these hours which followed the giving up of the big storm's last gasping breath. Slowly the sky cleared. Here and there a star burned through. But Jolly Roger and Peter, deep in the sleep of exhaustion, knew nothing of the change.

CHAPTER XVI

IT was Peter who roused Jolly Roger many hours later; Peter nosing about the still burning embers of the fire, and at last muzzling his master's face with increasing anxiety. McKay sat up out of his nest of balsam boughs and blankets and caught the bright glint of sunlight through the treetops. He rubbed his eyes and stared again to make sure. Then he looked at his watch. It was ten o'clock and peering in the direction of the open he saw the white edge of it glistening in the unclouded blaze of a sun. It was the first sun— the first real sun—he had seen for many days, and with Peter he went to the rim of the barren a hundred yards distant. He wanted to shout. As far as he could see the white plain was ablaze with eye-blinding light, and never had the sky at Cragg's Ridge been clearer than the sky that was over him now.

He returned to the fire, singing. Back through the months leapt Peter's memory to the time when his master had sung like that. It was in Indian Tom's cabin, with Cragg's Ridge just beyond the creek, and it was in those days before Terence Cassidy had come to drive them to another hiding place; in the happy days of Nada's visits and of their trysts under the Ridge, when even the little gray mother mouse lived in a paradise with her nest of babies in the box on their cabin shelf. He had almost forgotten but it came back to him now. It was the old Jolly Roger—the old master come to life again.

In the clear stillness of the morning one might have heard that shouting song half a mile away. But McKay was no longer afraid. As the storm seemed to have cleaned the world so the sun cleared his soul of its last shadow of doubt. It was not merely an omen or a promise, but for him proclaimed a certainty. God was with him. Life was with him. His world was opening its arms to him again— and he sang as if Nada was only a mile away from him instead of a thousand.

When he went on, after their breakfast, he laughed at the thought of Breault discovering their trail. The Ferret would be more than human to do that after what wind and storm and fire had done for them.

This first day of their pilgrimage into the southland was a day of glory from its beginning until the setting of the sun. There was no cloud in the sky. And it grew warmer, until Jolly Roger flung back the hood of his parkee and turned up the fur of his cap. That night a million stars lighted the heaven.

After this first day and night nothing could break down the hope and confidence of Jolly Roger and his, dog. Peter knew they were going south, in which direction lay everything he had ever yearned for; and each night beside their campfire McKay made a note with pencil and paper and measured the distance they had come and the distance they had yet to go. Hope in a little while became certainty. Into his mind urged no thought of changes that might have taken place at Cragg's Ridge; or, if the thought did come, it caused him no uneasiness. Now that Jed Hawkins was dead Nada would be with the little old Missioner in whose care he had left her, and not for an instant did a doubt cloud the growing happiness of his anticipations. Breault and the hunters of the law were the one worry that lay ahead and behind him. If he outwitted them he would find Nada waiting for him.

Day after day they kept south and west until they struck the Thelon; and then through a country unmapped, and at times terrific in its cold and storm, they fought steadily to the frozen regions of the Dubawnt waterways. Only once in the first three weeks did they seek human company. This was at a small Indian camp where Jolly Roger bartered for caribou meat and moccasins for Peter's feet. Twice between there and God's Lake they stopped at trappers' cabins.

It was early in March when they struck the Lost Lake country, three hundred miles from Cragg's Ridge.

And here it was, buried under a blind of soft snow, that Peter nosed out the frozen carcass of a disemboweled buck which Boileau, the French trapper, had poisoned for wolves. Jolly Roger had built a fire and was warming half a pint of deer tallow for a baking of bannock, when Peter dragged himself in, his rear legs already stiffening with the palsy of strychnine. In a dozen seconds McKay had the warm

tallow down Peter's throat, to the last drop of it; and this he followed with another dose as quickly as he could heat it, and in the end Peter gave up what he had
eaten.

Half an hour later Boileau, who was eating his dinner, jumped up in wonderment when the door of his cabin was suddenly opened by a grim and white-faced
man who carried the limp body of a dog in his arms.

For a long time after this the shadow of death hung over the Frenchman's
trapping-shack. To Boileau, with his brotherly sympathy and regret that his poison-
bait had brought calamity, Peter was "just dog." But when at last he saw the strong
shoulders of the grim-faced stranger shaking over Peter's paralyzed body and listened to the sobbing grief that broke in passionate protest from his white lips, he
drew back a little awed. It seemed for a time that Peter was dead; and in those moments Jolly Roger put his arms about him and buried his despairing face in Peter's
scraggly neck, calling in a wild fit of anguish for him to come back, to live, to open
his eyes again. Boileau, crossing himself, felt of Peter's body and McKay heard his
voice over him, saying that the dog was not dead, but that his heart was beating
steadily and that he thought the last stiffening blow of the poison was over. To
McKay it was like bringing the dead back to life. He raised his head and drew away
his arms and knelt beside the bunk stunned and mutely hopeful while Boileau took
his place and began dropping warm condensed milk down Peter's throat. In a little
while Peter's eyes opened and he gave a great sigh.

Boileau looked up and shrugged his shoulders.

"That was a good breath, m'sieu," he said. "What is left of the poison has done
its worst. He will live."

A bit stupidly McKay rose to his feet. He swayed a little, and for the first time
sensed the hot tears that had blinded his eyes and wet his cheeks. And then there
came a sobbing laugh out of his throat and he went to the window of the Frenchman's shack and stared out into the white world, seeing nothing. He had stood in
the presence of death many times before but never had that presence choked up his
heart as in this hour when the soul of Peter, his comrade, had stood falteringly for
a space half-way between the living and the dead.

When he turned from the window Boileau was covering Peter's body with
blankets and a warm bear skin. And for many days thereafter Peter was nursed

through the slow sickness which followed.

An early spring came this year in the northland. South of the Reindeer water-way country the snows were disappearing late in March and ice was rotting the first week in April. Winds came from the south and west and the sun was warmer and clearer than Boileau had ever known it at the winter's end in Lost Lake country. It was in this first week of April that Peter was able to travel, and McKay pointed his trail once more for Cragg's Ridge

He left a part of his winter dunnage at Boileau's shack and went on light, figuring to reach Cragg's Ridge before the new "goose moon" had worn itself out in the west. But for a week Peter lagged and until the darker red in the rims of his eyes cleared away Jolly Roger checked the impetus of his travel so that the goose moon had faded out and the "frog moon" of May was in its full before they came down the last slope that dipped from the Height of Land to the forests and lakes of the lower country.

And now, in these days, it seemed to Jolly Roger that a great kindness, and not tragedy, had delayed him so that his "home coming" was in the gladness of spring. All about him was the sweetness and mystic whispering of new life just awakening. It was in the sky and the sun; it was underfoot, in the fragrance of the mold he trod upon, in the trees about him, and in the mate- chirping of the birds flocking back from the southland. His friends the jays were raucous and jaunty again, bullying and bluffing in the warmth of sunshine; the black glint of crows' wings flashed across the opens; the wood-sappers and pewees and big-eyed moose-birds were aflutter with the excitement of home planning; partridges were feasting on the swelling poplar buds— and then, one glorious sunset, he heard the chirruping evening song of his first robin.

And the next day they would reach Cragg's Ridge!

Half of that last night he sat up, awake, or smoked in the glow of his fire, waiting for the dawn. With the first lifting of darkness he was traveling swiftly ahead of Peter and the morning was only half gone when he saw far ahead of him the great ridge which shut out Indian Tom's swamp, and Nada's plain, and Cragg's Ridge beyond it.

It was noon when he stood at the crest of this. He was breathing hard, for to reach this last precious height from which he might look upon the country of Nada's home he had half run up its rock- strewn side. There, with his lungs gasping for air, his eager eyes shot over the country below him and for a moment the significance of the thing which he saw did not strike him. And then in another instant it seemed that his heart choked up, like a fist suddenly tightened, and stopped its beating.

Reaching away from him, miles upon miles of it, east, west and south—was a dead and char-stricken world.

Up to the foot of the ridge itself had come the devastation of flame, and where it had swept, months ago, there was now no sign of the glorious spring that lay behind him.

He looked for Indian Tom's swamp, and where it had been there was no longer a swamp but a stricken chaos of ten thousand black stubs, the shriven corpses of the spruce and cedar and jackpines out of which the wolves had howled at night.

He looked for the timber on Sucker Creek where the little old Missioner's cabin lay, and where he had dreamed that Nada would be waiting for him. And he saw no timber there but only the littleness and emptiness of a blackened world.

And then he looked to Cragg's Ridge, and along the bald crest of it, naked as death, he saw blackened stubs pointing skyward, painting desolation against the blue of the heaven beyond.

A cry came from him, a cry of fear and of horror, for he was looking upon the fulfilment of Yellow Bird's prediction. He seemed to hear, whispering softly in his ears, the low, sweet voice of the sorceress, as on the night when she had told him that if he returned to Cragg's Ridge he would find a world that had turned black with ruin and that it would not be there he would ever find Nada.

After that one sobbing cry he tore like a madman dawn into the valley, traveling swiftly through the muck of fire and under-foot tangle with Peter fighting behind him. Half an hour later he stood where the Missioner's cabin had been and he found only a ruin of ash and logs burned down to the earth. Where the trail had run there was no longer a trail. A blight, grim and sickening, lay upon the earth that had been paradise.

Peter heard the choking sound in his master's throat and chest. He, too, sensed the black shadow of tragedy and cautiously he sniffed the air, knowing that at last they were home—and yet it was not home. Instinctively he had faced Cragg's Ridge and Jolly Roger, seeing the dog's stiffened body pointing toward the break beyond which lay Nada's old home, felt a thrill of hope leap up within him. Possibly the farther plain had escaped the scourge of fire. If so, Nada would be there, and the Missioner—

He started for the break, a mile away. As he came nearer to it his hope grew less for he could see where the flames had swept in an inundating sea along Cragg's Ridge. They passed over the meadow where the thick young jackpines, the red strawberries and the blue violets had been and Peter heard the strange sob when they came to the little hollow—the old trysting place where Nada had first given herself into his master's arms. And there it was that Peter forgot master and caution and sped swiftly ahead to the break that cut the Ridge in twain.

When Jolly Roger came to that break and ran through it he was staggering from the mad effort he had made. And then, all at once, the last of his wind came in a cry of gladness. He swayed against a rock and stood there staring wild-eyed at what was before him. The world was as black ahead of him as it was behind. But Jed Hawkins' cabin was untouched! The fire had crept up to its very door and there it had died.

He went on the remaining hundred yards and before the closed door of Nada's old home he found Peter standing stiff-legged and strange. He opened the door and a damp chill touched his face. The cabin was empty. And the gloom and desolation of a grave filled the place.

He stepped in, a moaning whisper of the truth coming to his lips. He heard the scurrying flight of a starved wood-rat, a flutter of loose papers, and then the silence of death fell about him. The door of Nada's little room was open and he entered through it. The bed was naked and there remained only the skeleton of things that had been.

He moved now like a man numbed by a strange sickness and Peter followed gloomily and silently in the footsteps of his master. They went outside and a distance away Jolly Roger saw a thing rising up out of the char of fire, ugly and foreboding, like the evil spirit of desolation itself. It was a rude cross made of saplings, up which the flames had licked their way, searing it grim and black.

His hands clenched slowly for he knew that under the cross lay the body of Jed Hawkins, the fiend who had destroyed his world.

After that he re-entered the cabin and went into Nada's room, closing the door behind him; and for many minutes thereafter Peter remained outside guarding the outer door, and hearing no sound or movement from within.

When Jolly Roger came out his face was set and white, and he looked where the thick forest had stood on that stormy night when he ran down the trail toward Mooney's cabin. There was no forest now. But he found the old tie-cutters' road, cluttered as it was with the debris of fire, and he knew when he came to that twist in the trail where long ago Jed Hawkins had lain dead on his back. Half a mile beyond he came to the railroad. Here it was that the fire had burned hottest, for as far as his vision went he could see no sign of life or of forest green alight in the waning sun.

And now there fell upon him, along with the desolation of despair, a something grimmer and more terrible—a thing that was fear. About him everywhere reached this graveyard of death, leaving no spot untouched. Was it possible that Nada and the Missioner had not escaped its fury? The fear settled upon him more heavily as the sun went down and the gloom of evening came, bringing with it an unpleasant chill and a cloying odor of things burned dead.

He did not talk to Peter now. There was a lamp in the cabin and wood behind the stove, and silently he built a fire and trimmed and lighted the wick when darkness came. And Peter, as if hiding from the ghosts of yesterday, slunk into a corner and lay there unmoving and still. And McKay did not get supper nor did he smoke, but after a long time he carried his blankets into Nada's room, and spread them out upon her bed. Then he put out the light and quietly laid himself down where through the nights of many a month and year Nada had slept in the moon glow.

The moon was there tonight. The faint glow of it rose in the east and swiftly it climbed over the ragged shoulder of Cragg's Ridge, flooding the blackened world with light and filling the room with a soft and golden radiance. It was a moon un-dimmed, full and round and yellow; and it seemed to smile in through the window as if some living spirit in it had not yet missed Nada, and was embracing her in its glory. And now it came upon Jolly Roger why she had loved it even more than she had loved the sun; for through the little window it shut out all the rest of the world, and sitting up, he seemed to hear her heart beating at his side and clearly he saw her face in the light of it and her slim arms out- reaching, as if to gather it to her breast. Thus—many times, she had told him—had she sat up in her bed to greet the moon and to look for the smiling face that was almost always there, the face of the Man in the Moon, her friend and playmate in the sky.

For a space his heart leapt up; and then, as if discovery of the usurper in her room had come, a cloud swept over the face of the moon like a mighty hand and darkness crowded him in. But the cloud sailed on and the light drove out the gloom again. Then it was that Jolly Roger saw the Old Man in the Moon was up and awake tonight, for never had he seen his face more clearly. Often had Nada pointed it out to him in her adorable faith that the Old Man loved her, telling him how this feature changed and that feature changed, how sometimes the Old Man looked sick and at others well, and how there were times when he smiled and was happy and other times when he was sad and stern and sat there in his castle in the sky sunk in a mysterious grief which she could not understand.

"And always I can tell whether I'm going to be glad or sorry by the look of the Man in the Moon," she had said to him. "He looks down and tells me even when the clouds are thick and he can only peep through now and then. And he knows a lot about you, Mister— Jolly Roger—because I've told him everything."

Very quietly Jolly Roger got up from the bed and very strange seemed his manner to Peter as he walked through the outer room and into the night beyond. There he stood making no sound or movement, like one of the lifeless stubs left by fire; and Peter looked up, as his master was looking, trying to make out what it was he saw in the sky. And nothing was there—nothing that he had not seen many times before; a billion stars, and the moon riding King among them all, and fleecy clouds as if made of web, and stillness, a great stillness that was like sleep in the lap of the world.

For a little Jolly Roger was silent and then Peter heard him saying,

"Yellow Bird was right—again. She said we'd find a black world down here and we've found it. And we're going to find Nada where she told us we'd find her, in that place she called The Country Beyond—the country beyond the forests, beyond the tall trees and the big swamps, beyond everything we've ever known of the wild and open spaces; the country where God lives in churches on Sunday and where people would laugh at some of our queer notions, Pied-Bot. It's there we'll find Nada, driven out by the fire, and waiting for us now in the settlements."

He spoke with a strange and quiet conviction, the haggard look dying out of his face as he stared up into the splendor of the sky.

And then he said.

"We won't sleep tonight, Peter. We'll travel with the moon."

Half an hour later, as the lonely figures of man and dog headed for the first settlement a dozen miles away, there seemed to come for an instant the flash of a satisfied smile in the face of the Man in the sky.

CHAPTER XVII

FROM the cabin McKay went first to the great rock that jutted from the broken shoulder of Cragg's Ridge, and as they stood there Peter heard the strange something that was like a laugh, and yet was not a laugh, on his master's lips. But his scraggly face did not look up. There was an answering whimper in his throat. He had been slow in sensing the significance of the mysterious thing that had changed his old home since months ago. During the hours of afternoon, and these moonlit hours that followed, he tried to understand. He knew this was home. Yet the green grass was gone, and a million trees had changed into blackened stubs. The world was no longer shut in by deep forests. And Cragg's Ridge was naked where he and Nada had romped in sunshine and flowers, and out of it all rose the mucky death-smell of the flame-swept earth. These things he understood, in his dog way. But what he could not understand clearly was why Nada was not in the cabin, and why they did not find her, even though the world was changed.

He sat back on his haunches, and Jolly Roger heard again the whimpering grief in his throat. It comforted the man to know that Peter remembered, and he was not alone in his desolation. Gently he placed a soot-grimed hand on his comrade's head.

"Peter, it was from this rock—right where we're standing now— that I first saw her, a long time ago," he said, a bit of forced cheer breaking through the huskiness of his voice. "Remember the little jackpine clump down there? You climbed up onto her lap, a little know-nothing thing, and you pawed in her loose curls, and growled so fiercely I could hear you. And when I made a noise, and she looked up, I thought she was the most beautiful thing I had ever seen—just a kid, with those eyes like the flowers, and her hair shining in the sun, an' tear stains on her cheeks. Tear stains, Pied-Bot—because of that snake who's dead over there. Remember how you growled at me, Peter?"

Peter wriggled an answer.

"That was the beginning," said Jolly Roger, "and this—looks like the end. But—"

He clenched his fists, and there was a sudden fierceness in the grotesque movement of his shadow on the rock.

"We're going to find her before that end comes," he added defiantly. "We're going to find her, Pied-Bot, even if it takes us to the settlements—right up into the face of the law."

He set out over the rocks, his boots making hollow sounds in the deadness of the world about them. Again he followed where once had been the trail that led to Mooney's shack, over on the wobbly line of rail that rambled for eighty miles into the wilderness from Fort William. The P. D. & W. it was named—Port Arthur, Duluth & Western; but it had never reached Duluth, and there were those who had nicknamed it Poverty, Destruction & Want. Many times Jolly Roger had laughed at the queer stories Nada told him about it; how a wrecking outfit was always carried behind on the twice-a-week train, and how the crew picked berries in season, and had their trapping lines, and once chased a bear half way to Whitefish Lake while the train waited for hours. She called it the "Cannon Ball," because once upon a time it had made sixty-nine miles in twenty- four hours. But there was nothing of humor about it as Jolly Roger and Peter came out upon it tonight. It stretched out both ways from them, a thin, grim line of tragedy in the moonlight, and from where they stood it appeared to reach into a black and abysmal sea.

Once more man and dog paused, and looked back at what had been. And the whine came in Peter's throat again and something tugged inside him, urging him to bark up into the face of the moon, as he had often barked for Nada in the days of his puppyhood, and afterward.

But his master went on and Peter followed him, stepping the uneven ties one by one. And with the black chaos of the world under and about them, and the glorious light of the moon filling; the sky over their heads, the journey they made seemed weirdly unreal. For the silver and gold of the moon and the black muck of the fire refused to mingle, and while over their heads they could see the tiniest clouds and beyond to the farthest stars, all was black emptiness when they looked about them upon what once had been a living earth. Only the two lines of steel caught the moon-glow and the charred ends of the fire-shriven stubs that rose up out of the earth shroud and silhouetted themselves against the sky.

To Peter it was not what he failed to see, but what he did not hear or smell that oppressed him and stirred him to wide-eyed watchfulness against impending evil. Under many moons he had traveled with his master in their never-ending flight from the law, and many other nights with neither moon nor stars had they felt out their trails together. But always, under him and over him on all sides of him, there had been LIFE. And tonight there was no life, nor smell of life. There was no chirp of night bird, or flutter of owl's wing, no plash of duck or cry of loon. He listened in vain for the crinkling snap of twig, and the whisper of wind in treetops. And there was no smell—no musk of mink that had crossed his path, no taste in the air of the strong scented fox, no subtle breath of partridge and rabbit and fleshy porcupine. And even from the far distances there came no sound, no howl of wolf, no castanet clatter of stout moose horns against bending saplings—not even the howl of a trapper's dog.

The stillness was of the earth, and yet unearthly. It was even as if some fearsome thing was smothering the sound of his master's feet. To McKay, sensing these same things that Peter sensed, came understanding that brought with it an uneasiness which changed swiftly into the chill of a growing fear. The utter lifelessness told him how vast the destruction of the fire had been. Its obliteration was so great no life had adventured back into the desolated country, though the conflagration must have passed in the preceding autumn, many months ago. The burned country was a grave and the nearest edge of it, judged from the sepulchral stillness of the night, was many miles away.

For the first time came the horror of the thought that in such a fire as this people must have died. It had swept upon them like a tidal wave, galloping the forests with the speed of a race horse, with only this thin line of rail leading to the freedom of life outside. In places only a miracle could have made escape possible. And here, where Nada had lived, with the pitch-wood forests crowding close, the fire must have burned most fiercely. In this moment, when fear of the unspeakable set his heart trembling, his faith fastened itself grimly to the little old gray Missioner, Father John, in whose cabin Nada had taken refuge many months ago, when Jed Hawkins lay dead in the trail with his one-eyed face turned up to the thunder and lightning in the sky. Father John, on that stormy night when he fled north, had promised to care for Nada, and in silence he breathed a prayer that the Missioner had saved her from the red death that had swept like an avalanche upon them. He told himself it must be so. He cried out the words aloud, and Peter heard him, and followed closer, so that his head touched his master's leg as he walked.

But the fear was there. From a spark it grew into a red-hot spot in Jolly Roger's heart. Twice in his own life he had raced against death in a forest fire. But never had he seen a fire like this must have been. All at once he seemed to hear the roar of it in his ears, the rolling thunder of the earth as it twisted in the cataclysm of flame, the hissing shriek of the flaming pitch-tops as they leapt in lightning fires against the smoke-smothered sky. A few hours ago he had stood where Father John's Cabin had been and the place was a ruin of char and ash. If the fire had hemmed them in and they had not escaped—

His voice cried out in sudden protest.

"It can't be, Peter. It can't be! They made the rail—or the lake —and we'll find them in the settlements. It couldn't happen. God wouldn't let her die like that!"

He stopped, and stared into the moon-broken gloom on his left. Something was there, fifty feet away, that drew him down through the muck which lay knee deep in the right-of-way ditch. It was what was left of the cutter's cabin, a clutter of burned logs, a wind scattered heap of ash. Even there, within arm's reach of the railroad, there had been no salvation from the fire.

He waded again through the muck of the ditch, and went on. Mentally and physically he was fighting the ogre that was striving to achieve possession of his brain. Over and over he repeated his faith that Nada and the Missioner had escaped and he would find them in the settlements. Less than ever he thought of the law in these hours. What happened to himself was of small importance now, if he could find Nada alive before the menace caught up with him from behind, or ambushed him ahead. Yet the necessity of caution impinged itself upon him even in the recklessness of his determination to find her if he had to walk into the arms of the law that was hunting him.

For an hour they went on, and as the moon sank westward it seemed to turn its face to look at them; and behind them, when they looked back, the world was transformed into a black pit, while ahead—with the glow of it streaming over their shoulders—ghostly shapes took form, and vision reached farther. Twice they caught the silvery gleam of lakes through the tree-stubs, and again they walked with the rippling murmur of a stream that kept for a mile within the sound of their ears. But even here, with water crying out its invitation to life, there was no life.

Another hour after that Jolly Roger's pulse beat a little faster as he strained his eyes to see ahead. Somewhere near, within a mile or two, was the first settlement with its sawmill and its bunkhouses, its one store and its few cabins, with flat mountains of sawdust on one side of it, and the evergreen forest creeping up to its doors on the other. Surely they would find life here, where there had been man power to hold fire back from the clearing. And it was here he might find Nada and the Missioner, for more than once Father John had preached to the red-cheeked women and children and the clear-eyed men of the Finnish community that thrived there.

But as they drew nearer he listened in vain for the bark of a dog, and his eyes quested as futilely for a point of light in the wide canopy of gloom. At last, close together, they rounded a curve in the road, and crossed a small bridge with a creek running below, and McKay knew his arm should be able to send a stone to what he was seeking ahead. And then, a minute later, he drew in a great gasping breath of unbelief and horror.

For the settlement was no longer in the clearing between him and the rim-glow of the moon. No living tree raised its head against the sky, no sign of cabin or mill shadowed the earth, and where the store had been, and the little church with its white-painted cross, was only a chaos of empty gloom.

He went down, as he had gone to the tie cutter's cabin, and for many minutes he stared and listened, while Peter seemed to stand without breathing. Then making a wide megaphone of his hands, he shouted. It was an alarming thing to do and Peter started as if struck. For there were only ghosts to answer back and the hollowness of a shriven pit for the cry to travel in. Nothing was there. Even the great sawdust piles had shrunk into black scars under the scourge of the fire.

A groaning agony was in the breath of Jolly Roger's lips as he went back to the railroad and hurried on Death must have come here, death sudden and swift. And if it had fallen upon the Finnish settlement, with its strong women and its stronger men, what might it not have done in the cabin of the little old gray Missioner—and Nada?

For a long time after that he forgot Peter was with him. He forgot everything but his desire to reach a living thing. At times, where the road-bed was smooth, he almost ran, and at others he paused for a little to gather his breath and listen. And it was Peter, in one of these intervals, who caught the first message of life. From a long distance away came faintly the barking of a dog.

Half a mile farther on they came to a clearing where no stubs of trees stood up like question marks against the sky, and in this clearing was a cabin, a dark blotch that was without light or sound. But from behind it the dog barked again, and Jolly Roger made quickly toward it. Here there was no ash under his feet, and he knew that at last he had found an oasis of life in the desolation. Loudly he knocked with his fist at the cabin door and soon there was a response inside, the heavy movement of a man's body getting out of bed, and after that the questioning voice of a woman. He knocked again and the flare of a lighted match illumined the window. Then came the drawing of a bar at the door and a man stood there in his night attire, a man with a heavy face and bristling beard, and a lamp in his hand.

"I beg your pardon for waking you," said Jolly Roger, "but I am just down from the north, hoping to find my friends back here and I have seen nothing but destruction and death. You are the first living soul I have found to ask about them."

"Where were they?" grunted the man.

"At Cragg's Ridge."

"Then God help them," came the woman's voice from back in the room.

"Cragg's Ridge," said the man, "was a burning hell in the middle of the night."

Jolly Roger's fingers dug into the wood at the edge of the door.

"You mean—"

"A lot of 'em died," said the man stolidly, as if eager to rid himself of the one who had broken his sleep. "If it was Mooney, he's dead. An' if it was Robson, or Jake the Swede, or the Adams family—they're dead, too."

"But it wasn't," said Jolly Roger, his heart choking between fear and hope. "It was Father John, the Missioner, and Nada Hawkins, who lived with him—or with her foster-mother in the Hawkins' cabin."

The man shook his head, and turned down the wick of his lamp.

"I dunno about the girl, or the old witch who was her mother," he said, "but the Missioner made it out safe, and went to the settlements."

"And no girl was with him?"

"No, there was no girl," came the woman's voice again, and Peter jerked up his ears at the creaking of a bed. "Father John stopped here the second day after the fire had passed, and he said he was gathering up the bones of the dead. Nada Hawkins wasn't with him, and he didn't say who had died and who hadn't. But I think—"

She stopped as the bearded man turned toward her.

"You think what?" demanded Jolly Roger, stepping half into the room.

"I think," said the woman, "that she died along with the others. Anyway, Jed Hawkins' witch-woman was burned trying to make for the lake, and little of her was left."

The man with the lamp made a movement as if to close the door.

"That's all we know," he growled.

"For God's sake—don't!" entreated Jolly Roger, barring the door with his arm. "Surely there were some who escaped from Cragg's Ridge and beyond!"

"Mebby a half, mebby less," said the man. "I tell you it burned like hell, and the worst of it came in the middle of the night with a wind behind it that blew a hurricane. We've twenty acres cleared here, with the cabin in the center of it, an' it singed my beard and burned her hair and scorched our hands, and my pigs died out there from the heat of it. Mebby it's a place to sleep in for the night you want, stranger?"

"No, I'm going on," said Jolly Roger, the blood in his veins running with the chill of water. "How far before I come to the end of fire?"

"Ten miles on. It started this side of the next settlement."

Jolly Roger drew back and the door closed, and standing on the railroad once more he saw the light go out and after that the occasional barking of the settler's dog grew fainter and fainter behind them.

He felt a great weariness in his bones and body now. With hope struck down the exhaustion of two nights and a day without sleep seized upon him and his feet plodded more and more slowly over the uneven ties of the road. Even in his weariness he fought madly against the thought that Nada was dead and he repeated the word "impossible—impossible" so often that it ran in sing-song through his brain. And he could not keep away from him the white, thin face of the Missioner, who had promised on his faith In God to care for Nada, and who had passed the settler's cabin ALONE.

Another two hours they went on and then came the first of the green timber. Under the shelter of some balsams Jolly Roger found a resting place and there they waited for the break of dawn. Peter stretched out and slept. But Jolly Roger sat with his head and shoulders against the bole of a tree, and not until the light of the moon was driven away by the darkness that preceded dawn by an hour or two did his eyes close in restless slumber. He was roused by the wakening twitter of birds and in the cold water of a creek that ran near he bathed his face and hands. Peter wondered why there was no fire and no breakfast this morning.

The settlement was only a little way ahead and it was very early when they reached it. People were still in their beds and out of only one chimney was smoke rising into the clear calm of the breaking day. From this cabin a young man came, and stood for a moment after he had closed the door, yawning and stretching his arms and looking up to see what sort of promise the sky held for the day. After that he went to a stable of logs, and Jolly Roger followed him there.

He was unlike the bearded settler, and nodded with a youthful smile of cheer.

"Good morning," he said. "You're traveling early, and—"

He looked more keenly as his eyes took in Jolly Roger's boots and clothes, and the gray pallor in his face.

"Just get in?" he asked kindly. "And—from the burnt country?"

"Yes, from the burnt country. I've been away a long time, and I'm trying to find out if my friends are among the living or the dead. Did you ever hear of Father John, the Missioner at Cragg's Ridge?"

The young man's face brightened.

"I knew him," he said. "He helped me to bury my brother, three years ago. And if it's him you seek, he is safe. He went up to Fort William a week after the fire, and that was in September, eight months past."

"And was there with him a girl named Nada Hawkins?" asked Jolly Roger, trying hard to speak calmly as he looked into the other's face.

The youth shook his head.

"No, he was alone. He slept in my cabin overnight, and he said nothing of a girl named Nada Hawkins."

"Did he speak of others?"

"He was very tired, and I think he was half dead with grief at what had happened. He spoke no names that I remember."

Then he saw the gray look in Jolly Roger's face grow deeper, and saw the despair which could not hide itself in his eyes.

"But there were a number of girls who passed here, alone or with their friends," he said hopefully. "What sort of looking girl was Nada Hawkins?"

"A—kid. That's what I called her," said Jolly Roger, in a dead, cold voice. "Eighteen, and beautiful, with blue eyes, and brown hair that she couldn't keep from blowing in curls about her face. So like an angel you wouldn't forget her if you'd seen her—just once."

Gently the youth placed a hand on Jolly Roger's arm.

"She didn't come this way," he said, "but maybe you'll find her somewhere else. Won't you have breakfast with me? I've a stranger in the cabin, still sleeping, who's going into the fire country from which you've come. He's hunting for some one, and maybe you can give him information. He's going to Cragg's Ridge."

"Cragg's Ridge!" exclaimed Jolly Roger. "What is his name?"

"Breault," said the youth. "Sergeant Breault, of the Royal Northwest Mounted Police."

Jolly Roger turned to stroke the neck of a horse waiting for its morning feed. But he felt nothing of the touch of flesh under his hand. Cold as iron went his heart, and for half a minute he made no answer. Then he said:

"Thanks, friend. I breakfasted before it was light and I'm hitting out into the brush west and north, for the Rainy River country. Please don't tell this man Breault that you saw me, for he'll think badly of me for not waiting to give him information he might want. But—you understand—if you loved the brother who died—that it's hard for me to talk with anyone just now."

The young man's fingers touched his arm again.

"I understand," he said, "and I hope to God you'll find her."

Silently they shook hands, and Jolly Roger hurried away from the cabin with the rising spiral of smoke.

Three days later a man and a dog came from the burned country into the town of Fort William, seeking for a wandering messenger of God who called himself Father John, and a young and beautiful girl whose name was Nada Hawkins. He stopped first at the old mission, in whose shadow the Indians and traders of a century before had bartered their wares, and Father Augustine, the aged patriarch who talked with him, murmured as he went that he was a strange man, and a sick one, with a little madness lurking in his eyes.

And it was, in fact, a madness of despair eating out the life in Jolly Roger's heart. For he no longer had hope Nada had escaped the fire, even though at no place had he found a conclusive evidence of her death. But that signified little, for there were many of the missing who had not been found between the last of September and these days of May. What he did find, with deadly regularity, was the fact that Father John had escaped—and that he had traveled to safety ALONE.

And Father Augustine told him that when Father John stopped to rest for a few days at the Mission he was heading north, for somewhere on Pashkokogon Lake near the river Albany.

There was little rest for Peter and his master at Fort William town. That Breault must be close on their trail, and following it with the merciless determination of the ferret from which he had been named, there was no shadow of doubt in the mind of Jolly Roger McKay. So after outfitting his pack at a little corner shop, where Breault would be slow to enquire about him, he struck north through the bush toward Dog Lake and the river of the same name. Five or six days, he thought, would bring him to Father John and the truth which he dreaded more and more to hear.

The despondency of his master had sunk, in some mysterious way, into the soul of Peter. Without the understanding of language he sensed the oppressive gloom of tragedy behind and about him and there was a wolfish slinking in the manner of his travel now, and his confidence was going as he caught the disease of despair of the man who traveled with him. But constantly and vigilantly his eyes and scent were questing about them, suspicious of the very winds that whispered in the treetops. And at night after they had built their little cooking fire in the deepest heart of the bush he would lie half awake during the hours of darkness, the watchfulness of his senses never completely dulled in the stupor of sleep.

Since the night they had stopped at the settler's cabin Jolly Roger's face had grown grayer and thinner. A number of times he had tried to assure himself what he would do in that moment which was coming when he would stand face to face with Breault the man- hunter. His caution, after he left Fort William, was in a way an automatic instinct that worked for self-preservation in face of the fact that he was growing less and less concerned regarding Breault's appearance. It was not in his desire to delay the end much longer. The chase had been a long one, with its thrills and its happiness at times, but now he was growing tired and with Nada gone there was only hopeless gloom ahead. If she were dead he wanted to go to her. That thought was a dawning pleasure in his breast, and it was warm in his heart when he tied in a hard knot the buckskin string which locked the flap of his pistol holster. When Breault overtook him the law would know, because of the significance of this knot, that he had welcomed the end of the game.

Never in the northland had there come a spring more beautiful than this of the year in which McKay and his dog went through the deep wilds to Pashkokogon Lake. In a few hours, it seemed, the last chill died out of the air and there came the soft whispers of those bridal-weeks between May and Summer, a month ahead of their time. But Jolly Roger, for the first time in his life, failed to respond to the wonder and beauty of the earth's rejoicing. The first flowers did not fill him with the old joy. He no longer stood up straight, with expanding chest, to drink in the rare sweetness of air weighted with the tonic of balsams and cedar spruce. Vainly he tried to lift up his soul with the song and bustle of mating things. There was no longer music for him in the flood-time rushing of spring waters. An utter loneliness filled the cry of the loon. And all about him was a vast emptiness from which the spirit of life had fled for him.

Thus he came at last to a stream in the Burntwood country which ran into Pashkokogon Lake; and it was this day, in the mellow sunlight of late afternoon, that they heard coming to them from out of the dense forest the chopping of an axe.

Toward this they made their way, with caution and no sound, until in a little clearing in a bend of the stream they saw a cabin. It was a newly built cabin, and smoke was rising from the chimney.

But the chopping was nearer them, in the heart of a thick cover of evergreen and birch. Into this Jolly Roger and Peter made their way and came within a dozen steps of the man who was wielding the axe. It was then that Jolly Roger rose up with a cry on his lips, for the man was Father John the Missioner.

In spite of the tragedy through which he had passed the little gray man seemed younger than in that month long ago when Jolly Roger had fled to the north. He dropped his axe now and stood as if only half believing, a look of joy shining in his face as he realized the truth of what had happened. "McKay," he cried, reaching out his hands. "McKay, my boy!"

A look of pity mellowed the gladness in his eyes as he noted the change in Jolly Roger's face, and the despair that had set its mark upon it.

They stood for a moment with clasped hands, questioning and answering with the silence of their eyes. And then the Missioner said:

"You have heard? Someone has told you?"

"No," said Jolly Roger, his head dropping a little. "No one has told me," and he was thinking of Nada, and her death.

Father John's fingers tightened.

"It is strange how the ways of God bring themselves about," he spoke in a low voice. "Roger, you did not kill Jed Hawkins!"

Dumbly, his lips dried of words, Jolly Roger stared at him.

"No, you didn't kill him," repeated Father John. "On that same night of the storm when you thought you left him dead in the trail, he stumbled back to his cabin, alive. But God's vengeance came soon.

"A few days later, while drunk, he missed his footing and fell from a ledge to his death. His wife, poor creature, wished him buried in sight of the cabin door—"

But in this moment Roger McKay was thinking less of Breault the Ferret and the loosening of the hangman's rope from about his neck than he was of another thing. And Father John was saying in a voice that seemed far away and unreal:

"We've sent out word to all parts of the north, hoping someone would find you and send you back. And she has prayed each night, and each hour of the day the same prayer has been in her heart and on her lips. And now—"

Someone was coming to them from the direction of the cabin— someone, a girl, and she was singing,

McKay's face went whiter than the gray ash of fire.

"My God," he whispered huskily. "I thought—she had died!"

It was only then Father John understood the meaning of what he had seen in his face.

"No, she is alive," he cried. "I sent her straight north through the bush with an Indian the day after the fire. And later I left word for you with the Fire Relief Committee at Fort Wiliam, where I thought you would first enquire."

"And it was there," said Jolly Roger, "that I did not enquire at all!"

In the edge of the clearing, close to the thicket of timber, Nada had stopped. For across the open space a strange looking creature had raced at the sound of her voice; a dog with bristling Airedale whiskers, and a hound's legs, and wild-wolf's body hardened and roughened by months of fighting in the wilderness. As in the days of his puppyhood, Peter leapt up against her, and a cry burst from Nada's lips, a wild and sobbing cry of PETER, PETER, PETER—and it was this cry Jolly Roger heard as he tore away from Father John.

On her knees, with her arms about Peter's shaggy head, Nada stared wildly at the clump of timber, and in a moment she saw a man break out of it, and stand still, as if the mellow sunlight blinded him, and made him unable to move. And the same choking weakness was at her own heart as she rose up from Peter, and reached out her arms toward the gray figure in the edge of the wood, sobbing, trying to speak and yet saying no word.

And a little slower, because of his age, Father John came a moment later, and peered out with the knowledge of long years from a thicket of young banksians, and when he saw the two in the open, close in each other's arms, and Peter hopping madly about them, he drew out a handkerchief and wiped his eyes, and went back then for the axe which he had dropped in the timber clump.

There was a great drumming in Jolly Roger's head, and for a time he failed even to hear Peter yelping at their side, for all the world was drowned in those moments by the breaking sobs in Nada's breath and the wild thrill of her body in his arms; and he saw nothing but the upturned face, crushed close against his breast, and the wide-open eyes, and the lips to kiss. And even Nada's face he seemed to see through a silvery mist, and he felt her arms strangely about his neck, as if it was all half like a dream—a dream of the kind that had come to him beside his campfire. It was a little cry from Nada that drove the unreality away.

"Roger—you're—breaking me," she cried, gasping for her breath in his arms, yet without giving up the clasp of her own arms about his neck in the least; and at that he sensed the brutality of his strength, and held her off a little, looking into her face.

Pride and happiness and the courage in his heart would have slunk away could he have seen himself then, as Father John saw him, coming from the edge of the bush, and as Nada saw him, held there at the end of his arms. Since the day he had come with Peter to Cragg's Ridge the blade of a razor had not touched his face, and his beard was like a brush, and with it his hair unkempt and straggling; and his eyes were red from sleeplessness and the haunting of that grim despair which had dogged his footsteps.

But these things Nada did not see. Or, if she did, there must have been something beautiful about them for her. For it was not a little girl, but a woman who was standing there before Jolly Roger now—Nada grown older, very much older it seemed to McKay, and taller, with her hair no longer rioting free about her, but gathered up in a wonderful way on the crown of her head. This change McKay discovered as she stood there, and it swept upon him all in a moment, and with it the prick of something swift and terrorizing inside him. She was not the little girl of Cragg's Ridge. She was a WOMAN. In a year had come this miracle of change, and it frightened him, for such a creature as this that stood before him now Jed Hawkins would never have dared to curse or beat, and he—Roger McKay—was afraid to gather her back into his arms again.

And then, even as his fingers slowly drew themselves away from her shoulders, he saw that which had not changed—the wonder-light in her eyes, the soul that lay as open to him now as on that other day in Indian Tom's cabin, when Mrs. Captain Kidd had bustled and squeaked on the pantry shelf, and Peter had watched them as he lay with his broken leg in the going down of the sun. And as he hesitated it was Nada herself who came into his arms, and laid her head on his breast, and trembled and laughed and cried there, while Father John came up and patted her shoulder, and smiled happily at McKay, and then went on to the cabin in the clearing. For a time after that Jolly Roger crushed his face in Nada's hair, and neither said a word, but there was a strange throbbing of their hearts together, and after a little Nada reached up a hand to his cheek, and stroked it tenderly, bristly beard and all.

"I'll never let you run away from me again—Mister—Jolly Roger," she said, and it was the little Nada of Cragg's Ridge who whispered the words, half sobbing;

but in the voice there was also something very definite and very sure, and McKay felt the glorious thrill of it as he raised his face from her hair, and saw once more the sun-filled world about him.

CHAPTER XVIII

FOLLOWING this day Peter was observant of a strange excitement in the cabin on the Burntwood. It was not so much a thing of physical happening, but more the mysterious FEEL of something impending and very near. The day following their arrival in the Pashkokogon country his master seemed to have forgotten him entirely. It was Nada who noticed him, but even she was different; and Father John went about, overseeing two Indians whom he kept very busy, his pale, thin face luminous with an anticipation which roused Peter's curiosity, and kept him watchful. He was puzzled, too, by the odd actions of the humans about him. The second morning Nada remained in her room, and Jolly Roger wandered off into the woods without his breakfast, and Father John ate alone, smiling gently as he looked at the tightly closed door of Nada's bedroom. Even Oosimisk, the Leaf Bud, the sleek-haired Indian woman who cared for the house, was nervously expectant as she watched for Nada, and Mistoos, her husband, grunted and grimaced as he carried in from the edge of the forest many loads of soft evergreens on his shoulders.

Into the forest Jolly Roger went alone, puffing furiously at his pipe. He was all a-tremble and his blood seemed to quiver and dance as it ran through his veins. Since the first rose-flush of dawn he had been awake, fighting against this upsetting of every nerve that was in him.

He felt pitiably weak and helpless. But it was the weakness and helplessness of a happiness too vast for him to measure. It was Nada in her ragged shoes and dress, with the haunting torture of Jed Hawkins' brutality in her eyes and face, that he had expected to find, if he found her at all; someone to fight for, and kill for if nec-

essary, someone his muscle and brawn would always protect against evil. He had
not dreamed that in these many months with Father John she would change from
"a little kid goin' on eighteen" into—A WOMAN.

He tried to recall just what he had said to her last night—that he was still an
outlaw, and would always be, no matter how well he lived from this day on; and
that she, now that she had Father John's protection, was very foolish to care for
him, or keep her troth with him, and would be happier if she could forget what had
happened at Cragg's Ridge.

"You're a WOMAN now," he said. "A WOMAN—" he had emphasized that
—"and you don't need me any more."

And she had looked at him, without speaking, as if reading what was inside him; and then, with a sudden little laugh, she swiftly pulled her hair down
about her shoulders, and repeated the very words she had said to him a long time
ago—"Without you—I'd want to die—Mister—Jolly Roger," and with that she
turned and ran into the cabin, her hair flying riotously, and he had not seen her
again since that moment.

Since then his heart had behaved like a thing with the fever, and it was beating
swiftly now as he looked at his watch and noted the quick passing of time.

Back in the cabin Peter was sniffing at the crack under Nada's door, and listening to her movement. For a long time he had heard her, but not once had she
opened the door. And he wondered, after that, why Oosimisk and her husband and
Father John piled evergreens all about, until the cabin looked like the little jackpine
trysting-place down at Cragg's Ridge, even to the soft carpet of grass on the floor,
and flowers scattered all about.

Hopeless of understanding what it meant, he went outside, and waited in the
warm May-day sun until his master came back through the clearing. What happened after that puzzled him greatly. When he followed Jolly Roger into the cabin
Mistoos and the Leaf Bud were seated in chairs, their hands folded, and Father John
stood behind a small table on which lay an open book, and he was looking at his
watch when they came in. He nodded, and smiled, and very clearly Peter saw his
master gulp, as if swallowing something that was in his throat. And the ruddiness
had gone completely out of his smooth-shaven cheeks. It was the first time Peter had
seen his master so clearly afraid, and from his burrow in the evergreens he growled

under his breath, eyeing the open door with sudden thought of an enemy.

And then Father John was tapping at Nada's door.

He went back to the table and waited, and as the knob of the door turned very slowly Jolly Roger swallowed again, and took a step toward it. It opened, and Nada stood there. And Jolly Roger gave a little cry, so low that Peter could just hear it, as he held out his hands to her.

For Nada was no longer the Nada who had come to him in Father John's clearing. She was the Nada of Cragg's Ridge, the Nada of that wild night of storm when he had fled into the north. Her hair fell about her, as in the old days when Peter and she had played together among the rocks and flowers, and her wedding dress was faded and torn, for it was the dress she had worn that night of despair when she sent her message to Peter's master, and on her little feet were shoes broken and disfigured by her flight in those last hours of her mighty effort to go with the man she loved. In Father John's eyes, as she stood there, was a great astonishment; but in Jolly Roger's there came such a joy that, in answer to it, Nada went straight into his arms and held up her lips to be kissed.

Her cheeks were very pink when she stood beside McKay, with Father John before them, the open book in his hands; and then, as her long lashes drooped over her eyes, and her breath came a little more quickly, she saw Peter staring at her questioningly, and made a little motion to him with her hand. He went to her, and her fingers touched his head as Father John began speaking. Peter looked up, and listened, and was very quiet in these moments. Jolly Roger was staring straight at the balsam-decked wall opposite him, but there was something mighty strong and proud in the way he held his head, and the fear had gone completely out of his eyes. And Nada stood very close to him, so that her brown head lightly touched his shoulder and he could see the silken shimmer of loose tresses which with sweet intent she had let fall over his arm. And her little fingers clung tightly to his thumb, as on that blessed night when they had walked together across the plain below Cragg's Ridge, with the moon lighting their way.

Peter, in his dog way, fell a-wondering as he stood there, but kept his manners and remained still. When it was all over he felt a desire to show his teeth and growl, for when Father John had kissed Nada, and was shaking Jolly Roger's hand, he saw his mistress crying in that strange, silent way he had so often seen her crying in his puppyhood days. Only now her blue eyes were wide open as she looked at Jolly Roger, and her cheeks were flushed to the pink of wild rose petals, and her lips were trembling a little, and there was a tiny something pulsing in her soft white throat. And all at once there came a smile with the tears, and Jolly Roger—turning from Father John to find her thus—gathered her close in his arms, and Peter wagged his tail and went out into the sun-filled day, where he heard a red squirrel challenging him from a stub in the edge of the clearing.

A little later he saw Nada and his master come out of the cabin, and walk hand in hand across the open into the sweet-smelling timber where Father John had been chopping with his axe.

On a fresh-cut log Nada sat down, and McKay sat beside her, still holding her hand. Not once had he spoken in crossing the open, and it seemed as though little devils were holding his lips closed now.

With her eyes looking down at the greening earth under their feet, Nada said, very softly,

"Mister—Jolly Roger—are you glad?"

"Yes," he said.

"Glad that I am—your wife?"

The word drew a great, sobbing breath from him, and looking up suddenly she saw that he was staring over the balsam-tops into the wonderful blue of the sky.

"Your WIFE," she whispered, touching his shoulder gently with her lips.

"Yes, I'm glad," he said. "So glad that I'm—afraid."

"Then—if you are glad—please kiss me again."

He stood up, and drew her to him, and held her face between his hands as he kissed her red lips; and after that he kissed her shining hair again and again, and when he let her go her eyes were a glory of happiness.

"And you will never run away from me again?" she demanded, holding him at arm's length. "Never?"

"Never!"

"Then—I want nothing more in this life," she said, nestling against him again. "Only you, for ever and ever."

Jolly Roger made no answer, but held her a long time in his arms, with the soft beating of her heart against him, and listened to the twitter and song of nesting and mating things about them. In this silence she lay content, until Peter—growing restless— started quietly into the golden depths of the forest.

It was Pied-Bot's going, cautious and soft-footed, as if danger and menace might lurk just ahead of him, that brought another look into McKay's eyes as Nada's hand crept to his cheek, and rested there.

"You love me—very much?"

"More than life," he answered, and as he spoke he was watching Peter, questing the soft wind that came whispering from the south.

Her finger touched his lips, gentle and sweet.

"And wherever you go, I go—forever and always?" she questioned.

"Yes, forever and always"—and his eyes were looking through miles upon miles of deep forest, and at the end he saw the thin and pitiless face of a man who was following his trail, Breault the Ferret.

His arms closed more tightly about her, and he pressed her face against him.

"And I pray God you will never be sorry," he said, still looking through the miles of forest.

"No, no—sorry I shall never be," she cried softly. "Not if we fly, and go hungry, and fight— and die. Never shall I be sorry— with you," and he felt the tightening of her arms.

And then, as he remained silent, with his lips on the velvety smoothness of her hair, she told him what Father John had already told him—of her wild effort to overtake him in that night of storm when he had fled from the Missioner's cabin at Cragg's Ridge; and in turn he told her how Peter came to him in the break of the morning with the treasure which had saved him heart and soul, and how he had given that treasure into the keeping of Yellow Bird, on the shores of Wollaston.

And thereafter, for an hour, as they wandered through the May-time sweetness of the forest, she would permit him to talk of only Yellow Bird and Sun Cloud; and, one thing leading to another, she learned how it was that Yellow Bird had been his fairy in childhood days, and how he came to be an outlaw for her in later manhood. Her eyes were shining when he had finished, and her red lips were a-tremble with the quickness of her breathing.

"Some day—you'll take me there," she whispered. "Oh, I'm so proud of you, my Roger. And I love Yellow Bird. And Sun Cloud. Some day —we'll go!"

He nodded, happiness overshadowing the fear of Breault that had grown in his heart.

"Yes, we'll go. I've dreamed it, and the dream helped to keep me alive—"

And then he told her of Cassidy, and of the paradise he had found with Giselle and her grandfather on the other side of Wollaston.

And so it happened the hours passed swiftly, and it was afternoon when they returned to Father John's cabin, and Nada went into her room.

In the early waning of the sun the feast which the Leaf Bud had been preparing was ready, and not until then did Nada appear again.

And once more the lump rose up in Roger's throat at the wonder of her, for very completely she had transformed herself into a woman again, from the softly shining coils of hair on the crown of her head to the coquettish little slippers that set off her dainty feet. And he saw the white gleam of soft shoulders and tender arms where once had been rags and bruises, and held there by the slim beauty and exquisite daintiness of her he stared like a fool, until suddenly she laughed joyously at his amaze, and ran to him with wide-open arms, and kissed him so soundly that Peter cocked up his ears a bit startled. And then she kissed Father John, and after that was mistress at the table, radiant in her triumph and her eyes starry with happiness.

And she was no longer shy in speaking his name, but called him Roger boldly and many times, and twice during that meal of marvelous forgetfulness—though long lashes covered her eyes when she spoke it—she called him 'my husband.'

In truth she was a woman and for the most part Roger McKay— fighting man and very strong though he was—looked at her in dumb worship, speaking little, his heart a-throb, and his brain reeling in the marvel of what at last had come into his possession.

And yet, even in this hour of supreme happiness that held him half mute, there was always lurking in the back of his brain a thought of Breault, the Ferret.

CHAPTER XIX

IN the star dusk of evening the time came when he spoke his fears to Father John.

Nada had gone into her room, taking Peter with her, and out under the cool of the skies Father John's pale face was turned up to the unending glory of the firmament, and his lips were whispering a prayer of gratitude and blessing, when Roger laid a hand gently on his arm.

"Father," he said, "it is a wonderful night."

"A night of gladness and omen," replied Father John. "See the stars! They seem to be alive and rejoicing, and it is not sacrilege to believe they are, giving you their benediction."

"And yet—I am afraid."

"Afraid?"

Father John looked into his eyes, and saw him staring off over the forest-tops.

"Yes—afraid for her."

Briefly he told him of what had happened on the Barren months ago, and how he had narrowly escaped Breault in coming away from the burned country.

"He is on my trail," he said, "and tonight he is not very far away."

The Missioner's hand rested in a comforting way on his arm.

"You did not kill Jed Hawkins, my son, and for that we have thanked God each day and night of our lives—Nada and I. And each evening she has prayed for you, kneeling at my side, and through every hour of the day I know she was praying for you in her heart —and I believe in the answer to prayer such as that, Roger. Her faith, now, is as deep as the sea. And you, too, must have faith."

"She is more precious to me than life—a thousand lives, if I had them," whispered Jolly Roger. "If anything should happen—now—"

"Yes, if the thing you fear should happen, what then?" cried Father John, faith ringing like a note of inspiration in his low voice. "What, then, Roger? You did not kill Jed Hawkins. If the law compels you to pay a price for the errors it believes you have committed, will that price be so terribly severe?"

"Prison, Father. Probably five years."

Father John laughed softly, the star-glow revealing a radiance in his face.

"Five years!" he repeated. "Oh, my boy, my dear boy, what are five years to pay for such a treasure as that which has come into your possession tonight? Five short years—only five. And she waiting for you, proud of you for those very achievements which sent you to prison, planning for all the future that lies beyond those five short years, growing sweeter and more beautiful for you as she waits—Roger, is that a very great sacrifice? Is it too great a price to pay? Five years, and after that—peace, love, happiness for all time? Is it, Roger?"

McKay felt his voice tremble as he tried to answer.

"But she, father—"

"Yes, yes, I know what you would say," interrupted Father John gently. "I argued with her, just as you would have argued, Roger. I appealed to her reason. I told her that if you returned it would mean prison for you, and strangely I said that same thing—five years. But I found her selfish, Roger, very selfish—and set upon her desire beyond all reason. And it was she who asked first those very questions I have asked you tonight. 'What are five years?' she demanded of me, defying my logic. 'What are five years—or ten—or twenty, IF I KNOW I AM TO HAVE HIM AFTER THAT?' Yes, she was selfish, Roger. Just that great is her love for you."

"Dear God in Heaven," breathed Jolly Roger, and stopped, his eyes staring wide at the stars.

"And after that, after I had given in to her selfishness, Roger, she planned how we—she and I—would live very near to the place where they imprisoned you, and how each day some sight or sign should pass between you, and the baby—"

"The baby, Father?"

"Thus it seems she dreams, Roger. She, in the wilfulness of her desire and selfishness—"

With a choking cry Roger bowed his face in his hands.

For a moment Father John was silent. And then he said, so very low that it was almost a whisper,

"I have passed many years in the wilderness, Roger, many years trying to look into the hearts of people—and of God. And this— this love of Nada's—is the greatest of all the miracles I have witnessed in a life that is now reaching to its three score and five. Do you see the wonder of it, son? And does it make you happy, and fearless now?"

He did not wait for an answer, but turned slowly and went in the direction of the cabin, leaving Roger alone under the thickening stars. And McKay's face was like Father John's, filled with a strange and wonderful radiance when he looked up. But with that light of happiness was also the fiercer underglow of a great determination. For Nada—for THE BABY—the worst should not happen; he breathed the thought aloud, and in the words was a prayer that God might help him, and make unnecessary the sacrifice from which Father John had taken the sting of fear. And yet, if that sacrifice came, he saw clearly now that it would not be a great tragedy but only a brief shadow cast over the undying happiness in his soul. For they—NADA AND THE BABY—would be waiting—waiting—

Suddenly he was conscious of a sound very near, and he beheld Nada, taller and slimmer and more beautiful than ever, it seemed to him, in the starlight.

"I have told him," Father John had whispered to her only a moment before. "I have told him, so that he will not fear prison—either for himself or for you."

And she had come to him quietly, all of the pretty triumph and playfulness gone, so that she stood like an angel in the soft glow of the skies, much older than he had ever seen her before, and smiled at him with a new and wonderful tenderness as she held out her hands to him.

Not until she lay in his arms, looking up at him from under her long lashes, did he dare to speak. And then,

"Is it true—what Father John has told me?" he asked.

"It is true," she whispered, and the silken lashes covered her eyes.

Her hand crept up to his face in the silence that followed, and rested there; and with no desire to hear more than the three words she had spoken he crushed his lips in the sweet coils of her hair, and together, in that peace ands understanding, they listened to the gentle whisperings of the night.

"Roger," she whispered at last.

"Yes, my NEWA—"

"What does that mean, Roger?"

"It means—beloved—wife"

"Then I like it. But I shall like the others—one of the others— best."

"My—WIFE."

"That—that makes me happiest, Roger. Your WIFE. Oh, it is the sweetest word in the world, that—and—"

He felt her warm face hide itself softly against his neck.

"Mother," he added.

"Yes—Mother," she repeated after him in an awed little voice. "Oh, I have dreamed of Mothers since I have been old enough to dream, Roger! My Mother—I never had one that I can remember, except in a dream. It must be wonderful to—to—have a Mother, Roger."

"And yet, I think, not quite so wonderful as to BE a Mother, my Nada."

"Listen!" she whispered.

"It is the Leaf Bud singing."

"A love song?"

"Yes, in Cree."

She raised her head, so that her eyes were wide open, and looking at him.

"Since we came up here all this wonderful world has been promising song for me, Roger. And since you came back to me it has been singing—singing—singing—every hour of night and day. Have you ever dreamed of leaving it, Roger—of going down into that world of towns and cities of which Father John has told me so much?"

"Would you like to go there, Nada?"

"Only to look upon it, and come away. I want to live in the forests, where I found you. Always and always, Roger."

She raised herself on tip-toe, and kissed him.

"I want to live near Yellow Bird and Sun Cloud—please—Mister Jolly Roger—I do. And Father John will go with us. And we'll be so happy there all together, Yellow Bird and Sun Cloud and Giselle and I—oh!"

His arms had tightened so suddenly that the little cry came from her.

"And yet—I may have to leave you for a little time, Nada. But it will not be for long. What are five years, when all life reaches out a paradise before us? They are nothing—nothing—and will pass swiftly—"

"Yes, they will pass swiftly," she said, so gently that scarce did he hear.

But on his breast she gave a little sob which would not choke itself back, a sob which bravely she smiled through a moment later, and which he—knowing that it was best—made as if he had not heard.

And so, this night, while Father John and Peter waited and watched in the cabin, did they plan their future in the company of the stars.

CHAPTER XX

T HE Sabbath was a day of glory and peace in the Burntwood country. The sun rose warm and golden, the birds were singing, and never had the air seemed sweeter to Father John when he came out quietly from the cabin and breathed it in the early break of dawn. Best of all he loved this very beginning of day, before darkness was quite gone, when the world seemed to be awakening mid sleepy whisperings and sounds came clearly from a long distance.

This morning he heard the barking of a dog, a mile away it must have been, and Peter, who followed close beside him, pricked up his ears at the sound of it. Father John had noted Peter's vigilance, the cautious expectancy with which he was always sniffing the air, and the keen alertness of his eyes and ears. McKay had explained the reason for it. And this morning, as they made their way down to the pool at the creekside, Peter's ceaseless watching for danger held a deeper significance for Father John. All through the night, in spite of his faith and his words of consolation, he was thinking of the menace which was following McKay, and which eventually must catch up with him.

And yet, how short a time was five years! Looking backward, each five years of his life seemed but a yesterday. It was eight times five years ago that a sweet-faced girl had first filled his life, as Nada filled Jolly Roger's now, and through the thirty years since he had lost her he could still hear her voice as clearly as though he had held her in his arms only a few hours ago, so swift had been the passing of time. But looking ahead, and not backward, five years seemed an eternity of time, and the dread of it was in Father John's heart as he stood at the side of the pool, with the first pink glow of sunrise coming to him over the forest-tops.

Five years, and he was an old man now. A long and dreary wait it would be for him. But for youth, the glorious youth of Roger and Nada, it would seem very short when in later years they looked back upon it. And for a time as he contemplated the long span of life that lay behind him, and the briefness of that which lay ahead, a yearning selfishness possessed the soul of Father John, an almost savage desire to hold those five years away from the violation of the law—not alone for Nada's sake and Roger McKay's —but for his own. In this twilight of a tragic life a great happiness had come to him in the love of these two, and thought of its menace, its desecration by a pitiless and mistaken justice, roused in him something that was more like the soul of a fighting man than the spirit of a missioner of God.

Vainly he tried to stamp out the evil of this resentment, for evil he believed it to be. And shame possessed him when he saw the sweet glory in Nada's face later that morning, and the happiness that was in Roger McKay's. Yet was that aching place in his heart, and the hidden fear which he could not vanquish.

And that day, it seemed to him, his lips gave voice to lies. For, being Sunday, the wilderness folk gathered from miles about, and he preached to them in the little mission house which they had helped him to build of logs in the clearing. Partly he spoke in Cree, and partly in English, and his message was one of hope and inspiration, pointing out the silver linings that always lay beyond the darkness of clouds. To McKay, holding Nada's hand in his own as they listened, Father John's words brought a great and comforting faith. And in Nada's eyes and voice as she led in Cree the song, "Nearer, My God, to Thee," he heard and saw the living fire of that faith, and had Breault come in through the open doorway then he would have accepted him calmly as the beginning of that sacrifice which he had made up his mind to make.

In the afternoon, when the wilderness people had gone, Father John heard again the story of Yellow Bird, for Nada was ever full of questions about her, and for the first time the Missioner learned of the inspiration which the Indian woman's sorcery had been to Jolly Roger.

"It was foolish," McKay apologized, in spite of the certainty and faith which he saw shining in Nada's eyes. "But—it helped me."

"It wasn't foolish," replied Nada quickly. "Yellow Bird DID come to me. And—SHE KNEW."

"No true faith is folly," said Father John, in his soft, low voice. "The great fact is that Yellow Bird believed. She was inspired by a great confidence, and confidence and faith give to the mind a power which it is utterly incapable of possessing without them. I believe in the mind, children. I believe that in some day to come it will reach those heights where it will unlock the mystery of life itself to us. I have seen many strange things in my forty-odd years in the wilderness, and not the least of these have been the achievements of the primitive mind. And it seems to me, Roger, that Yellow Bird told you much that has come true. And has it occurred to you—"

He stopped, knowing that the cloud of unrest which was almost fear in his heart was driving him to say these things.

"What, father," questioned Nada, bending toward him.

"I was about to express a thought which suggests an almost childish curiosity, and you will laugh at me, my dear. I am wondering if it has occurred to Roger the mysterious 'Country Beyond' of which Yellow Bird dreamed might be the great country down there—south—BEYOND THE BORDER—the United States?"

Something which he could not control seemed to drive the words from his lips, and in an instant he saw that Nada had seized upon their significance. Her eyes widened. The blue in them grew darker, and Roger observed her fingers grip suddenly in the softness of her dress as she turned from Father John to look at him.

"Or—it might be China, or Africa, or the South Seas," he tried to laugh, remembering his old visions. "It might be—anywhere."

Nada's lips trembled, as if she were about to speak; and then very quietly she sat, with her hands tightly clasped in her lap, and Father John knew she was not expressing the thought in her heart when she said,

"Someday I want to tell Yellow Bird how much I love her."

Now in these hours since he and his master had come to the Burntwood it seemed to Peter that he had lost something very great, for in his happiness McKay had taken but scant notice of him, and Nada seemed to have found a greater joy than that which a long time ago she had found in his comradeship. So now, as she saw him lying in his loneliness a short distance away, Nada suddenly ran to him, and together they went into the thick screen of the balsams, Peter yipping joyously, and Nada without so much as turning her head in the direction of Roger and Father John. But even in that bird-like swiftness with which she had left them, Father

John had caught the look in her eyes.

"I have made a mistake," he confessed humbly. "I have sinned, because in her I have roused the temptation to urge you to fly away with her—down there—south. She is a woman, and being a woman she has infinite faith in Yellow Bird, for Yellow Bird helped to give you to her. She believes—"

"And I—I—also believe," said McKay, staring at the green balsams.

"And yet—it is better for you to remain. God means that judgment and happiness should come in their turn."

Jolly Roger rose to his feet, facing the south.

"It is a temptation, father. It would be hard to give her up—now. If Breault would only wait a little while. But if he comes—NOW—"

He walked away slowly, following through the balsams where Nada and Peter had gone. Father John watched him go, and a trembling smile came to his lips when he was alone. In his heart he knew he was a coward, and that these young people had been stronger than he. For in their happiness and the faith which he had falsely built up in them they had resigned themselves to the inevitable, while he, in these moments of cowardice, had shown them the way to temptation. And yet as he stood there, looking in the direction they had gone, he felt no remorse because of what he had done, and a weight seemed to have lifted itself from his shoulders.

For a time the more selfish instincts of the man rose in him, fighting down the sacrificial humility of the great faith of which he was a messenger. The new sensation thrilled him, and in its thrill he felt his heart beating a little faster, and hope rising in him. Five years were a long time— FOR HIM. That was the thought which kept repeating itself over and over in his brain, and with it came that other thought, that self-preservation was the first law of existence, and therefore could not be a sin. Thus did Father John turn traitor to his spoken words, though his calm and smiling face gave no betrayal of it when Nada and Roger returned to the cabin an hour later, their arms filled with red bakneesh vines and early wildflowers.

Nada's cheeks were as pink as the bakneesh, and her eyes as blue as the rock-violets she wore on her breast.

And Father John knew that Jolly Roger was no longer oppressed by the fear of a menace which he was helpless to oppose, for there was something very confident in the look of his eyes and the manner in which they rested upon Nada

Peter alone saw the mysterious thing which happened in the early evening. He was with Nada in her room. And she was the old Nada again, hugging his shaggy head in her arms, and whispering to him in the old, excited way. And strange memory of a bundle came back to Peter, for very quietly, as if unseen ears might be listening to her, Nada gathered many things in a pile on the table, and made another bundle. This bundle she thrust under her bed, just as a long time ago she had thrust a similar bundle under a banksian clump in the meadowland below Cragg's Ridge.

Father John went to his bed very early, and he was thinking of Breault. The Hudson's Bay Company post was only twelve miles away, and Breault would surely go there before questing from cabin to cabin for his victim.

So it happened that a little after midnight he rose without making a sound, and by the light of a candle wrote a note for Nada, saying he had business at the post that day, and without wakening them had made an early start. This note Nada read to McKay when they sat at breakfast.

"Quite frequently he has gone like that," Nada explained. "He loves the forests at night—in the light of the moon."

"But last night there was no moon," said Roger.

"Yes—"

"And when Father John left the cabin the sky was clouded, and it was very dark."

"You heard him go?"

"Yes, and saw him. There was a worried look in his face when he wrote that note in the candle-glow."

"Roger, what do you mean?"

McKay went behind her chair, and tilted up her face, and kissed her shining hair and questioning eyes.

"It means, precious little wife, that Father John is hurrying to the post to get news of Breault if he can. It means that deep in his heart he wants us to follow Yellow Bird's advice to the end. For he is sure that he knows what Yellow Bird meant by 'The Country Beyond.' It is the great big world outside the forests. a world so big that if need be we can put ourselves ten thousand miles away from the trails of the mounted police. That is the thought which is urging him to the post to look for Breault."

Her arms crept up to his neck, and in a little voice trembling with eagerness she said,

"Roger, my bundle is ready. I prepared it last night—and it is under the bed."

He held her more closely.

"And you are willing to go with me—anywhere?"

"Yes, anywhere."

"To the end of the earth?"

Her crumpled head nodded against his breast.

"And leave Father John?"

"Yes, for you. But I think—sometime—he will come to us."

Her fingers touched his cheek.

"And there must be forests, big, beautiful forests, in some other part of the world, Roger"

"Or a desert, where they would never think of looking for us," he laughed happily.

"I'd love the desert, Roger."

"Or an uninhabited island?"

Against him her head nodded again.

"I'd love life anywhere—WITH YOU."

"Then—we'll go," he said, trying to speak very calmly in spite of the joy that was consuming him like a fire. And then he went on, steadying his voice until it was almost cold. "But it means giving up everything you've dreamed of, Nada—these forests you love, Father John, Yellow Bird, Sun Cloud—"

"I have only one dream," she interrupted him softly.

"And five years will pass very quickly," he continued. "Possibly it will not be as bad as that, and afterward all this land we love will be free to us forever. Gladly will I remain and take my punishment if in the end it will make us happier, Nada"

"I have only one dream," she repeated, caressing his cheek with her hand, "and that is you, Roger. Where-ever you take me I shall be the happiest woman in the world."

"WOMAN," he laughed, scarcely breathing the word aloud.

"Yes, I am a woman—now"

"And yet forever and ever the little girl of Cragg's Ridge," he cried with sudden passion, crushing her close to him. "I'd lose my life sooner than I would lose her, Nada—the little girl with flying hair and strawberry stain on her nose, and who believed so faithfully in the Man in the Moon. Always I shall worship her as the little goddess who came down to me from somewhere in heaven!"

Yet all through that day, as they waited for Father John's return, he saw more and more of the wonder of woman that had come to crown the glory of Nada's wifehood, and his heart trembled with joy at the miracle of it. There was something vastly sweet in the change of her. She was no longer the utterly dependent little thing, possibly caring for him because he was big and strong and able to protect her; she was a woman, and loved him as a woman, and not because of fear or helplessness. And then came the thrilling mystery of another thing. He found himself, in turn, beginning to depend upon her, and in their planning her calm decision and quiet reasoning strengthened him with new confidence and made his heart sing with gladness. With his eyes on the smooth and velvety coils of hair which she had twisted woman-like on her head, he said,

"With your hair like that you are my Margaret of Anjou, and the other way—with it down you are my little Nada of Cragg's Ridge. And I—I don't quite understand why God should be so good to me."

And this day Peter was trying in his dumb way to analyze the change. The touch of Nada's hand thrilled him, as it did a long time ago, and still he sensed the difference. Her voice was even softer when she put her cheek down to his whiskered face and talked to him, but in it he missed that which he could not quite bring back clearly through the lapse of time—the childish comradeship of her. Yet he began to worship her anew, even more fiercely than he had loved the Nada of old. He was content now to lie with his nose touching her foot or dress; but when in the sunset of early evening she went into her room, and came out a little later with her curling hair clouding her shoulders and breast, and tied with a faded ribbon she had brought from Cragg's Ridge, he danced about her, yelping joyously, and she accepted the challenge in a wild race with him to the edge of the clearing.

Panting and flushed she ran back to Jolly Roger, and rested in his arms.

And it was McKay, with his face half hidden in her riotous hair, who saw a figure come suddenly out of the forest at the far end of the clearing. It was Father John. He saw him pause for an instant, and then stagger toward them, swaying as if about to fall.

The sudden stopping of his breath—the tightening of his arms— drew Nada's shining eyes to his face, and then she, too, saw the little old Missioner as he swayed and staggered across the clearing. With a cry she was out of McKay's arms and running toward him.

Father John was leaning heavily upon her when McKay came up. His face was tense and his breath came in choking gasps. But he tried to smile as he clutched a hand at his breast.

"I have hurried," he said, making a great effort to speak calmly, "and I am—winded—"

He drew in a deep breath, and looked at Jolly Roger.

"Roger—I have hurried to tell you—Breault is coming. He cannot be far behind me. Possibly half a mile, or a mile—"

In the thickening dusk he took Nada's white face between his hands.

"I find—at last—that I was mistaken, child," he said, very calmly now. "I believe it is not God's will that you remain to be taken by Breault. You must go. There is no time to lose. If Breault does not stumble off the trail in this gloom he will be here in a few minutes. Come."

Not a word did Nada say as they went to the cabin, and McKay saw her tense face as pale as an ivory cameo in the twilight. But something in the up-tilt of her chin and the poise of her head assured him she was prepared, and unafraid.

In the cabin the Leaf Bud met them, and to her Nada spoke quickly. There was understanding between them, and Oosimisk dragged in a filled pack from the kitchen while Nada ran into her room and came out with the bundle.

Suddenly she was standing before McKay and Father John, her breast throbbing with excitement.

"There is nothing more to make ready," she said. "Yellow Bird has been with me all this day, and her spirit told me to prepare. We have everything we need."

And then she saw only Father John, and put her arms closely about his neck, and with wide, tearless eyes looked into his face.

"Father, you will come to us?" she whispered. "You promise that?"

The Missioner's arms closed about her, and he bowed his face against her lips and cheek.

"I pray God that it may be so," he said.

Nada's arms tightened convulsively, and in that moment there came a warning growl from outside the cabin door.

"Peter!" she cried.

In another moment Father John had extinguished the light.

"Go, my children," he commanded. "You must be quick. Twenty paces below the pool is a canoe. I had one of my Indians leave it there yesterday, and it is ready. Roger—Nada—"

He groped out, and the hands of the three met in the darkness.

"God bless you—both! And go south—always south. Now go—go! I think I hear footsteps—"

He thrust them to the door, Nada with her bundle and Roger with his pack. Suddenly he felt Peter at his side, and reaching down he fastened his fingers in the scruff of his neck, and held him back.

"Good-bye," he whispered huskily. "Good-bye—Nada—Roger—"

A sob came back out of the gloom.

"Good-bye, father."

And then they listened, Peter and Father John, until the swift footsteps of the two they loved passed beyond their hearing.

Peter whimpered, and struggled a little, but Father John held him as he closed the door.

"It's best for you to stay, Peter," he tried to explain. "It's best for you to stay—with me. For I think they are going a far distance, and will come to a land where you would shrivel up and die. Besides, you could not go in the canoe. So be good, and remain with me, Peter—with me—"

And the Leaf Bud, standing wide-eyed and motionless, heard a strange little choking laugh come from Father John as he groped in darkness for a light.

CHAPTER XXI

A slow illumination filled the cabin, first the yellow flare of a match and then the light of a lamp, and as Father John's waxen face grew out of the darkness Peter whimpered and whined and scratched with, his paws at the closed door.

Oosimisk, the Leaf Bud, stood like a statue, with her wide, dark eyes staring at Father John, but scarcely seeming to breathe.

In the old Missioner's face came a trembling smile and a look of triumph as he read the fear-written question in her steady gaze

"All is well, Oosimisk," he said quietly, speaking in Cree. "They are safely away, and will not be caught. Continue with your duties and let no one see that anything unusual has happened. Breault will come very soon."

He straightened his shoulders, as if to give himself confidence and strength, and then he called Peter, and comforted the dog whose master and mistress were fleeing through the dark.

"They have reached the pool," he said, seating himself and holding Peter's shaggy head between his hands. "They have just about reached the pool, and Breault must be entering the clearing on the other side. Roger cannot miss the canoe—twenty paces down and with nothing to shadow it overhead; I think he has found it by this time, and in another half minute they will be off. And it is very black down the Burntwood, with deep timber close to the water, and for many miles no man can follow by night along its shores. "Suddenly his hands tightened, and the Leaf Bud, watching him slyly, saw the last of suspense go out of his face. "And now— they are safe," he cried exultantly. "They must be on their way— and Breault has not come across the clearing!"

He rose to his feet, and began pacing back and forth, while Peter sniffed yearn-ingly at the door again. Oosimisk, with the caution of her race in moments of danger, was drawing the curtains at the windows, and Father John smiled his approbation. He did not want Breault, the man-hunter, peering through one of the windows at him. Even as he walked back and forth he listened intently for Breault's footsteps. Peter, with a sigh, gave up his scratching and settled himself on his haunches close to Nada's door.

Father John, in passing him, paused to lay a hand on his head.

"Some day it may please God to let us go to them," he consoled, speaking for himself even more than for Peter. "Some day, when they are far away—and safe."

He felt Peter suddenly stiffen under his hand, and from the Leaf Bud came a low, swift word of warning.

She began singing softly, and dishes and pans already clean rattled under her hands in the kitchen, and she continued to sing even as the cabin door opened and Breault the man-hunter stood in it.

The unexpectedness of his appearance, without the sound of a warning foot-step outside, was amazing even to Peter. In the open door he stood for a moment, his thin, ferret-like face standing out against the black background of the night, and his strange eyes, apparently half closed yet bright as diamonds, sweeping the inte-rior without effort but with the quickness of lightning.

There was something deadly and foreboding about him as he stood here, and Peter growled low in his throat. Recognition flashed upon him in an instant. It was the man of the snow-dune, away up on the Barren, the man whom he had mis-trusted from the beginning, and from whom they had fled into the face of the Big Storm months ago. His mind worked swiftly, even as swiftly as Breault's in its way, and without any process of reasoning he sensed menace and enmity in this man's appearance, and associated with it the mysterious flight of Jolly Roger and Nada.

Breault had nodded, without speaking. Then his eyes rested on Peter, and his face broke into a twisted sort of smile. It was not altogether unpleasant, yet was there something about it which made one shiver. It spoke the character of the man, pitiless, determined, omniscient almost, as if the spirit of a grim and unrelenting fate walked with him.

Again he nodded, and held out a hand.

"Peter," he called. "Come here, Peter!"

Peter flattened his ears a fraction of an inch, but did not move. Even that fraction of an inch caught Breault's keen eyes.

"Still a one-man dog," he observed, stepping well inside the cabin, and facing Father John. "Where is McKay, Father?"

He had not closed the door, and Peter saw his chance. The Leaf Bud saw him pass like a shot out into the night, but as he went she made no effort to call him back, for her ears were wide open as Breault repeated his question,

"Where is McKay, Father?"

Peter heard the man-hunter's voice from the darkness outside. For barely an instant he paused, picking up the fresh scent of Nada and Jolly Roger. It was easy to follow—straight to the pool, and from the pool twenty paces down-stream, where a little finger of sand and pebbles had been formed by the eddies. In this bar was fresh imprint of the canoe, and here the footprints ended.

Peter whimpered, peering into the tunnel of darkness between forest trees, where the water rippled and gurgled softly on its way into a deeper and more tangled wilderness. He waded belly-deep into the current, half determined to swim; and then he waited, listening intently, but could hear no sound of voice or paddle stroke.

Yet he knew Jolly Roger and Nada could not be far away.

He returned to the edge of the pool, and began sniffing his way down-stream, pausing every two or three minutes to listen. Now and then he caught the presence of those he sought, in the air, but those intervals in which he stopped to catch sound of voice or paddle lost him time, so the canoe was traveling faster than Peter.

Half way between himself and the bow of that canoe McKay could dimly make out Nada's pale face in the star glow that filtered like a mist through the tops of the close-hanging trees.

Scarcely above his breath he laughed in joyous confidence.

"At last my dream is coming true, Nada," he whispered. "You are mine. And we are going into another world. And no one will ever find us there—no one but Father John, when we send him word. You are not afraid?"

Her voice trembled a little in the gloom.

"No, I am not afraid. But it is dark—so dark—"

"The moon will be with us again in a few nights—your moon, with the Old Man smiling down on us. I know how the Man in the Moon must feel when he's on the other side of the world, and can't see you, Nada."

Her silence made him lean toward her, striving to get a better view of her face where the starlight broke through an opening in the tree-tops.

And in that moment he heard a little breath that was almost a sob.

"It's Peter," she said, before he could speak. "Oh, Roger, why didn't we bring Peter?"

"Possibly—we should have," he replied, skipping a stroke with his paddle. "But I think we have done the best thing for Peter. He is a wilderness dog, and has never known anything different. Over there, where we are going—"

"I understand. And some day, Father John will bring him?"

"Yes. He has promised that. Peter will come to us when Father John comes."

She had turned, looking into the pit-gloom ahead of them, so dark that the canoe seemed about to drive against a wall. Under its bow the water gurgled like oil.

"We are entering the big cedar swamp," he explained. "It is like Blind Man's Buff, isn't it? Can you see?"

"Not beyond the bow of the canoe, Roger."

"Work back to me," he said, "very carefully."

She came, obediently.

"Now turn slowly, so that you face the bow, and lean back with your head against my knees."

This also, she did.

"This is much nicer," she whispered, nestling her head comfortably against him. "So much nicer."

By leaning over until his back nearly cracked he was able to find her lips in the darkness.

"I was thinking of the brush that overhangs the stream," he explained when he had straightened himself. "Sitting up as you were it might have caused you hurt."

There was a little silence between them, in which his paddle caught again its slow and steady rhythm. Then,

"Were you thinking only of the brush, Roger—and of the hurt it might cause me?"

"Yes, only of that," and he chuckled softly.

"Then I don't think it nice here at all," she complained. "I shall sit up straight so the brush may put my eyes out!"

But her head pressed even closer against him, and careful not to interrupt his paddle-stroke she touched his face for an instant with her hand.

"It's there," she purled, as if utterly comforted. "I wanted to be sure—it is so dark!"

With cimmerian blackness on all sides of them, and a chaotic tunnel ahead, they were happy. Staring straight before him, though utterly unable to see, McKay sensed in every movement he made and in every breath he drew the exquisite thrill of a miracle. And the same thrill swept into him and through him from the softly breathing body of Nada. Light or darkness made no difference now. Together, inseparable from this time forth, they had started on the one great adventure of their lives, and for them fear had ceased to exist. The night sheltered them. Its very blackness held in its embrace a warmth of welcome and of unending hope. Twice in the next half hour he put his hand to Nada's face, and each time she pressed her lips against it, sweet with that confidence which so completely possessed her soul.

Very slowly they moved through the swamp, for because of the gloom his paddle-strokes were exceedingly short, and he was feeling his way. Frequently he ran into brush, or struck the boggy shore, and occasionally Nada would hold lighted matches while he extricated the canoe from tree-tops and driftwood that impeded the way. He loved the brief glimpses he caught of her face in the match-glow, and twice he deliberately wasted the tiny flares that he might hold the vision of her a little longer.

At last he began to feel the pulse of a current against his paddle, and soon after that the star-mist began filtering through the thinning tree-tops again, so that he knew they were almost through the swamp. Another half-hour and they were free of it, with a clear sky overhead and the cheering song of running water on both sides of them.

Nada sat up, and it was now so light that he could see the soft shimmer of her hair in the starlight. He also saw a pretty little grimace in her face, even as she smiled at him.

"I—I can't move," she exclaimed. "UGH! my feet are asleep—"

"We'll go ashore and stretch ourselves," said McKay, who had looked at his watch in the light of the last match. "We've two hours the start of Breault, and there is no other canoe."

He began watching the shore closely, and it was not long before he made out the white smoothness of a sandbar on their right. Here they landed and for half an hour rested their cramped limbs.

Then they went on, and in his heart McKay blessed the deep swamp that lay between them and Breault.

"I don't think he can make it without a canoe, even if he guesses we went this way," he explained to Nada. "And that means—we are safe."

There was a cheery ring in his voice which would have changed to the deadness of cold iron could he have looked back into that sluggish pit of the Burntwood through which they had come, or could he have seen into the heart of the still blacker swamp.

For through the swamp, feeling his way in the black abysses and amid the monster-ghosts of darkness, came Peter.

And down the Burntwood, between the boggy mucklips of the swamp, a man followed with slow but deadly surety, guiding with a long pole two light cedar timbers which he had lashed together with wire, and which bore him safely and in triumph where the canoe had gone before him.

This man was Breault, the man-hunter.

"The swamp will hold him!" McKay was saying again, exultantly. "Even if he guesses our way, the swamp will hold him back, Nada."

"But he won't know the way we have come," cried Nada, the faith in her voice answering his own. "Father John will guide him in another direction."

Back in the pit-gloom, with a grim smile now and then relaxing the tight-set compression of his thin lips, and with eyes that stared like a night-owl's into the gloom ahead of him, Breault poled steadily on.

CHAPTER XXII

DRIPPING from the bog-holes and lathered with mud, it was the mystery of Breault's noiseless presence somewhere near him in the still night that drew Peter continually deeper into the swamp.

Half a dozen times he caught the scent of him in a quiet air that seemed only now and then to rise up in his face softly, as if stirred by butterflies' wings. Always it came from ahead, and Peter's mind worked swiftly to the decision that where Breault was there also would be Nada and Jolly Roger. Yet he caught the scent of neither of these two, and that puzzled him.

Many times he found himself at the edge of the black lip of water, but never quite at the right time to see a shadow in its darkness, or hear the sound of Breault's pole.

But in the swamp, as he went on, he saw nothing but shadow, and heard weird and nameless sounds which made his blood creep, even though his courage was now full-grown within him.

He was not frightened at the ugly sputter of the owls, as in the days of old. Their throaty menace and snapping beaks did not stop him nor turn him aside. The slashing scrape of claws in the bark of trees and the occasional crackling of brush were matters of intimate knowledge, and he gave but little attention to them in his eagerness to reach those who had gone ahead of him. What troubled him, and filled his eyes with sudden red glares, were the oily gurgles of the pitfalls which tried to suck him down; the laughing madness of muck that held him as if living things were in it, and which spluttered and coughed when he freed himself.

Half blinded at times, so that even the black shadows were blotted out, he went on. And at last, coming again to the edge of the stream, he heard a new kind of sound—the slow, steady dipping of Breault's pole.

He hurried on, finding harder ground under his feet, and came noiselessly abreast of the man on his raft of cedar timbers. He could almost hear his breathing. And very faintly he could see in the vast gloom a shadow—a shadow that moved slowly against the background of a still deeper shadow beyond.

But there was no scent of Nada or Jolly Roger, and whatever desire had risen in him to make himself known was smothered by caution and suspicion. After this he did not go ahead of Breault, but kept behind him or abreast of him, within sound of the dipping pole. And every minute his heart thumped expectantly, and he sniffed the new air for signs of those he most desired to find.

Dawn was breaking in the sky when they came out of the swamp, and the first flush of the sun was lighting up the east when Breault headed his improvised craft for the sandbar upon which Nada and McKay had rested many hours before.

Breault was tired, but his eyes lighted up when he saw the footprints in the sand, and he chuckled—almost good humoredly. As a matter of fact he was in a good humor. But one would not have reckoned it as such in Breault. A hard man, the forests called him; a man with the hunting instincts of the fox and the wolf and the merciless persistency of the weazel—a man who lived his code to the last letter of the law, without pity and without favoritism. At least so he was judged, and his hard, narrow eyes, his thin lips and his cynically lined face seldom betrayed the better thoughts within him, if he possessed any at all. In the Service he was regarded as a humanly perfect mechanism, a bit of machinery that never failed, the dreaded Nemesis to be set on the trail of a wrong-doer when all others had failed.

But this morning, with every bone and muscle in him aching from his long night of tedious exertion, the chuckle grew into a laugh as he looked upon the tell-tale signs in the sand.

He stretched himself and his tired bones cracked.

Breault did not think aloud. But he was saying to himself.

"There, against that rock, Jolly Roger McKay sat There is the imprint of only one person sitting. The girl was in his arms. Here are little holes where her outstretched heels rested in the sand. She is wearing shoes and not moccasins."

He grinned as he drew his service pack from the two-log cedar raft.

"Plenty of time now," he continued to think. "They are mine this time—sure. They believe they have fooled me, and they haven't. That's fatal. Always."

Not infrequently, when entirely alone, Breault let a little part of himself loose, as if freeing a prisoner from bondage for a short time. For instance, he whistled. It was not an unpleasant whistle, but rather oddly reminiscent of tender things he remembered away back somewhere; and as he fried his bacon and steamed a handful of desiccated potatoes he hummed a song, also rather pleasant to ears that were as closely attentive as Peter's.

For Peter had crept up through a tangle of ground-scrub and lay not twenty paces away, smelling of the bacon hungrily, and watching intently from his concealment.

Peter knew the fox and the wolf, but he did not know Breault, and he did not guess why the man's whistling grew a little louder, nor why his humming voice grew stronger. But after a time, with his back and not his face toward Peter, Breault called in the most natural and matter-of-fact voice in the world,

"Come on, Peter. Breakfast is ready!"

Peter's jaws dropped in amazement. And as Breault turned toward him, his thin face a-grin, and continued to invite him in a most companionable way, he forgot his concealment entirely and stood up straight, ready either to fight or fly.

Breault tossed him a dripping slice of bacon which he held in his hand. It fell within a foot of Peter's nose, and Peter was ravenously hungry. The delicious odor of it demoralized his senses and his caution. For a few seconds he resisted, then thrust himself out toward it an inch at a time, made a sudden grab, and swallowed it at one gulp

Breault laughed outright, and with the first of the sun striking into his face he did not look like an enemy to Peter.

A second slice of bacon followed the first, and then a third— until Breault was frying another mess over the fire.

"That's partial payment for what you did up on the Barren," he was saying inside himself. "If it hadn't been for you—"

He didn't even imagine the rest. Nor after that did he pay the slightest attention to Peter. For Breault knew dogs possibly even better than he knew men, and not by the smallest sign did he give Peter to understand that he was interested in him at all. He washed his dishes, whistling and humming, reloaded his pack on the raft, and once more began poling his way downstream.

Peter, still in the edge of the scrub, was not only puzzled, but felt a further sense of abandonment. After all, this man was not his enemy, and he was leaving him as his master and mistress had left him. He whined. And Breault was not out of sight when he trotted down to the sandbar, and quickly found the scent of Nada and McKay. Purposely Breault had left a lump of desiccated potato as big as his fist, and this Peter ate as ravenously as he had eaten the bacon. Then, just as Breault knew he would do, he began following the raft.

Breault did not hurry, and he did not rest. There was something almost mechanically certain in his slow but steady progress, though he knew it was possible for the canoe to outdistance him three to one. He was missing nothing along the shore. Three times during the forenoon he saw where the canoe had landed, and he chuckled each time, thinking of the old story of the tortoise and the hare. He stopped for not more than two or three minutes at each of these places, and was then on his way again.

Peter was fascinated by the unexcited persistency of the man's movement. He followed it, watched it, and became more and more interested in the unvarying monotony of it. There were the same up-and-down strokes of the long pole, the slight swaying of the upstanding body, the same eddy behind the cedar logs—and occasionally wisps of smoke floating behind when the pursuer smoked his pipe. Not once did Peter see Breault turn his head to look behind him. Yet Breault was seeing everything. Five times that morning he saw Peter, but not once did he make a sign or call to him.

He drove his raft ashore at twelve o'clock to prepare his dinner, and after he had built a fire, and his cooking things were scattered about, he straightened himself up and called in that same matter-of-fact way, as if expecting an immediate response,

"Here, Peter!—Peter!—Come in, Boy!"

And Peter came. Fighting against the last instinct that held him back he first thrust his head out from the brush and looked at Breault. Breault paid no attention to him for a few moments, but sliced his bacon. When the perfume of the cooking meat reached Peter's nose he edged himself a little nearer, and with a whimpering sigh flattened himself on his belly.

Breault heard the sigh, and grunted a reply,

"Hungry again, Peter?" he inquired casually.

He had saved for this moment a piece of cooked bacon held over from break-fast, and tearing this with his fingers he tossed the strips to Peter. As he did this he was thinking to himself,

"Why am I doing this? I don't want the dog. He will be a nuisance. He will eat my grub. But it's fair. I'm paying a debt. He helped to save me up on the Barren."

Thus did Breault, the man without mercy, the Nemesis, briefly analyze the matter. And he cooked five pieces of bacon for Peter.

During the rest of that day Peter made no effort to keep himself in concealment as he followed Breault and his raft. This afternoon Breault shot a fawn, and when he made camp that night both he and Peter feasted on fresh meat. This broke down the last of Peter's suspicion, and Breault laid a hand on his head. He did not particularly like the feel of the hand, but he tolerated it, and Breault grunted aloud, with a note of commendation in his hard voice.

"A one-man dog—never anything else."

Half a dozen times during the day Peter had found the scent of Nada and Roger where they had come ashore, and from this night on he associated Breault as a nec-essary agent in his search for them. And with Breault he went, instinctively guess-ing the truth.

The next day they found where Nada and McKay had abandoned the canoe, and had struck south through the wilderness. This pleased Breault, who was tired of his poling. This third night there was a new moon, and something about it stirred in Peter an impulse to run ahead and overtake those he was seeking. But a still strong instinct held him to Breault.

Tonight Breault slept like a dead man on his cedar boughs. He was up and had a fire built an hour before dawn, and with the first gray streaking of day was on the trail again. He made no further effort to follow signs of the pursued, for that was a hopeless task. But he knew how McKay was heading, and he traveled swiftly, fig-uring to cover twice the distance that Nada might travel in the same given time. It was three o'clock in the afternoon when he came to a great ridge, and on its highest pinnacle he stopped.

Peter had grown restless again, and a little more suspicious of Breault. He was not afraid of him, but all that day he had found no scent of Nada or Jolly Roger, and slowly the conviction was impinging itself upon him that he should seek for himself in the wilderness.

Breault saw this restlessness, and understood it.

"I'll keep my eye on the dog," he thought. "He has a nose, and an uncanny sixth sense, and I haven't either. He will bear watching. I believe McKay and the girl cannot be far away. Possibly they have traveled more slowly than I thought, and haven't passed this ridge; or it may be they are down there, in the plain. If so I should catch sign of smoke or fire—in time."

For an hour he kept watch over the plain through his binoculars, seeking for a wisp of smoke that might rise at any time over the treetops. He did not lose sight of Peter, questing out in widening circles below him. And then, quite unexpectedly, something happened. In the edge of a tiny meadow an eighth of a mile away Peter was acting strangely. He was nosing the ground, gulping the wind, twisting eagerly back and forth. Then he set out, steadily and with unmistakable decision, south and west.

In a flash Breault was on his feet, had caught up his pack, and was running for the meadow. And there he found something in the velvety softness of the earth which brought a grim smile to his thin lips as he, too, set out south and west.

The scent he had found, hours old, drew Peter on until in the edge of the dusk of evening it brought him to a foot-worn trail leading to the Hudson's Bay Company post many miles south. In this path, beaten by the feet of generations of forest dwellers, the hard heels of McKay's boots had made their imprint, and after this the scent was clearer under Peter's nose. But with forest-bred caution he still traveled slowly, though his blood was burning like a pitch-fed fire in his veins. Almost as swiftly followed Breault behind him.

Again came darkness, and then the moon, brighter than last night, lighting his way between the two walls of the forest

CHAPTER XXIII

DAWN came softly where the quiet waters of the Willow Bud ran under deep forests of evergreen out into the gold and silver birch of the Nelson River flats. A veiling mist rose out of the earth to meet the promise of day, gentle and sweet, like scented raiment, stirring sleepily to the pulse of an awakening earth. Through it came the first low twitter of birdsong, a sound that seemed to swell and grow until it filled the world. Yet was it still a sound of sleep, of half wakefulness, and the mist was thinning away when, a ruffled little breast sent out its full throat-song from the tip of a silver birch that overhung the stream.

The little warbler was looking down, as if wondering why there was no stir of life beneath him, where in last night's sunset there had been much to wonder at and a new kind of song to thrill him. But the girl was no longer there to sing back at him. The cedar and balsam shelter dripped with morning dew, the place where fire had been was black and dead, and ruffling his feathers the warbler continued his song in triumph.

Nada, hidden under her shelter, and still half dreaming, heard him. She lay with her head nestled in the crook of Roger's arm, and the birdsong seemed to come to her from a great distance away. She smiled, and her lips trembled, as if even in sleep she—was about to answer it. And then the song drifted away until she could no longer hear it, and she sank back into an oblivion of darkness in which she seemed lost for a long time, and out of which some invisible force was struggling to drag her.

There came at last a sudden irresistible pull at her senses, and she opened her eyes, awake. Her head was no longer in the crook of Jolly Roger's arm. She could see him sitting up straight, and he was not looking at her. It must be late, she thought, for the light was strong in his face, warm with the first golden flow of the sun. She smiled, and sat up, and shook her soft curls with a happy little laugh.

"Roger—"

And then she, too, was staring, wide-eyed and speechless. For she saw Peter under Jolly Roger's hand. But it was not Peter who drew her breath short and sent fear cutting like a sharp knife through her heart.

Facing them, seated coldly on a log which McKay had dragged in from the timber, was a thin-faced sharp-eyed man who was studying them with an odd smile on his lips, and instantly Nada knew this man was Breault.

There was something peculiarly appalling about him as he sat there, in spite of the fact that for a few moments he neither spoke nor moved. His eyes, Nada thought, were not like human eyes, and his lips were like the blades of two knives set together. Yet he was smiling, or half smiling, not in a comforting or humorous way, but with exultation and triumph. From looking at him one would never have guessed that Breault loved his joke.

He nodded.

"Good morning, Jolly Roger McKay! And—good morning, Mrs. Jolly Roger McKay! Pardon me for watching you like this, but duty is duty. I am Breault, of the Royal Northwest Mounted Police."

McKay wet his lips. Breault saw him, and the grin on his thin face widened.

"I know, it's hard," he said. "But you've got Peter to thank for it. Peter led me to you."

He stood up, and in a most casual fashion covered Jolly Roger with his automatic.

"Would you mind stepping out, McKay?" he asked.

In his other hand he dangled a pair of handcuffs. McKay stood up, and Nada rose beside him, gripping his arms with both hands.

"No need of those things, Breault," he said. "I'll go peaceably."

"Still—it's safer," argued Breault, a wicked glitter in his eyes. "Hold out one hand, please—"

The manacle snapped over Jolly Roger's wrist.

"I'm Breault—not Terence Cassidy," he chuckled. "Never take a chance, you know. Never!"

Swift as a flash was his movement then, as the companion bracelet snapped over Nada's wrist. He stepped back, facing them with a grin.

"Got you both now, haven't I?" he gloated. "Can't get away, can you?" He put his gun away, and bowed low to Nada. "How do you like married life, Mrs. Jolly Roger?"

McKay's face was whiter than Nada's.

"You coward!" he spoke in a low, quiet voice. "You low-down miserable coward. You're a disgrace to the Service. Do you mean you are going to keep my wife ironed like this?"

"Sure," said Breault. "I'm going to make you pay for some of the trouble I've had over you. I believe in a man paying his debts, you know. And a woman, too. And probably you've lied to her like the very devil."

"He hasn't!" protested Nada fiercely. "You're a—a—"

"Say it," nodded Breault good humoredly. "By all means say it, Mrs. Jolly Roger. If you can't find words, let me help you," and while he waited he loaded his pipe and lighted it.

"You see I don't exactly live up to regulations when I'm with good friends like you," he apologized cynically. "In other words you're a couple of hard cases. Cassidy has turned in all sorts of evidence about you. He says that you, McKay, should be hung the moment we catch you. He warned me not to take a chance—that you'd slit my throat in the dark without a prick of conscience. And I'm a valuable man in the Service. It can't afford to lose me."

McKay shut his lips tightly, and did not answer.

"Now, while you're helpless, I want to tell you a few things," Breault went on. "And while I'm talking I'll start the fire, so we can have breakfast. Peter and, I are hungry. A good dog, McKay. He saved us up on the Barren. Have you told Mrs. Jolly Roger about that?"

He expected no answer, and whistled as he lighted a pile of birchbark which he had already placed under dry cedar wood which McKay had gathered the preceding evening.

"That's where MY trouble began—up there on the Barren, Mrs. Jolly Roger," he continued, ignoring McKay. "You see the three of us, Superintendent Tavish, and Porter—who is now his son-in-law—and I had a splendid chance to die like martyrs, and go down forever in the history of the Service, if it hadn't been for this fool of a husband of yours, and Peter. I can't blame Peter, because he's only a dog. But McKay is responsible. He robbed us of a beautiful opportunity of dying in an unusual way by hunting us up and dragging us into his shelter. A shabby trick, don't you think? And inasmuch as Superintendent Tavish is about the biggest man in the Service, and Porter is his son-in-law, and Miss Tavish was saved along with us—why, they reckoned something ought to be done about it."

Breault did not look up. With, exasperating slowness he added fuel to the fire. "And so—"

He rose and stood before them again.

"And so—they assigned me to the very unpleasant duty of running you down with a pardon, McKay—a pardon forgiving you for all your sins, forever and ever, Amen. And here it is!"

He had drawn an official-looking envelope from inside his coat, and held it out now—not to McKay—but to Nada.

Neither reached for it. Standing there with the cynical smile still on his lips, his strange eyes gimleting them with a cold sort of laughter, it was as if Breault tortured them with a last horrible joke. Then, suddenly, Nada seized the envelope and tore it open, while McKay stared at Breault, believing, and yet not daring to speak.

It was Nada's cry, a cry wild and sobbing and filled with gladness, that told him the truth, and with the precious paper clutched in her hand she smothered her face against McKay's breast, while Breault came up grinning behind them, and Jolly Roger heard the click of his key in the handcuffs.

"I am also loaded down with a number of foolish messages for you," he said, attending to the fire again. "For instance, that red- headed good-for-nothing, Cassidy, says to tell you he is building a four-room bungalow for you in their clearing, and that it will be finished by the time you arrive. Also, a squaw named Yellow Bird, and a redskin who calls himself Slim Buck, sent word that you will always be welcome in their hunting grounds. And a pretty little thing named Sun Cloud sent as many kisses as there are leaves on the trees—"

He paused, chuckling, and did not look up to see the wide, glorious eyes of the girl upon him.

"But the funniest thing of all is the baby," he went on, preparing to slice bacon. "They're going to have one pretty soon—Cassidy's wife, I mean. They've given it a name already. If it's a boy it's Roger—if it's a girl it's Nada. They wanted me to tell you that. Silly bunch, aren't they? A couple of young fools—"

Just then something new happened in the weirdly adventurous life of Frangois Breault. Without warning he was suddenly smothered in a pair of arms, his head was jerked back, and against his hard and pitiless mouth a pair of soft red lips pressed for a single thrilling instant. "Well, I'll be damned," he gasped, dropping his bacon and staggering to his feet like a man who had been shot. "I'll be—CUSSED!"

And he picked up his pack and walked off into the thick young spruce at the edge of the timber, without saying another word or once looking behind him. And breakfast waited, and Nada and Jolly Roger and Peter waited, but Frangois Breault did not return. For a strange and unaccountable man was he, a hard and pitiless man and a deadly hunter who knew no fear. Yet the wilderness swallowed him, a coward at last—running away from the two red lips that had kissed him.

So went Breault, for the first time in his life a messenger of mercy; and at the top of the silver birch the little warbler knew that something glad had happened, and offered up its gratitude in a sudden burst of song.

THE END

The Codes Of Hammurabi And Moses
W. W. Davies

QTY

The discovery of the Hammurabi Code is one of the greatest achievements of archaeology, and is of paramount interest, not only to the student of the Bible, but also to all those interested in ancient history...

Religion   **ISBN:** *1-59462-338-4*   **Pages:132**
MSRP $12.95

The Theory of Moral Sentiments
Adam Smith

QTY

This work from 1749. contains original theories of conscience amd moral judgment and it is the foundation for systemof morals.

Philosophy   ISBN: *1-59462-777-0*   **Pages:536**
MSRP $19.95

Jessica's First Prayer
Hesba Stretton

QTY

In a screened and secluded corner of one of the many railway-bridges which span the streets of London there could be seen a few years ago, from five o'clock every morning until half past eight, a tidily set-out coffee-stall, consisting of a trestle and board, upon which stood two large tin cans, with a small fire of charcoal burning under each so as to keep the coffee boiling during the early hours of the morning when the work-people were thronging into the city on their way to their daily toil...

Pages:84

Childrens   ISBN: *1-59462-373-2*   **MSRP $9.95**

My Life and Work
Henry Ford

QTY

Henry Ford revolutionized the world with his implementation of mass production for the Model T automobile. Gain valuable business insight into his life and work with his own auto-biography... "We have only started on our development of our country we have not as yet, with all our talk of wonderful progress, done more than scratch the surface. The progress has been wonderful enough but..."

Pages:300

Biographies/   ISBN: *1-59462-198-5*   **MSRP $21.95**

The Art of Cross-Examination
Francis Wellman

QTY

I presume it is the experience of every author, after his first book is published upon an important subject, to be almost overwhelmed with a wealth of ideas and illustrations which could readily have been included in his book, and which to his own mind, at least, seem to make a second edition inevitable. Such certainly was the case with me; and when the first edition had reached its sixth impression in five months, I rejoiced to learn that it seemed to my publishers that the book had met with a sufficiently favorable reception to justify a second and considerably enlarged edition. ..

Reference   ISBN: *1-59462-647-2*

Pages:412

MSRP *$19.95*

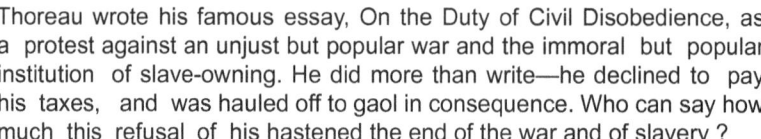

On the Duty of Civil Disobedience
Henry David Thoreau

QTY

Thoreau wrote his famous essay, On the Duty of Civil Disobedience, as a protest against an unjust but popular war and the immoral but popular institution of slave-owning. He did more than write—he declined to pay his taxes, and was hauled off to gaol in consequence. Who can say how much this refusal of his hastened the end of the war and of slavery ?

Law   ISBN: *1-59462-747-9*

Pages:48

MSRP *$7.45*

Dream Psychology Psychoanalysis for Beginners
Sigmund Freud

QTY

Sigmund Freud, born Sigismund Schlomo Freud (May 6, 1856 - September 23, 1939), was a Jewish-Austrian neurologist and psychiatrist who co-founded the psychoanalytic school of psychology. Freud is best known for his theories of the unconscious mind, especially involving the mechanism of repression; his redefinition of sexual desire as mobile and directed towards a wide variety of objects; and his therapeutic techniques, especially his understanding of transference in the therapeutic relationship and the presumed value of dreams as sources of insight into unconscious desires.

Psychology   ISBN: *1-59462-905-6*

Pages:196

MSRP *$15.45*

The Miracle of Right Thought
Orison Swett Marden

QTY

Believe with all of your heart that you will do what you were made to do. When the mind has once formed the habit of holding cheerful, happy, prosperous pictures, it will not be easy to form the opposite habit. It does not matter how improbable or how far away this realization may see, or how dark the prospects may be, if we visualize them as best we can, as vividly as possible, hold tenaciously to them and vigorously struggle to attain them, they will gradually become actualized, realized in the life. But a desire, a longing without endeavor, a yearning abandoned or held indifferently will vanish without realization.

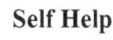

Self Help   ISBN: *1-59462-644-8*

Pages:360

MSRP *$25.45*

www.**bookjungle**.com *email: sales@bookjungle.com fax: 630-214-0564 mail: Book Jungle PO Box 2226 Champaign, IL 61825*

QTY

The Rosicrucian Cosmo-Conception Mystic Christianity by *Max Heindel*   ISBN: *1-59462-188-8*   **$38.95**
The Rosicrucian Cosmo-conception is not dogmatic, neither does it appeal to any other authority than the reason of the student. It is: not controversial, but is: sent forth in the, hope that it may help to clear...   New Age/Religion Pages 646

Abandonment To Divine Providence by *Jean-Pierre de Caussade*   ISBN: *1-59462-228-0*   **$25.95**
"The Rev. Jean Pierre de Caussade was one of the most remarkable spiritual writers of the Society of Jesus in France in the 18th Century. His death took place at Toulouse in 1751. His works have gone through many editions and have been republished...   Inspirational/Religion Pages 400

Mental Chemistry by *Charles Haanel*   ISBN: *1-59462-192-6*   **$23.95**
Mental Chemistry allows the change of material conditions by combining and appropriately utilizing the power of the mind. Much like applied chemistry creates something new and unique out of careful combinations of chemicals the mastery of mental chemistry...   New Age Pages 354

The Letters of Robert Browning and Elizabeth Barret Barrett 1845-1846 vol II   ISBN: *1-59462-193-4*   **$35.95**
by *Robert Browning* and *Elizabeth Barrett*   Biographies Pages 596

Gleanings In Genesis (volume I) by *Arthur W. Pink*   ISBN: *1-59462-130-6*   **$27.45**
Appropriately has Genesis been termed "the seed plot of the Bible" for in it we have, in germ form, almost all of the great doctrines which are afterwards fully developed in the books of Scripture which follow...   Religion/Inspirational Pages 420

The Master Key by *L. W. de Laurence*   ISBN: *1-59462-001-6*   **$30.95**
In no branch of human knowledge has there been a more lively increase of the spirit of research during the past few years than in the study of Psychology, Concentration and Mental Discipline. The requests for authentic lessons in Thought Control, Mental Discipline and...   New Age/Business Pages 422

The Lesser Key Of Solomon Goetia by *L. W. de Laurence*   ISBN: *1-59462-092-X*   **$9.95**
This translation of the first book of the "Lemegeton" which is now for the first time made accessible to students of Talismanic Magic was done, after careful collation and edition, from numerous Ancient Manuscripts in Hebrew, Latin, and French...   New Age/Occult Pages 92

Rubaiyat Of Omar Khayyam by *Edward Fitzgerald*   ISBN: *1-59462-332-5*   **$13.95**
Edward Fitzgerald, whom the world has already learned, in spite of his own efforts to remain within the shadow of anonymity, to look upon as one of the rarest poets of the century, was born at Bredfield, in Suffolk, on the 31st of March, 1809. He was the third son of John Purcell...   Music Pages 172

Ancient Law by *Henry Maine*   ISBN: *1-59462-128-4*   **$29.95**
The chief object of the following pages is to indicate some of the earliest ideas of mankind, as they are reflected in Ancient Law, and to point out the relation of those ideas to modern thought.   Religion/History Pages 452

Far-Away Stories by *William J. Locke*   ISBN: *1-59462-129-2*   **$19.45**
"Good wine needs no bush, but a collection of mixed vintages does. And this book is just such a collection. Some of the stories I do not want to remain buried for ever in the museum files of dead magazine-numbers an author's not unpardonable vanity..."   Fiction Pages 272

Life of David Crockett by *David Crockett*   ISBN: *1-59462-250-7*   **$27.45**
"Colonel David Crockett was one of the most remarkable men of the times in which he lived. Born in humble life, but gifted with a strong will, an indomitable courage, and unremitting perseverance...   Biographies/New Age Pages 424

Lip-Reading by *Edward Nitchie*   ISBN: *1-59462-206-X*   **$25.95**
Edward B. Nitchie, founder of the New York School for the Hard of Hearing, now the Nitchie School of Lip-Reading, Inc, wrote "LIP-READING Principles and Practice". The development and perfecting of this meritorious work on lip-reading was an undertaking...   How-to Pages 400

A Handbook of Suggestive Therapeutics, Applied Hypnotism, Psychic Science   ISBN: *1-59462-214-0*   **$24.95**
by *Henry Munro*   Health/New Age/Health/Self-help Pages 376

A Doll's House: and Two Other Plays by *Henrik Ibsen*   ISBN: *1-59462-112-8*   **$19.95**
Henrik Ibsen created this classic when in revolutionary 1848 Rome. Introducing some striking concepts in playwriting for the realist genre, this play has been studied the world over.   Fiction/Classics/Plays 308

The Light of Asia by *sir Edwin Arnold*   ISBN: *1-59462-204-3*   **$13.95**
In this poetic masterpiece, Edwin Arnold describes the life and teachings of Buddha. The man who was to become known as Buddha to the world was born as Prince Gautama of India but he rejected the worldly riches and abandoned the reigns of power when...   Religion/History/Biographies Pages 170

The Complete Works of Guy de Maupassant by *Guy de Maupassant*   ISBN: *1-59462-157-8*   **$16.95**
"For days and days, nights and nights, I had dreamed of that first kiss which was to consecrate our engagement, and I knew not on what spot I should put my lips..."   Fiction/Classics Pages 240

The Art of Cross-Examination by *Francis L. Wellman*   ISBN: *1-59462-309-0*   **$26.95**
Written by a renowned trial lawyer, Wellman imparts his experience and uses case studies to explain how to use psychology to extract desired information through questioning.   How-to/Science/Reference Pages 408

Answered or Unanswered? by *Louisa Vaughan*   ISBN: *1-59462-248-5*   **$10.95**
Miracles of Faith in China   Religion Pages 112

The Edinburgh Lectures on Mental Science (1909) by *Thomas*   ISBN: *1-59462-008-3*   **$11.95**
This book contains the substance of a course of lectures recently given by the writer in the Queen Street Hall, Edinburgh. Its purpose is to indicate the Natural Principles governing the relation between Mental Action and Material Conditions...   New Age/Psychology Pages 148

Ayesha by *H. Rider Haggard*   ISBN: *1-59462-301-5*   **$24.95**
Verily and indeed it is the unexpected that happens! Probably if there was one person upon the earth from whom the Editor of this, and of a certain previous history, did not expect to hear again...   Classics Pages 380

Ayala's Angel by *Anthony Trollope*   ISBN: *1-59462-352-X*   **$29.95**
The two girls were both pretty; but Lucy who was twenty-one who supposed to be simple and comparatively unattractive, whereas Ayala was credited, as her Bombwhat romantic name might show, with poetic charm and a taste for romance. Ayala when her father died was nineteen...   Fiction Pages 484

The American Commonwealth by *James Bryce*   ISBN: *1-59462-286-8*   **$34.45**
An interpretation of American democratic political theory. It examines political mechanics and society from the perspective of Scotsman James Bryce   Politics Pages 572

Stories of the Pilgrims by *Margaret P. Pumphrey*   ISBN: *1-59462-116-0*   **$17.95**
This book explores pilgrims religious oppression in England as well as their escape to Holland and eventual crossing to America on the Mayflower, and their early days in New England...   History Pages 268

QTY

The Fasting Cure *by Sinclair Upton*   ISBN: *1-59462-222-1* **$13.95**
In the Cosmopolitan Magazine for May, 1910, and in the Contemporary Review (London) for April, 1910, I published an article dealing with my experiences in fasting. I have written a great many magazine articles, but never one which attracted so much attention... New Age/Self Help/Health Pages 164

Hebrew Astrology *by Sepharial*   ISBN: *1-59462-308-2* **$13.45**
In these days of advanced thinking it is a matter of common observation that we have left many of the old landmarks behind and that we are now pressing forward to greater heights and to a wider horizon than that which represented the mind-content of our progenitors... Astrology Pages 144

Thought Vibration or The Law of Attraction in the Thought World   ISBN: *1-59462-127-6* **$12.95**
by William Walker Atkinson   *Psychology/Religion Pages 144*

Optimism *by Helen Keller*   ISBN: *1-59462-108-X* **$15.95**
Helen Keller was blind, deaf, and mute since 19 months old, yet famously learned how to overcome these handicaps, communicate with the world, and spread her lectures promoting optimism. An inspiring read for everyone... Biographies/Inspirational Pages 84

Sara Crewe *by Frances Burnett*   ISBN: *1-59462-360-0* **$9.45**
In the first place, Miss Minchin lived in London. Her home was a large, dull, tall one, in a large, dull square, where all the houses were alike, and all the sparrows were alike, and where all the door-knockers made the same heavy sound... Childrens/Classic Pages 88

The Autobiography of Benjamin Franklin *by Benjamin Franklin*   ISBN: *1-59462-135-7* **$24.95**
The Autobiography of Benjamin Franklin has probably been more extensively read than any other American historical work, and no other book of its kind has had such ups and downs of fortune. Franklin lived for many years in England, where he was agent... Biographies/History Pages 332

Name	
Email	
Telephone	
Address	
City, State ZIP	

☐ **Credit Card**   ☐ **Check / Money Order**

Credit Card Number	
Expiration Date	
Signature	

Please Mail to: Book Jungle
                              PO Box 2226
                              Champaign, IL 61825
or Fax to: 630-214-0564

ORDERING INFORMATION

web: *www.bookjungle.com*
email: *sales@bookjungle.com*
fax: *630-214-0564*
mail: *Book Jungle PO Box 2226 Champaign, IL 61825*
or PayPal *to sales@bookjungle.com*

Please contact us for bulk discounts

DIRECT-ORDER TERMS

**20% Discount if You Order
Two or More Books**
Free Domestic Shipping!
Accepted: Master Card, Visa,
Discover, American Express

www.ingramcontent.com/pod-product-compliance
Lightning Source LLC
Chambersburg PA
CBHW080903020726
47502CB00008B/2327